The Christmas Kite

GAIL
GAYMER
MARTIN

The Christmas Kite

Steeple Hill®

Published by Steeple Hill Books™

STEEPLE HILL BOOKS

ISBN 0-373-78508-9

THE CHRISTMAS KITE

This edition published by arrangement with Steeple Hill Books.

Visit us at www.steeplehill.com

Printed in U.S.A.

With much love, to Andrea,
the inspiration for my poem, "The Kite Flyers."
May she always remember to bend with the wind.

Thanks to Jo Ferguson and Linda Windsor,
fellow authors who introduced me
to families with Down Syndrome children.
And a huge thanks to authors Deb Stover
and April Kihlstrom and to Jenni, who willingly shared
their stories. I hope I did your openness justice.

My grace is sufficient for you, for my power is made perfect in weakness. Therefore I will boast all the more gladly about my weaknesses, so that Christ's power may rest on me.

—2 *Corinthians* 12:9

THE KITE FLYERS

The heart, like a kite, is tugged
By the winds of change.
Fragments of color, dipping and soaring,
The kite flyers hold in their hands
The string, giving more to the wind
Or holding back in the softer silence.
With eager hearts they watch their kites
Soar in harmony, in a sweep of colored
Stillness.
Tugging too hard on the cord, it may break
And the lovely kite
                    flutters lifeless
                                    to the ground.
Its spirit silenced like a whimper,
Or the string may slip from the hands
And the kite caught on the wind
                    sails away
                                    a memory.
Patience and love is the cord.
Learn to bend with the wind,
To understand when to give
And when to hold back,
So your kites will soar on any wind
Independent, yet together.

Gail Gaymer Martin
1988

Chapter One

"Be careful, Mac." Meara Hayden's heart rose to her throat as her son wandered toward the white-capped waves. "Stay back."

He turned toward her, his mouth bent into a gleeful smile. "Birds." He pointed upward where seagulls curled and dipped above the rolling waters of Lake Huron.

"Yes," she yelled, forcing her soft voice above the dashing waves, fear gripping her heart. "Come back, Mac."

A new crest rose, its frothy cap arching high above the surface. Meara dashed forward. But too late.

The surging water thundered upward, crashing to the shore, then siphoned back in a powerful undertow. Mac staggered against its strength, and as the swell washed the earth from beneath his feet, the water dragged driftwood, debris and Mac into its roiling depths.

As a heart-wrenching gasp tore from Meara's throat, she dashed into the retreating wave, grabbed him by one flailing arm and lifted him to safety.

"Mac," she whispered, her voice quaking with fear. She clutched him to her side and guided him back to the dry sand.

"Wet," he moaned, pulling at his soggy shorts. Tears brimmed in his eyes.

"It's all right. They'll dry." To distract him, Meara pulled a wrapped cookie from her blouse pocket. "Here, Mac." Her ploy worked.

"Cookie," he said, brushing his moist eyes with a finger before grasping the treat.

Meara captured his free hand and continued their journey along the warm sandy beach. Glancing over her shoulder, she estimated the distance they'd wandered from the rough, rented cabin. Obviously her choice was a poor one. She hadn't considered the inherent dangers of the water… and her son.

Mac paused and gazed above his head. "Birds," he said again, waving the sugar cookie in the air.

"They're seagulls. You'll see lots of them around the water."

"Sea…gulls," he repeated, his face lifted upward toward her watchful eyes. He waved the cookie again in the birds' direction.

Without warning, a cluster of gulls soared over them and swooped down. His body shaking, Mac gasped, grabbed the leg of her slacks, and buried his face against the denim, knocking his glasses to the ground. She held him tightly as the birds gathered on the ground around them and fluttered toward the sweet clutched in his fingers.

"Drop the cookie, Mac. That's what they're after."

It fell to the ground, and she snatched up his glasses and pulled the child away. The birds flapped their wings and screeched at one another, pecking and vying for bits of the scattered pieces.

She knelt at his side and pulled a tissue from her pocket to wipe his tear-filled eyes. "It's okay, Mac. Mama should have thought. The birds like cookies and bread, all kinds of food. We'll be more careful next time."

He nodded, dragging his arm across his dripping nose. "Next time," he agreed.

Meara pulled his arm away from his face and wiped the moisture with a tissue. "What about your hankie? What does Mama tell you?"

He looked thoughtfully, his dark brown almond-shaped eyes squinting into hers. "Use a hankie."

"That's right. Not your arm, remember?" She used another tissue to clean the sand from his glasses and popped them onto his blunt, upturned nose.

He grinned, and, having forgotten his fear of the birds, he scuttled off ahead of her.

Waves. Birds. She hesitated, wondering if they should return to the gloom of their cabin. The late-spring sun lit the sky, but did not quite penetrate the foliage of their small rental—two rooms and a bath—that lay hidden amidst the heavy pines. Only a few small windows allowed the sun's rays in, and they were situated too high to enjoy a relaxed view of the lake. Their only entertainment was a fuzzy-picture television—nothing really to occupy Mac's time. She looked ahead at the shoreline. We'll walk to the bend and see what's around the corner, she thought.

A warm gust whipped off the water, and she lifted her eyes to the blue sky dotted with a smattering of puffy white clouds. She felt free for the first time in her life. Free, but frightened. How could she survive alone with Mac? When she first left her deceased husband's parents, the thoughts of where she would go or what she would do barely skittered through her mind. Freedom was what she'd longed for. Freedom and a chance to raise her son as she wanted, not chained by the Hayden family's shame.

Meara focused again on her son. Mac's short, sturdy legs struggled through the sand, his curiosity as strong as her sense of release. He neared the bend in the shoreline, and she hurried to shorten the distance between them.

But a large island in the distance, rising into hills above the green water, caught her eye, and she paused to enjoy its lush expanse and the miniature-appearing village that grazed the shoreline. Mackinaw Island, she told herself, a Michigan landmark. She'd heard of it but had never been there.

On the left hillside a long ribbon of white drew her interest. The hotel? She narrowed her eyes, gazing at the pale splotch against the green landscape. The name edged into her memory. Yes, the Grand Hotel. So many places she had never seen.

Meara looked ahead and her pulse lurched. Mac was no longer in sight. "Mac," she called, dashing along the curve of the beach.

When she rounded the evergreens that grew close to the shoreline, Mac appeared far ahead of her, rushing away as fast as his awkward legs would carry him. His arm was extended, his finger pointing toward the sky. Expecting to see more birds, she looked up, but instead she saw what had lured him. A kite. An amazing kite, dipping and soaring above the water. The brilliant colors glinted in the sun, and a long, flowing yellow-and-red tail curled and waved like pennants in a parade.

She halted to catch her breath, clasping her fist against her pounding heart. Her fear subsided. Mac was safe, a generous distance from the water's edge. He turned toward her, waving his arms above his head. She waved back, pointing toward the kite, letting him know she saw the lovely sight.

He turned again and trudged forward toward the distant figure of a man who apparently held the invisible string.

Jordan Baird grasped the cord, fighting the wind. If he tugged too hard, the string would break and send his kite swooping into the water. If he released his grip, the wind could snatch it from his hand. With expert control, he eased and pulled, knowing when to let the wind take control and when to hold it back. Pride rose in him. If he knew anything, he understood the aerodynamics of a kite.

A shadow fell across his line of sight and, surprised, he glanced at its origin. A child with soggy shorts and an eager face tripped through the sand toward him.

"Whoa, there, young man. What do you think you're doing?" He glowered down at the boy, pointing to the sign stuck haphazardly into the grassy sand above the beach. "Can't you read? This is private property."

The boy skidded to a halt, and a pair of frightened eyes shifted upward. "I can…read…some words."

"Can't you read those? It says, Private Property."

The child squinted at the sign and shook his head.

Jordan peered down—the child was maybe five or six—and reality set in. Perhaps he couldn't read.

The child's smile returned. Faltering, he lifted his finger, pointing to the soaring colors. "Look!"

"Haven't you seen a kite before?" He frowned at the boy, studying his face. The child's expression amazed him.

The boy's innocent grin met his scowl. "Kite," the boy repeated, gazing at him with huge almond-shaped eyes behind thick glasses.

"Yes, a kite."

The boy giggled. "Kite," he said again.

He peered at the child. Something wasn't quite right.

The child's mouth opened in an uncontrolled laugh.

Jordan's curiosity ebbed as his awareness rose. Down Syndrome. He should have realized sooner. But certainly, the boy would not be walking this lonely stretch of beach alone.

He looked beyond the child's head and saw, nearing them, a woman hurrying across the sand. For a fleeting moment his thoughts flew back in time. A knifing ache tore through him, and he closed his eyes, blocking the invading, painful memory.

Despite his defense the child's intrusion penetrated Jordan's iron wall, a wall he'd built to keep the torment out. Memories flooded over its barrier, and Jordan struggled to gather the horrible images and push them away behind the crumbling stones of protection.

Yet the boy rattled the door of Jordan's curiosity and, wall or no wall, questions jutted into his mind. Where had he come from? And the woman. Who was she? "What's your name, son?"

The child pulled his gaze from the kite long enough to answer the question. "Dunstan Mac...Auley Hayden." He punched the last syllable of each name as he faltered over the three words.

"That's quite a label for a young man."

The boy giggled and poked a fist toward him. "I don't have a label."

An unnatural grin pulled at Jordan's mouth. "I mean your name. That's a powerful name for a boy." His gaze shifted. "Is that lady your mother?" He tilted his head in the direction of the woman, keeping his eye on the kite.

The lad glanced over his shoulder and nodded, a wide grin stretching his blotchy red cheeks.

"What does *she* call you? Certainly not Dunstan MacAuley, I hope."

"Mac." He poked himself in the chest. "I'm Mac. What's your name?" He stuck his hand forward, offering a handshake.

Amused, Jordan shifted the kite string and grasped the child's hand but didn't answer. Instead, he eyed the slender, fragile-looking woman who came panting to his side.

"I'm sorry," she said, gazing at him with doleful, emerald-green eyes. "He saw your kite and got away from me." Her voice rose and fell in a soft lilt.

"You need to keep a better eye on him. The water can be dangerous." The muscles tightened in his shoulders at the thought, and he tugged on the kite string to right it.

"Yes, I know. I'm sorry. He's never seen a kite. Everything is new to him, and—"

Jordan's chest tightened. How could a child never have seen a kite? "How old is he?" Eyeing the boy, the throbbing sadness filled his heart.

A flush rose to her ivory cheeks, and her eyes darkened. "Eight," she mumbled. "He's small for his age."

Jordan shifted his gaze from the woman to his kite, then to the child. "You need to watch him."

"I said I'm sorry."

She lowered her eyes, and he wished he hadn't sounded so harsh. But then, she'd never lost a son.

"Mac," she called, "let's go."

The child gave a hesitant look, but the kite seemed to mesmerize him and he didn't move.

"Mac, I said let's go." She stepped toward him, then spun around to face Jordan. "I'm sorry we intruded."

Longing and grief pitched in his mind and muddied his thoughts like a stick stirring a rain puddle. "Yes, well, this is private property." The words marched undaunted from his mouth, and he gestured to the makeshift sign.

And so is my life.

"But anyone can make a mistake," he added, feeling the need to ease his sharp words. His emotions knotted—pity for himself and sadness for the mother and son.

"That's private," she snapped, pointing to the grass above the sand. "Not the beach." She glared at him, her eyes shooting sparks like gemstones. "It's public." The fire in her voice matched her blazing red hair tied back in a long, thick tail. She grabbed Mac's hand and spun away, heading back the way she'd come. The boy twisted in her grasp, his eyes riveted to the kite sailing above the water.

Watching the woman and boy vanish around the bend, Jordan closed his eyes. She was right. He didn't own the beach, though he wished he did. He would put up a fence to keep the few stragglers from invading his world.

After a final glance at the retreating figures, he turned his attention to the kite. With measured motion, he reeled in his paper creation. He'd lost his spirit. The intrusion settled on his enthusiasm like an elephant on a turtle's back.

As the kite neared the shore, he shifted farther from the

lake and turned to avoid a water landing. Before the fragile construction hit the ground, he caught it in his hand and then toted it up the incline to the house.

Inside, Jordan placed the kite on the enclosed back porch with the others he'd made over the past few days, then stopped in the kitchen. He'd forgotten to turn off the coffeepot, and the acrid smell caught in his throat. He pulled the wall plug and poured the thick, black liquid into a mug. Wandering to the screened front porch, Jordan took a sip, grimacing at its pungent taste.

He looked toward the beach. The waves, stirred by the wind, rolled forward in frothy caps, spilling debris along the sand. He let his gaze wander to the bend in the shoreline and wondered about the mother and child. Were they visiting someone? Jordan had never seen them before. Few people, especially strangers, wandered this stretch of the beach. Miles of the wooded, weedy acreage was state owned, without a cottage or house.

Jordan remembered a few ramshackle cabins up the road a mile or two. Had they wandered from there? If so, they'd be gone in the morning and leave him to his peace and quiet. He snorted. Quiet, yes, but peace? Never. Since the fiery death of Lila and Robbie, peace had evaded him.

He raised his arm and ran his hand across the back of his neck. Tension knotted along his shoulders, always, when he thought about them. The woman had said Mac was eight years old. The round impish face of Jordan's son filled his thoughts. Robbie was eight, too, when he died. Tears stung the back of Jordan's eyes, and a deep moan rumbled from his throat. Its impact quaked along his spine. Why did he allow these strangers to wrench his memories from hiding? Three years. Hadn't he suffered enough? Hadn't he paid his dues?

But Jordan knew the answer. He had nothing more with which to pay the price, nothing to heal the wounds, nothing to smooth the scars. He slapped his hand against the rickety table and shook his head. "Enough!" he cried out to the heavens. "Why not my life? If You're really up there, Lord, why not me? I'll never forgive You. Never."

Tears escaped his tight control and lay in the corner of his eye. His hand shot upward, catching the single fleeting drop, halting it before it rolled down his cheek. He had promised himself he would no longer cry. He had thought he'd shed every tear possible. Yet one had lived, laughing at him behind his eye, waiting to foil his masquerade.

But he'd won. He'd snuffed it out with the swipe of his fingers—as quickly as a life could end.

Meara poured the cold cereal into a bowl, then sloshed in the milk. The blurry television filled the quiet morning with local news, and Mac stared into the dish, singing one of his incessant tunes.

"Mac, let's say the blessing." Meara held out her hand, and he grasped her fingers and bowed his head, the tune undaunted. When the song ended, he recited the prayer, then spooned into the cereal.

Meara sipped her tea, wishing she had coffee. Gazing out the small window, she watched the glimmer of sunlight play on the nearby birch trees. The pungent smell of mildew and disinfectant that clung to the old cabin infested her lungs, and she longed to be outside in the fresh air.

Leaning her elbows against the high windowsill, she

peered through the foliage toward the beach. The water dragged visions of her homeland, her lovely green Erin, from her smothered memories. Dingle and Kenmare bays and the deepest cobalt blue of the Kerry Loughs waved through her thoughts.

Shades of green and blue swirled in her memory—the Emerald Isle. How had her American visit, so long ago, become this nightmare? The question was foolish. She knew how the nightmare began. But now, it had ended. She prayed it had. She would carve out a new life for Mac and her. With love pushing against her chest, she turned to study the child intent on his cereal bowl and his song.

A deep sense of grief stabbed her. How long would she have her son? How long would God grant him life on this earth? Deep love charged through her—despite the trials, despite the incessant songs. Meara smiled as Mac's singsong voice penetrated her thoughts. Despite everything, she'd give the world for her son to have a long life.

Meara clapped her hands. "Mac, let's get outside in the sunshine. You ready?"

His beaming smile met hers. "The kite." He ate the last of his cereal. "Let's see the kite."

"Not today, Mac. We'll gather shells on the beach. I'll bring a plastic bag along to hold them, okay?"

"I want…the kite," Mac said. "You have shells."

Meara chuckled. "You're a generous laddie, all right. And remember, no food, no cookies."

Mac sat deathly still, finally giving a resolute nod. He slid off the chair and made his way to her. "No birds, Mama." He rested his head on her leg, then slyly lifted his face with a grin. "You have…the birds."

Playfully she tousled his hair. After grabbing a plastic bag, she locked the cabin and they headed down the path to the beach.

When they left the shade of the woods, the sun beat against Meara's cool skin. She pulled her sweater off and tied it around her waist. Searching the sky ahead of him, Mac tore off down the beach in the direction that he had seen the kite the day before.

"Hold up, Mac."

He slowed and turned toward her.

"How about if we take off our shoes. We can walk in the water."

Mac plopped in the sand and tugged at his canvas shoes. Meara stepped out of her sandals and tossed them farther up on the beach, toward the grassy edge. Mac followed her lead. With the shoes safely stowed, they stepped into the frigid morning lake. With a shuddering laugh, they trudged along, halting for an occasional shell, but no matter what she said, Mac's mind seemed focused on the bend in the shoreline.

Though the strange man had rankled her the day before, his image rose in her thoughts. Handsome, he was. Tall and lean, six-foot-plus, she guessed, with ash-brown hair streaked with wisps of gray. But mostly, she remembered his eyes, sad eyes of the palest blue, and his full, shapely lips, closed and unsmiling.

Why? filled her mind. He seemed a paradox, a grim, brooding man flying a bright, beautiful kite. The picture didn't mix, like Scrooge tossing hundred-dollar bills to the poor.

Curiosity drove her forward, and her breath faltered in anticipation as she rounded the bend. Releasing a ragged blast of air, she paused. The sky ahead was empty. No kite. Nothing but the great expansion of the Mackinaw Bridge connecting the two peninsulas.

"No kite," Mac said, halting ahead of her. He turned and disappointment filled his face. "Where's…the kite man?"

"The man's not there, Mac."

Tears rose in his eyes. "He died?"

Her stomach knotted and she drew him closer. "No, maybe he's working…or busy today."

Mac didn't move. "My daddy died."

"Yes, he's in heaven." But she wondered if he were. Such a coldhearted man. Would God open His arms to a man who had rejected his son?

A new smile brightened Mac's face. "Two fathers in heaven."

She knelt and wrapped her arms around him, wanting to hold him forever. "That's right, and don't forget that." She gave him a squeeze, forcing the hurtful memories from her thoughts. "I'll race you," she said, changing the subject. She needed to run, to clear her mind. Self-pity was a horrible thing, and she was filled with it.

She hurried ahead, half running, allowing Mac to gain some distance before she pressed nearer. He giggled and pushed his short legs ahead of him. A dog's sharp bark drew him to an unplanned stop, and he tumbled to the sand.

"Are you okay?" She rushed forward, but he rolled over with a grin and pushed himself up. A door slam jolted her attention, and, turning, she caught sight of the ranch-style house set off the beach. Barking wildly, a dog pressed its muzzle against the front screen, and the shadow of a figure moved inside the screened porch.

Mac grabbed her hand and stared at the house through his sand-spattered glasses. A man's voice calmed the dog to silence.

"The kite man," Mac said, releasing Meara's hand and pointing toward the shadowy figure. He stepped toward the house.

Meara caught his hand. "Maybe, son, but he's busy today. Let's go back to the cabin. We'll take a ride into town. Mom needs a newspaper and some groceries. And—"

"Ice cream," Mac added.

She breathed a relieved sigh. "And an ice-cream cone." She turned and took a step in the direction they'd come. "Ready?"

He stared up at the shadow for a moment, then waved. Without a complaint, Mac turned and followed her.

Chapter Two

Jordan sank back against the wicker chair, feeling a mixture of relief and longing. At first he had thought the boy might be hurt, but his concern seemed foolish now, as he watched them retreat. The child had tripped in the sand, nothing more.

Jordan was relieved they'd turned back. His heart skipped at the thought. For a moment he had feared the boy might run up to his door. What would he do? Ignoring the child was one solution, but could he do that?

Longing shivered through him. Mac tugged at Jordan's repressed emotions—the desire to be a father, to teach a son about manhood. Jordan had never had the opportunity to share those things with his young son.

He pushed the thought from his mind. Where was this boy's father? Back at the cabin, perhaps. He had thought they'd be gone today, but obviously he'd been wrong. Anxiety filled him. Had the family rented the place for a week? Perhaps more? He leaned his head against the chair back, forcing the thoughts from his mind. He had work to do. *Con-*

centrate on the kite. He grabbed a piece of bamboo he'd whittled and began to sand. Softened by water, the bamboo dowel curved as he attached it to the other bonded pieces in an intricate design, then glued and tied each side with strong linen thread. He checked the rounded form against the washi paper's woodblock image of Fukusuke, a Japanese gnome. It fit perfectly.

As he grasped another dowel, a voice drifted from the side of the house.

"Anybody home?"

Jordan dropped the bamboo and rose, stepping to the door. "I'm in the front, Otis."

Otis Manning appeared at the side of the screened enclosure and nodded. Dooley, Jordan's Irish setter, raced onto the porch, his tail lashing like a whip.

"Come in," Jordan said, pushing open the door.

The elderly man stepped inside. "Thought you weren't here," he said. Dooley pressed against his leg, and Otis nuzzled the dog's head. "I rang the doorbell in the back. You didn't hear it?"

Jordan shook his head. "I don't think it's working. Never bothered to fix it."

"You got yourself a great watchdog, here, Jordan. Dooley just grinned at me and wagged his tail."

"He knows you." Jordan clapped his hands, and the dog left the man's side and curled beside Jordan. "Next time knock. I'll hear you then." He gestured toward the small sofa. "Have a seat."

"Thanks." He sat on the wicker settee and folded his hands on his knees. "Just come by for the new kites."

"They're on the back porch. I'll help you with them."

Otis eyed the unfinished kite. "Looks like a beauty, that one." He nodded toward the washi-paper gnome.

"Thanks," Jordan said, shifting in his chair. Though he knew Otis well, he'd lost the art of adult conversation. He'd held one-sided chats with the dog occasionally, but the longest conversation he'd had in days was with the child on the beach. "Care for a soda, Otis? I was about to get one myself."

"Sure. That'd be nice."

Jordan dashed into the safety of the house. Only three years earlier, he'd paraded in a lecture hall, teaching Shakespeare to two hundred college students. Today he couldn't come up with a single thread of casual conversation.

He screwed the caps off two sodas and grabbed one glass from the cupboard. Taking a deep breath, he returned to the porch. "Here you go." He handed Otis the soda and glass.

"Don't need no glass. Thanks. I'm a bottle baby myself." His eyes glinted with amusement.

Jordan slid the tumbler onto the table and sank back into the chair. A blast of air rushed from his chest. "So how's the store?"

"Still no clerk. Sign's in the window, but no bites yet. I'm surprised."

"You'll get someone soon," Jordan said.

"Hope so. The tourists are already pouring into town."

"Is business okay otherwise?"

"Pretty good." Otis's gaze shifted to Dooley, and he ran his fingers through his graying hair. "But I'm afraid we're going to run into a problem." Slowly, he raised his eyes to Jordan's. "I been meaning to talk to you about that investor, Donald Hatcher. Told you about him a while back. Remember?"

Jordan nodded, sensing something coming but not sure what.

"He's putting pressure on the shops along the strip there. I've been thinkin' maybe you'd want to get involved. Some of them might be ready to sell, and if one does, then the next will…and pretty soon, you got no business. Right now, the kite shop's in a prime location."

"I'm not sure I can do any more than the others. Who's giving up? The bakery?"

"Naw, Scott's tough as nails. He's ready for a fight. So's the fast-food place. Hatcher's been hanging around the gift shop. I talked to Bernard Dawson, the manager. He thinks the owner might be thinking about selling. The T-shirt shop's still stickin' to their guns." He took a long swig of soda.

"I'm not going to sweat it, Otis. The land is valuable. I hope the others know that and don't sell it off for half its worth."

"That's what I mean. Maybe we could hold a meetin'. You know, Jordan, it's not just losin' the shop that bothers me. It's what he's plannin' to put in its place. A saloon. One of those skimpy-dressed waitress bars. That's askin' for trouble. Booze and half-naked women. We have no place for that here. This is a family vacation spot, and we want to keep it that way."

"Who told you that's what he's planning to build?"

"Oh, word gets out. And I believe it. He's after that strip of land. It's right on the water, butted up to the ferry parking. All the Mackinaw Island traffic. He couldn't find a better spot for a bar."

Jordan's stomach knotted. Otis was right, but he had no

desire to get himself involved in city politics and battles. He hadn't years ago, either, when life felt normal...and real. And now he'd settled into his life just as it was. Right here on the water, building his kites.

"So, Jordan, what do you think? You don't want to see a joint like that in the city, do you?"

Jordan looked at the man's serious expression. "You know I don't, Otis. Let me think about it. I'm not sure you need to worry yet. Anyway, what about zoning? I wonder if anyone's checked with the zoning board. Isn't that Congregational church just down the street?"

Otis nodded. "Sure is. I wonder..." He ran his finger around the mouth of the bottle. "Let me check that out. Maybe the zoning board can save our necks."

"Do that. Then let me know what they say." Jordan rose and gave Otis a firm pat on the back. "Come out to the back porch, and I'll help you load up the kites."

Meara steered the coupe down Main Street, searching for a parking space. Tourists, pushing the summer season, thronged the streets and hung in shop doorways or gazed into colorful souvenir-filled windows. She stopped to give room to a van pulling away in the middle of the block. As he drove off, she nosed her car into the wide space.

She breathed a deep sigh. Though she knew how to drive, she'd had little practice in years. Her husband, Dunstan, or her father-in-law had driven her the few places she went. Most of the time she lived in the upper floors of the big rambling house, in her own sitting room with Mac playing by her side.

"Ice cream," Mac called, pointing to the ice-cream parlor sign embellished with a colorful triple-dip cone.

"That's a sure fact about you, Mac. You never forget a thing, do you? At least, nothing like ice cream." She smiled at him as they climbed out from the car.

He stuck close to her side, and she gazed in the shop windows, stopping to buy two local newspapers and a net bag filled with tiny cars and trucks. She watched the pity-filled faces of people who glanced at her and Mac, then, in discomfort, looked away. She cringed at their lack of understanding.

Mac let out a gleeful chortle when they neared the ice-cream shop, and hastily, she quieted him as they marched through the door. As they waited their turn, she and Mac studied the menu.

The clerk dipped the ice-cream scoop into the cold water and turned toward them. "And what will you have, young—" His head jerked upright. "What would he like, ma'am?" he asked, stumbling over his words.

Her automatic defense yanked her response. "Mac, tell the young man what you'd like."

A light flush rose on the teen's face.

"One...dip of double chocolate," Mac answered, sending the young man a spirited grin.

The clerk grabbed a cone and dug out a scoop. He glanced at the other workers behind the counter, dipped back into the barrel, slid an extra portion of ice cream onto the cone and smiled.

"Thank you," Meara said, understanding his apology. "I'll have a dip of peanut butter swirl."

He added an extra measure to hers, too, and with napkins wrapped around the cones, they made their way past customers to the sidewalk. She kept an eye on Mac's cone, guarding against unsightly drips, but he licked the edge and seemed in control.

"I saw a bakery across the street. Let's take a look."

They followed the sidewalk to the end of the block and crossed the road. Passing a fast-food restaurant, she drew in the smell of oil permeating the air, followed by the rich, taunting aroma of freshly baked bread. Beside the bakery, Meara studied the pastries and breads displayed in the window.

As she pulled open the screen door of the bakery, Mac's strident voice bellowed in her ear.

"Kites!" He rambled past her to the window of the shop next door.

Meara closed the bakery door and followed Mac. Unique kites filled the storefront window, and in one corner, a small Help Wanted sign was taped to the glass. Her stomach tightened. She wanted a job…needed a job, but how could she work and care for Mac? She'd wait until school began and pray her money lasted.

Mac pressed his nose against the window, and Meara joined him, peeking through the glass. Magnificent kites of every shape and design hung from the ceiling and clung to the walls—dragons, birds and other shapes she'd never seen before.

Mac pulled open the screen, but before entering, he glanced at Meara. She nodded and grinned at the smear of ice cream on his mouth, then followed him inside.

"Can I…have a kite?" he asked, marveling at the myriad of designs surrounding them.

Kites mesmerized him, and she saw no reason not to buy him a small, inexpensive paper one. She looked around for the cheaper models. "We'll see what they have, Mac." He accepted her remark.

The shop seemed empty, but a door slammed in the back. Meara looked up to see a huge kite held by a pair of stubby hands come through the storage room doorway. The person owning the hands was hidden behind the colorful paper design with the long yellow-and-red tail.

Mac gazed with awe at the huge creation until he swung around and grabbed Meara's arm. "The kite man." He pointed to the doorway. An elderly face peeked around the unique kite.

"Well, hello there." He grinned. "I'm just bringin' in some new stock. I'll be with you in a minute." Placing the kite against the wall, he turned and headed back through the doorway.

Meara bent down to Mac's level and whispered, "That's not the kite man, Mac. This man is too old."

Mac grinned. "No, the kite." He pointed. "That's the...kite man's...kite." His head punctuated every other word.

As Meara studied the paper-covered frame, her gaze drifted to the long tail. She could envision the yellow and red ribbons curling through the sky. "It is, Mac. You're right. This must be where the man sells his kites."

"Nice, huh?" The clerk's voice interrupted their quiet conversation. He stepped toward them. "Now, may I help you?"

"Oh, yes," Meara said, pulling her gaze to the storekeeper. "I'd like to get a paper kite for my son. You know, one of the little diamond-shaped ones."

He chuckled. "I'm afraid you'll have to go to the shop next door. We only have the kind yer lookin' at here. Handcrafted, they are."

"And expensive," Meara added.

"I'm afraid so. At least, lots more expensive than those little paper toys. You like kites, son?"

Mac grinned at the man. "Yep." His pudgy hand jutted outward. "My name's Mac. What's your name?"

The clerk leaned forward and took his hand in a broad handshake. "Nice to meet you, Mac. I'm Otis Manning." He straightened his back. "Just a couple steps next door, ma'am. They have lots of kites for this young fella."

Meara's heart lifted, observing the gentleman with Mac. He didn't gawk at the boy's disability or treat him like a second-rate citizen. His reaction warmed her heart. "Thank you. Ready, Mac? Let's go next door and get your kite."

With a broad grin, Mac took her hand and they left the shop. Outside, the smell from the bakery tempted her taste buds. But that could wait. Instead she turned in the opposite direction to buy Mac's kite. As she passed the display window, her gaze fell again on the Help Wanted sign. She paused. This would be a nice place to work. But reality tugged at her conscience, and she moved forward. She'd already decided to wait. By that time, the shop would have all the help it needed. Too bad.

Glancing at the sign again with longing, she gave a wave through the glass at the elderly gentleman who watched them leave.

Skimming the newspaper for rentals, Meara nibbled on a fresh oatmeal cookie from the bakery. She chided herself for the sweets—ice cream and now a cookie.

"You know, Mac, we can't keep eating all these treats. We'll both be as big as elephants."

Mac giggled, dropping one of the new miniature trucks to the floor, and ran to her side. "I love you, Mama."

"I love you, too, Mac." She gave him a big hug. Discouraged, Meara tossed the newspaper on the small table. Most rentals were summer cottages only meant for a one- or two-week vacation. One apartment seemed too expensive and was unfurnished. Only one held promise. Maybe later they would take a ride and check it out.

Mac wandered to the sofa and picked up the yardstick-shaped package. "Make my kite, please," he said, handing it to Meara.

She unrolled the flimsy tissue paper and thin dowels, and, following the instructions, constructed the kite.

Mac hung over her shoulder, watching, his eyes wide with wonder. "Can I…make it…fly?"

"That, we'll have to see," Meara said, wondering what she owned to make the tail. She looked around the room, mentally assessed her wardrobe, and finally remembered a few pieces of ragged cloth in her trunk, kept there to clean her windows or wipe up spills.

She went to the bedroom, and returned with the cloth, tearing it into strips. After she tied the pieces together, she fastened them to the end of the kite, and Mac herded her to the beach.

A light breeze stirred the trees near the cabin, but closer to shore a gusty wind blew, whisking the shimmering water into rolling whitecaps. Meara struggled to keep the paper kite from ripping away from her. She'd never flown a kite before, though she'd seen it done in movies or by others when she was a child. She prayed she wouldn't disappoint her son.

As if considering her the expert, Mac followed her every move. She unrolled a host of cord and let it fall to the ground.

"Now, hold the ball of string, and I'll run ahead with the kite."

Having no idea what she should do, she bit her lip and waited to make sure Mac appeared ready. While the wind pushed against her, she ran along the beach holding the kite in the air. Suddenly an air mass caught the paper and lifted it from her hands.

"Hang on to the string," she called, rushing back to Mac. But before she returned to him, the lengthy measure of string coiled on the ground offered no resistance to the aerodynamics, and the kite rose, then nose-dived into the water.

Mac let out a cry, but she was helpless. The kite lay on top of the water, rising and falling with the waves. She looked at Mac's downhearted expression, and disappointment coursed through her. She should have asked the shop clerk for tips on flying a kite. The "kite man" had made it look so easy.

With her eyes on Mac's disappointed face, she stepped forward to offer a consoling hug just as a huge red dog bounded between them. She struggled to keep her footing in the loose sand, wavering between success and failure, but the ground rose up to meet her. Though startled, she and Mac both laughed as the dog hovered above them, panted for a moment, then stayed long enough to lick her cheek.

When the large, rambunctious dog settled into Mac's awareness, his laughter faded. He let out a cry and dashed behind Meara, sending out sounds—a confused mixture of giggles and whimpers. With one hand, Meara patted Mac's arm wrapped around her neck, and with the other, she held the dog at bay.

A voice rose on the wind and she looked down the beach. The kite man raced forward toward her while she sprawled, pinioned to the spot by Mac and the big Irish setter.

"Come, Dooley," the man called. The dog lifted its head and turned toward him. "I'm sorry. Did he hurt you?"

Dooley. The dog's name. "No," Meara said, a grin curling her lips, thinking of what she must look like. "Just my dignity, a little."

He grabbed the dog's collar, pulling him away. "I'm usually more careful. I was maneuvering a kite through the door, and he shot out between my legs. He only does that when he sees the ducks."

"Ducks," Mac repeated. "I want…to see…the ducks." He punched the final word, tilting his head upward with a wide-mouthed smile.

"Dooley scared them away, I'm afraid." His gaze shifted from Mac to Meara, still sitting in the sand. "Let me help you." He held the dog back with one hand and reached down for her.

She felt like a downy pillow when he lifted her with ease. "Thank you," she said, brushing the sand from her slacks and hands.

His brooding eyes seemed friendly this afternoon, perhaps altered by the embarrassing situation Dooley had caused. His tight-pressed lips of yesterday looked more relaxed and the flicker of a grin curled the edge of his mouth.

Meara's gaze drifted to the thick cords of muscle that ribbed his arms as he controlled Dooley's exuberance. The vision brought warmth to her cheeks. She realized Mac still clung to her side.

"Mac, the dog won't hurt you. That's his way of being

friendly." Looking at her child, Meara saw the beads of tears in his eyes.

He took one step backward, but his grip on her arm tightened.

"Would you like to pet the dog?" the man asked, his gaze searching Mac's face. "I'm sorry Dooley frightened you."

"It's not just the dog," Meara said, noticing he had seen Mac's tears. "It's the kite." She gestured toward the lake.

He followed the motion of her hand. "Oh, I see."

Lapping against the sand, Meara spied the crossed dowels splotched with fragments of torn, soggy tissue. The rag tail advanced and ebbed in the undulating waves. "Not very successful, was I?"

A wry grin teased his mouth. "It takes a knack." He reached forward as if to touch Mac's head, but drew back. "I'll tell you what, pal. If your mother buys another kite, I'll show you how to fly it."

Mac's eyes widened, and he dragged his arm across his moist eyes. Apparently he'd forgotten the dog, because he stepped forward, his grin spreading from ear to ear. "Okay," he said.

Dooley's tail flagged the air as he strained forward. When Mac noticed he stepped away, but the new promise seemed to give him courage, and he edged closer, eyeing the large dog.

"He likes you, lad," the man said.

Mac eased nearer, inching his hand toward the dog's shiny red coat. Finally his fingers touched the setter's fur.

Though his action was fleeting, Meara reveled in the progress Mac had made and the kindness of the man. The man. She had not introduced herself. Before she could follow through with the amenities, he turned and stepped away.

"When you buy the kite, let me know," he said, his face darkening as he distanced himself.

"Thank you, Mr...." But he was out of earshot.

Down the beach, he gave the dog free rein.

Meara held Mac's hand and watched the man following the dog until he disappeared around the bend in the shoreline.

Jordan raced through the sand with Dooley a long stretch ahead of him. He sensed the woman watched, but he didn't turn around to see if he was correct. Earlier she'd studied him, and he had watched her lovely face shift from laughter to concern to curiosity. So much life in one delicate face. Lila's face had been round and sturdy, but this woman— He snapped his thoughts closed like a book he'd finally waded through and finished. No more of that. The child and his mother pressed against his thoughts too often. Talk about curiosity. He was as inquisitive about the child's mother as she appeared to be about him.

He skidded to a stop in front of the house and drew in a deep calming breath. Dooley had run a good race, but Jordan's heart hammered for more reason than the swift dash along the sand. Mac had pierced his barricade. Why had he offered to teach the child to fly a kite? He should have escaped immediately. Instead his fatherly instinct had led him to open his foolish mouth. Now he would pay.

Jordan remembered years earlier when he built Robbie his first kite. The boy had a knack—like father, like son, as they say. With little help, Robbie ran through the field, the bright yellow tissue billowing, diving and soaring toward the clouds. A warm summer day, it was. And he'd thought then that they had so many bright sunny days to share.

His chest tightened, holding back the emotion that burned his throat. His gaze lifted to the cerulean-blue sky, and he longed to shake his fist at Lila's God. But the gesture was useless.

No fist, no anger, no cursing could bring Robbie or Lila back.

Chapter Three

The following day, Meara drove Mac past the apartment listed in the newspaper. The location was near town, but the building needed paint and the grounds needed trimming. Was the inside as badly in need of care? She hesitated. Saying nothing to her son, she continued down the road. Maybe she'd check the newspaper one more time for another option before looking at this apartment.

In town, Meara found parking and headed for the gift shop. Two kites seemed safer than one, after their last fiasco, and she let Mac select the ones he wanted. When she paid and stepped outside, the bakery lured her again, and she headed that way with the wavering promise she would only buy bread.

Passing the kite shop, the Help Wanted sign rose to meet her. She paused. Closing her eyes, she asked God for a hint of what to do. When she opened them again, the elderly gentleman smiled through the store window and waved them in. Before moving she looked heavenward. Was this God's doing, or just an older man's friendly bidding?

She pulled open the door, and Mac stepped in ahead of her.

"Good morning," Otis said. "I see you got a couple more kites today. No luck with the last one?"

Meara chuckled. "'No experience' is the best way of putting it. I should have asked for a hint about launching one of these things. I'm grateful it was the two-dollar-and-fifty-cent version and not one of these."

Otis nodded. "Yep, you don't wanna spend your money on one of these gems unless you know what you're doin'. Now, that's for sure."

Otis bent down and gave Mac a hearty smile. "How's things goin', sonny?"

"Good. I like...kites. They're high in the sky."

"They sure are." He patted Mac's head as the child's focus swept the kite-filled ceiling. "You want to look at all the kites, boy? You can wander around if you want."

Mac looked at Meara, who gave an agreeable nod. "But not too long," she added. "And don't get into anything."

He wandered away, his mouth gaping at the colorful creations.

"That's a nice boy you got there."

"Thank you." Flustered, she wondered if the comment was meant to open the door to questions about Mac.

"I had a cousin with a Down Syndrome boy. He threw temper tantrums till you could hardly bear it. Your son seems easier goin'."

Her question had been answered. "Mac's no problem. He frightens easily. You know—dogs, birds, anything that comes up on him too quickly. But he's a good boy."

"You're a visitor in town. Tourist, I suppose."

Meara glanced down the aisle, checking on Mac. He stood near the back of the shop, staring at the kite they'd watched sailing over the lake. "No, we're staying in a cabin up the road. I'm looking for a place to rent for a while."

"You and the boy are alone?"

Her stomach jolted. She'd not been asked the question before and the reality shivered through her. "Yes, my husband died a few months ago. We lived with my in-laws and..." She ran her fingers through her hair. "I guess you didn't ask for my life story." She managed a smile. "We need a furnished place. Do you know of any?"

He hesitated, pinching his lower lip between his thumb and finger. "So happens, there's an apartment over this shop. Not too big. Couple of bedrooms and bath."

"We don't need anything fancy for now. The cabin only has one bedroom, so most anything would be a mansion to us."

Dunstan's family home was a mansion. The thought slammed into the pit of her stomach. Never again would she want to live in a huge estate like his, especially not as a prisoner. That's how she'd felt. When she focused on the kite shop proprietor, he was studying her.

"I even think the place up there has a few pieces of furniture," he said, pointing his thumb toward the ceiling. "But it hasn't been rented out since I can remember. Might be a mess now, for all I know."

"I'd like to take a look. Could I contact the owner?"

"Let me talk to Mr. Baird. I'm not sure he's even interested in using it as a rental. Right now, this whole strip of shops is in a bit of trouble.... But then, you don't need to hear about that."

He gave her a friendly smile, just as she had given him. The "bit of trouble" phrase caught her curiosity.

"Drop back tomorrow," Otis said, "and I'll let you know what he says."

"Thanks. I'd really appreciate that."

Mac wandered back down the aisle, and she called to him. His grin stretched across his rosy cheeks. She held out her hand, and he rushed to her side. After thanking the man again, she and Mac left the shop, her spirit lifting with hope.

Jordan hung the last pieces of cotton to dry. For the past two days he'd worked with batik wax-painting to design patterns on the cloth for an Edo warrior kite. Though beautiful, the design work was arduous, and the buyer would pay dearly for the creation.

Dooley nuzzled his nose against Jordan's leg, then rushed toward the door. With the family down the beach, Jordan hated to give the dog free rein. Rather than taking a chance, he tucked the leash in his pocket, opened the door and stepped outside, needing some fresh air himself. Dooley darted toward the lake. Jordan scanned the water's surface for any poor, unsuspecting ducks that might be lolling on the waves, but none was in sight.

At the water's edge, Jordan turned left, then halted. Maybe today, for a change, he'd walk east along the beach.

Who are you kidding?

He shook his head. He knew full well why he was headed that way. Dooley sped off ahead, and he hurried behind the dog, glancing, now and again, into the woods, for the dilapidated cabins.

He slowed his gait as they reached what he suspected was

the area. A child's laugh drifted from the trees, and Jordan looked through the foliage. Mac waved and lurched down the inclined path toward him.

"Good morning," Jordan said as the boy reached his side.

Mac's gaze drifted from his to Dooley's, and he teetered backward, a look of fright rushing to his face.

"It's okay, Mac. Dooley won't hurt you. Only thing he might do is knock you down trying to give you a big wet kiss." He caught the dog's collar, keeping him close to his side.

"Dooley," Mac repeated, maintaining his distance.

The dog looked at the boy, his tongue hanging from his mouth in a rapid pant. Jordan tightened his hold, monitoring Dooley's movement as the dog strained toward the child.

With caution, Mac garnered courage and stepped toward the dog, his hand outstretched. Dooley shot his tongue forward, dragging a slobbery kiss across Mac's fingers.

The boy's eyes widened, and Jordan expected him to cry out, but instead he laughed and leaned forward. Dooley swiped his tongue along the child's cheek.

"A big wet kiss," Mac said, his eyes twinkling.

Jordan looked back toward the foliage. Would the woman let him play outside without keeping an eye on him? He saw nothing near the cabin. "Where's your mom?"

"Making a kite. Come and see." He grasped Jordan's hand and pulled him toward the grassy path.

"And your father? Where's your dad?"

Mac clung to his fingers with one hand while his free hand pointed skyward. "Up," Max answered. "In heaven. Two fathers...in heaven."

Two fathers? His mind spun, wondering what kind of life this young boy must have experienced. "Two?"

Mac gave an assuring nod. "Come." He beckoned with his free hand. "See my kite." He tugged at Jordan's arm, and, reluctant to hurt the boy's feelings, Jordan followed.

His memory of the cabins was correct. Though the word *ramshackle* had come to mind first, he altered that to *rustic,* out of kindness.

"Mama," Mac called as they neared a cabin nestled in the trees closest to the beach.

In a flash a screen door swung open and the woman faltered in the doorway. "Oh, it's...you." She grinned and stepped outside. "Good morning. Is something wrong?" Her gaze shifted to Mac and returned to Jordan's face.

"No. Mac invited me up to see the kite. I'm sorry. I don't believe I've introduced myself." He forced his hand forward. "Jordan Baird."

Meara chuckled and grasped his fingers. "Glad to learn your name. You've been only the 'kite man' to us, Mr. Baird. I'm Meara Hayden, and this is—"

"Mac. He told me his name the first day we met." He glanced behind her into the shadows of the cabin. "Mac tells me you bought another kite."

"Two kites." Her delicate features curved to a lovely full-lipped smile. "Just to be on the safe side, this time."

Two kites. Two fathers. And he deduced, *two* husbands. Her lilting voice unsettled him, almost like music, and he longed to ask her heritage but muzzled his curiosity. "Do you need any help?"

"I'm not sure." She glanced over her shoulder. "This place isn't elegant, but would you like to step in? You can give me your expert opinion." She pulled the door open. Mac skittered inside and he followed.

In the dusky light, he agreed. The place was not elegant. It was barely passable for this woman and child. He scanned the sagging upholstered sofa and rickety side table while an acrid smell of mildew and cleaning fluid hit his senses.

A bright yellow kite lay across the small Formica kitchen table. He picked it up and studied her amateur workmanship. "Not bad. Looks like you followed directions." He glanced around the room. "How about a tail?"

"I used an old cloth from my car trunk for the last one."

"Let's...fly the kite," Mac decreed, his smile flashing like neon.

"In a minute, Mac. I might have another rag," she continued, looking at Jordan. "Let me see." She stepped toward the door.

"No need." The boy's bright smile motivated Jordan's offer without thinking. "You and your mom follow me. I have plenty of tail cloth at the house." He could have bit his tongue, but it was too late. The boy tugged at his heart like wind caught on a kite. Mac grabbed his hand, leading him back down the trail, and the intriguing woman—Meara—followed them.

Dooley, minding his manners, trotted beside the boy as if he understood that he must behave. Mac's grin swiveled like a weather vane in a wavering wind between Jordan and the dog. The child captivated his spirit.

In the heat a sweet scent permeated the breeze. Jordan glanced for wildflowers along the way, but Meara stepped into his line of vision. And he knew. The scent was hers, a fascinating aroma lingering in the heated air. Delicate and sweet, the woman pried into his closed heart with a new awareness. How long had it been since he'd allowed a woman in his thoughts or wanted a woman in his arms? He pulled his attention to the sand and the water, anything to drive away the longing.

Relieved, Jordan watched the house appear, but as he neared, the Private Property sign glowed in the sun like chastening neon. With what he hoped was a subtle yank, he jerked it from the sand, tossing it into the tall grass. He'd retrieve it later for the trash. But a quick glance at Meara's grinning face told him she'd witnessed every embarrassing move.

At the door, he invited them onto the porch. "I'm thirsty. How about you? Can I offer you a soda?"

"No, thank you, I think—"

"Okay," Mac countered. "A soda."

Meara closed her open mouth and aimed a warning look at Mac.

A chuckle rose in Jordan's chest, but he clamped his lips.

She gave an embarrassed grin. "I guess we'll trouble you for a soda, if you don't mind."

"Have a seat," he said, and went inside for the soft drinks. Mac chattered behind him. Surprised, he glanced over his shoulder and saw Mac at his heels. Despite having the boy underfoot, he made quick work of the tumblers and soda cans. "Here," he said, pouring Mac's drink into the glass, "you can carry your own."

Obviously pleased, the boy concentrated on the liquid and headed back to the porch.

"Careful, Mac," Meara said when he reached her.

"He's okay," Jordan said, and handed her a glass. He set his drink on a small side table and, before joining her, grabbed a handful of colorful tails from a storage box.

When he turned, Mac stood nearby, gazing with his trusting eyes at the strips of cloth.

"Okay, Mac, here are all the colors I have," he said, dangling the strands in front of the child.

Mac's face filled with wonder as he gazed at the bright strips. "Yellow, red, blue, purpo—"

"That's purple, Mac," Meara corrected. "Pur…ple."

He repeated the word, mimicking her careful enunciation.

Selecting purple and yellow, Mac handed Jordan the cloth, who knotted and attached them to the end of the kite.

"Ready?"

Mac gave an emphatic nod and Jordan led his guests to the beach. He located a log and upended it to form a stool for Meara. Then, explaining as simply as he could, Jordan described the major issues of aerodynamics. Mac listened as if he understood while Jordan demonstrated.

Meara watched him, her face as animated as Mac's. Losing himself in the process, Jordan moved closer and wrapped his hands around the boy's to give him the feeling of the tug and pull of the wind on the string.

But time after time, with each attempt to launch it, Jordan saved the nose-diving kite from a watery death. "You know, Mac, maybe you need to be one more year older. This kite-flying isn't easy."

"Isn't…easy," Mac repeated, giving his trademark nod. Then he grinned, grabbing his mother's hand. "Mom can fly the kite."

"'Mom,'" Meara said. "What happened to 'Mama'?"

"Mom," Mac said again with a laugh, squeezing her hand.

"I think that's my fault," Jordan said, recalling he'd used the term earlier. "How about it? Can I show you what to do?"

Meara lifted her eyebrows as if questioning his confidence. "We shall see."

Quickly repeating the process, he held the ball of string and kite toward her, but she hesitated.

"Let me take off my shoes. I'll trip myself up, otherwise." Slipping off her sandals, she dug her feet into the sun-warmed sand. "Feels good," she said, reaching out for the kite and string.

In a moment she was rushing along the sand, the kite extended into the air. At a gleeful laugh from Mac, it lifted from her hand and sailed upward. The boy patted Jordan's arm, then clapped his hands and bounced with pleasure.

Jordan kept his eyes riveted to the kite while Meara released the string, but suddenly a gust of wind flipped the kite into a nosedive. Panic rose on her face, and he dashed forward, wrapping his arms around her from behind and manipulating the string. With a pull and release of tension, the kite righted itself and sailed skyward again.

Her sweet, fascinating aroma filled his senses, and her soft hair brushed against his cheek. He moved back quickly, though he longed to stay in the embrace, holding her close and feeling her warm skin against his arms.

She turned to him, a flush highlighting her ivory skin. "I almost lost it again," she said, her eyes bright with life and her lips posed in a rich smile so close he could almost taste the sweetness.

A deep breath escaped him as he attempted to control his thudding heart. *You're a fool, Jordan. What are you doing?* "There's no 'almost' in baseball or kite-flying. A save is a save." He forced a lighthearted look to his face, but panic rose in his chest.

"But if you hadn't been here, I'd be back in the cabin building Mac's third kite."

"Let me show you what to do when you have another problem like that." He moved in again, knowing he was working the situation, taking advantage of her nearness. He had to stop, but the sound of her voice covered the warnings that raged in his head.

He took her hand and the string, demonstrating the tug and pull of the wind, but most of all, he reveled in the warmth of her delicate hand against his and the sound of her laughter in his ear.

"Me," Mac called.

Jordan swung around, realizing they had all but forgotten the boy. The kite was his, not theirs. He chided himself on his self-centered urges. "Come here, Mac. You hold the string, and I'll help you."

Not thinking, Jordan opened his arms to the boy, and his heart all but plunged to the ground. Grief washed over him like the waves that covered the shining rocks on the beach. With Mac in his arms, Robbie's image rose before him like a living phantom—a moving, loving memory that wrenched his entire being. A sob rose in his throat, and he coughed to cover the horrible reality that battered his happiness to deepest pain.

Mac turned his head, giving him a curious look, and Jordan forced a smile to his lips—so compacted that they felt numb. "How you doing?"

"Good," he whispered.

"You sure are."

With Meara watching from her log stool, they let the kite soar overhead for a time, until Mac's attention wavered.

Then, with Jordan's help, they reeled in the string, bringing the kite to a safe landing. Meara clapped her hands, then opened her arms as Mac ran to her.

"Good job."

"Yep," he agreed. "I flew the kite."

"And one of these days, you'll do it all by yourself, Mac," Jordan said, standing above them. "Now remember, if you have any trouble, let me know. If there's one thing I know, it's kites." That's about it, too, he thought, angry at himself for allowing his emotions to reach the surface.

"It was kind of you, Mr. Baird. Mac and I both appreciate your help."

Meara's gentle face caught him off guard again.

"Jordan, please, and if you don't mind, I'll call you Meara."

"Not at all," she said as her lashes lowered shyly for a heartbeat.

"It's a beautiful name. Where did you get it?" He looked at her with longing, marveling at the mysterious aura that emanated from her.

A grin crept to her lips. "From my mother."

"Hmm?" he asked, not understanding.

"My name. My mother gave it to me." Her grin widened to a smile.

"Right, but I mean, what kind of a name is it?"

"I'm being silly. I knew what you meant." She drew her shoulders as if surprised she'd allowed herself the lighthearted moment. "It's Irish. My parents were born in Ireland like I was."

"Ah, so that's the lilt I hear in your voice."

She tilted her head upward. "Lilt? I didn't know I had one."

"It's lovely, really, like your name. Like music."

"Thank you. Meara means 'happy.'" A distant look rose in her eyes, and her face filled with a kind of sadness.

"Happy? And are you?" he asked, wondering why he had posed such a personal question. "I'm sorry. I shouldn't have spoken like that."

Her gaze drifted to the ground, then upward. "No, you're being honest. I am...sometimes...like today with the kites." She nodded. "Today, I was happy." She reached toward Mac, who held the kite close to his chest. "We need to be running along. You've given us too much of your time. Thank you."

She gazed at her son. "Say thank-you, Mac."

The child lifted his excited gaze. "Thank you," he said.

"You're welcome. And you, too, Mac."

They headed down the beach, hand in hand, and Jordan turned toward the house, tugging at every fiber of his good sense. How many times must he caution himself and still not listen? This woman and child needed too much, and he had nothing to give anyone. He was scarred, scarred to his core. His capacity for love had burned away the day God took his family, the day guilt and grief scorched every strand of his being...his spirit.

He tucked his thoughts back where they belonged, deep inside. No time for mourning now. He needed to face life, learn to live in the world again, not for love or family, but just to get through each day. He'd abandoned his career and lived like a hermit far too long. Good old Otis did the pickup and delivery, while he hid from the world building kites. And what was he hiding from? Memories? A person can't hide from those. He'd tried.

Raising his eyes, Jordan saw Otis standing outside the front door. He hailed him with a wave.

"Okay, this time I knocked," Otis said with a good-natured grin. "That didn't work any better than the doorbell." He chuckled, and Jordan patted him on the back.

"Sorry, I was down here helping a young man fly a kite."

"Now, why doesn't that surprise me?"

Jordan gave him a fleeting grin. "So what can I do for you? Hadn't expected you today."

"No, I was passin' by and thought I'd stop in. I have a question for ya. And by the way, I checked out the zoning board. Looks like the church is a few feet clear of the property restriction limit, so that doesn't help us one bit."

"I'm sorry to hear that." He'd hoped the board might solve the problem without further action. Now he'd have to give the issue more thought. "Come in," he said, holding open the screen.

Otis stepped inside but stayed by the door. "This won't take a minute."

"Sure you don't want to sit?"

"No, the wife's probably wondering where I am. She's expectin' me home. I had a question from this woman and son who came by the shop a couple times. First time lookin' for those cheap kites. I sent her to the gift shop. Anyway, she passed by again and came in. Her boy is a charmer and loves kites."

Curious, Jordan's stomach tightened.

"She's lookin' for a rental. Happened to mention it, and I thought about the apartment above the shop. You have any interest in renting out the place? She's alone with the boy and could probably use a cheap rental."

Jordan stuck his hands in his pockets, trying to decide how to ask the question. "Do you know her name?"

"Nope. The boy's name is Mac. He introduced himself to me like a little man. Down Syndrome boy, but bright as a new penny."

Jordan's tensed shoulders rose and relaxed as he released a blast of pent-up air. "Can you guess what boy I was helping with the kite a few minutes ago?"

Otis snapped to attention. "Mac?"

Jordan nodded.

"You don't say."

"They're renting a cabin down the beach. Those rustic ones."

"She said they were down the road. Never thought you'd know her. Funny thing, I mentioned your name. She didn't act like she knew you at all."

He shook his head. "We introduced ourselves today." Curious. She hadn't shown she recognized his name. He gave a mental shrug. "I met them one day when the boy saw me kite-flying. Then Dooley knocked the woman over on the beach yesterday and we chatted a minute."

"You sure know how to win friends and influence people, don't you."

Otis's words held more truth than he knew. "I don't seem to have the knack, Otis."

He gave a soft chuckle. "So what about the apartment? I haven't seen it in a long time. Not sure what shape it's in. I told her to drop by, and I'd let her know."

"How about checking it out. I don't want to rent a firetrap to anyone."

"Sure thing. Might even have the missus look it over. You know, from a woman's point of view."

"Do you have a key for the place?"

"I think so. It should be on the ring." Otis pulled a set of keys from his pocket and eyed them. "Check this one out if you would. I think that's it."

Jordan took the key and burrowed through a drawer until he found a set of tagged keys. He matched it against the other. "That's it, Otis."

"Good. By the way, I mentioned earlier that I posted the Help Wanted in the window. Nothin' yet. Darla can work only another week or so. I'll need at least a part-timer."

"Whatever you need, Otis. Run an ad in the paper if you want to."

Otis stepped backward, his hand against the screen-door handle. "I'll check the apartment in the morning."

Jordan gave him a nod, and Otis headed back to his car.

Standing with a full view of the lake, Jordan gazed out at the glinting sun hanging low in the sky. Sparkles of gold and copper bounced on the waves. If he thought Lila's God really cared one iota for him, he'd believe the Lord was working in his life. Meara and Mac had walked into his walled-up world, and for the first time in years, life seemed tolerable. More than tolerable. He found himself looking down the beach, wishing he'd see Mac's smiling face and hear Meara's soft, lilting voice.

Chapter Four

The next morning Meara sat on the beach, longing for Jordan to stroll past taking Dooley for a walk. But only squawking gulls and lapping waves—and Mac—disturbed her silence. She grinned at the child making fortlike mounds in the sand and singing in his sweet voice a repetitive tune with lyrics only a mother could love.

"Dig the sand and dig the sand. Dig the sand and make a hole. Dig the sand and make a hole. Make a hole and dig the sand," he sang.

Listening, she recognized the tune was one she'd taught him, "Jesus Loves Me." To laugh or scream was her only way to handle his repetitiveness. She chuckled at the endless monotony. How could she do otherwise? Mac enjoyed music and loved to sing. Though he was cheated in one way, God had given him a gift.

Her heart tugged as she studied her son. He'd been cheated, and she would be, too...one day when he was gone. *Life expectancy.* She reeled, remembering the doctor's words. It would be shortened, he had said. Tears found her eyes. She pushed them away with angry fingers.

Not her son. Not Mac. Life expectancy had nothing to do with God's will. If she had anything to do about it, God's will would be a long life for Mac, if...

Mac's clear voice crooned the words again. Meara dragged her saddened thoughts upward and glanced for the fourth time in the direction of Jordan's house, hoping. Her vision reached the curve in the shoreline. Nothing. Why he interested her, she had no idea. She recalled the day they met. He had been rude and abrupt. But since that day, he had softened and had shown kindness to Mac and to her. And beneath Jordan's rough exterior, she suspected he was as vulnerable as she. Though she'd tried to read the hidden message in his brooding eyes, he had blocked it behind a wall of silence.

She rose from the sand chair and took a cautious step into the water. The sun's warmth had yet to raise the temperature of the lake, and she shivered as her foot sank into the frigid surf, jolting her senses. Yet she needed a jolt. She had been protected too long from everything, including living.

"Mac, want to walk in the water?" she called.

He shook his head without a break in his song.

"Don't go anywhere, then. I'm going for a swim."

With one rapid motion, she dived into the water, her body tingling with exhilaration. It had been forever since she'd gone swimming—until this past week. How many empty years had passed since she'd walked along a beach and watched the sun sink into a deep purple horizon? Or watched the birds flying free—the way she felt today? Free and optimistic...and happy. She bounced to her feet, feeling the sandy bottom against her toes. She wanted to yell, sing out like Mac.

Seeing her son playing with contentment on the shore, she felt her heart squeeze and tears appear behind her eyes. They had lived like prisoners in the Hayden mansion. Their presence had brought discomfort and shame to the arrogant, wealthy family. Life had, for once, turned the tables on their elaborate plans.

Following the death of Dunstan's childless wife, his parents had pushed their only heir, Dunstan Alfred Hayden, to woo and marry Meara MacAuley for the sole purpose of an heir. And what did Meara give him? A child with Down Syndrome. And who did they blame? Her. Her Irish heritage, her lack of education and her awkward ways.

Had they considered Dunstan's age? He was more than twice her twenty-seven years. She had been foolishly flattered—encouraged by her cousin to marry the wealthy man. "You can stay in America," Alison had said. "We'll be such friends." But instead, she, too, had turned her back when Mac was born, perhaps feeling to blame for arranging Meara's introduction to Dunstan.

Often Meara wondered why God had allowed those terrible things to happen to her. She'd been strong in her faith back then. She'd convinced herself that Dunstan glided into her life because God had planned it. He offered her a world she'd never known: wealth, security...and love. Or so she had thought. But Meara had been entirely wrong. Without love and tenderness, a baby-making machine was what she had become. She'd been the means to procreate, and once the child lived inside her, Dunstan might as well have vanished from her life. Once Mac was born, things became worse. She'd prayed and asked God "why," but no answer came to her—until she looked at Mac. Her child was God's gift and her special challenge. Meara clung to that belief.

No matter. Those days were over. Never again would she put herself in that position. Never again would she fall in love and allow her son to be hurt and abandoned...and let herself be hurt and abandoned.

Meara had new experiences awaiting her, and she prayed they would be blessings. Meara lifted her gaze toward heaven, then pulled her thoughts to the present and dove again into the clear, calm water, this time feeling less chilled.

The pleasant afternoon sun lay upon her arms, and she gauged from its position that it was nearly noon. She dragged her legs through the water to shore. Today she would drive into town to check the apartment. Hopefully Otis Manning would have some information.

"Hello, there," Otis said with an easy smile as they came through the shop door.

Mac shot forward, extending his hand in greeting. Otis grinned and grasped the child's hand in a hearty shake. "And how's the kite-flying, son?"

Mac poked himself in the chest. "Me? Nope. But Mama's good."

"She is, huh? And why can't you fly a kite?" He bent his pleasant face toward Mac's.

"Too small. Mr....Baird said...maybe a year."

"Well, if anyone knows about kite-flying, he's your man. You were talking to the horse's mouth." Otis patted the child's head.

Mac let out a loud chortle. “Horse’s mouth.” He poked at Meara.

She rolled her eyes at Otis, and the elderly man grimaced.

“That’s only an expression, Mac,” Meara said. “He means Mr. Baird knows what he’s talking about.”

“Okay,” Mac said, eyeing the kites. The “horse’s mouth” was forgotten as he wandered through the shop.

“Sorry about that,” Otis whispered. “I’d better watch what slips off this tongue with that young ’un around.”

He looked so downtrodden, forgiveness was easy. “No problem. I do it myself.”

A relieved expression swept over his face. “So I s’pose you’re anxious to hear about the apartment.”

“Yes. Did you talk to the owner?”

“Sure did. Jordan told me to give the place a once-over and—”

“Jordan?” Hearing the name, she stopped breathing for a moment.

“The owner. Jordan Baird. I understand you’ve met.” He let loose a quiet chuckle. “Met head-on from what I’m told. He tells me Dooley gave you a topple. Jordan sure has amusing ways to knock a woman off her feet. Well, at least Dooley does.”

“Jordan owns this shop?” A contained breath burst from her lungs. “The other day Mac noticed a kite that we figured he had made. But I thought maybe he sold them to you.”

“Jordan made all the kites in this shop. Every last one of them.” His arm made a broad sweep of the surroundings. “Right pretty, aren’t they?”

Meara craned her neck, gazing around the room with a

new appreciation. "You mean every single kite is handmade...by him?"

"None other. He's got quite a talent, for a college professor."

College professor. She reeled again. What else would she learn about this man? Then her heart sank. No college campus was nearby that she knew about. "Then, he only lives here in the summer." She faltered while finding the breath to speak. "I didn't realize."

"Oh, no. He doesn't teach anymore. Something happened. He doesn't talk about it." He dragged his hand along his jaw and chin, then pressed his forefinger against his lips and shook his head. "Avoids the subject. I only figured it out putting bits and pieces together. Must have been a tragedy."

Like a fist, pity and sorrow smacked her in the stomach. "A tragedy? I'm so sorry. I can't imagine—"

"Nothin' we need talk about. It's his private affair, and I think that's the way he wants it. I shouldn't have said anything." He shook his head. "Me and my big mouth."

"Please, Otis, don't worry. I won't say anything." With her finger, she made a small cross over her heart. "I promise."

"Oh, I know you wouldn't want to hurt him." He quieted for a moment as if in thought. Then, rejuvenated, he clapped his hands and rubbed them together. "So, let's get on with business. He told me to go up and take a look-see. I even dragged the wife upstairs. It's not bad. Needs a cleaning, but otherwise, it just might work for you." He beckoned her to follow.

With her mind still sorting Jordan's possible tragedies, Meara stuck close to Otis's heels. As she reached the back of the congested shop, she waved to Mac, and they passed through the outside doorway and up an enclosed staircase to the second floor.

Through the windows of the enclosure, Meara viewed the wide parking lot of the ferry landing and the lake beyond. With the official summer still a month away, the lot held many empty spaces. She guessed that in the thick of summer when the public schools let out, the slots would be packed with sightseers.

As they neared the top landing, sounds came from the open doorway. Stepping inside, Meara was greeted by a smiling, rosy face framed by a halo of white hair.

"So, this must be Meara and Mac." The woman scurried across the room, one arm spread open wide and the other sporting a broom. "I'm Nettie, Otis's wife. Come in and see the place."

Meara gazed at the bright, cozy kitchen with apricot walls lined with cabinets, a long Formica counter and a small maple table surrounded by four chairs.

"The kitchen is nice," Nettie said. "Lots of cupboards. Someone must have remodeled not too many years ago. Go ahead. Go inside." She shooed them through the next doorway.

Meara stepped into the large living room. Tall windows in front looked out on the busy street below. An arch opened on the right to a hallway with a front and back bedroom and bath in between. Exactly what they needed…at least, for the time being.

"You've cleaned," Meara said, looking at the gleaming table next to a love seat and the shiny windows.

"Oh, not much. Just dusted and swept," she said.

Meara chuckled, adding, "And ran the vacuum, washed

the windows and…" She stepped into the bathroom. "You cleaned the tub, sink, everything."

"Makes a place look more homey when it's not covered with dust."

"Well, thank you so much." Meara longed to give her a hug.

Otis stepped beside his wife and slid an arm around her shoulder. "I've got quite a woman here. Always doin' somethin' for someone. Over at the church, she's got her nose in every committee. Visits the sick, cares for the altar, attends Bible study, works on the dinners. You name it."

"You're a blessed man, Otis," Meara agreed.

"S'pose I am." He gave Nettie a loving hug and strode across the room to the front windows.

"What do you think?" Nettie asked.

"I think it'll do fine for us," Meara said. "But I need to pick up a few things before we can move in. I'll make a list of necessities before I leave."

"Now, you check with us first," Otis offered. "We got a pile of furniture sittin' in the basement and all just lookin' for a home."

"He means that, Meara." Nettie gave her a warm smile. "Such a pretty name," she added.

"Thank you," Meara said. "Both of you are too kind." Recalling the years she had rarely heard a kind or loving word, she felt about to bust with gratitude. She looked across the room at Mac and a twinge of sadness ran through her. He'd never experienced a loving father or grandfather.

A sound drew her attention. Mac had his nose pressed against the single window that overlooked the other single-story shops. "Kites," he called, pointing wildly through the pane.

Meara joined him and witnessed a multitude of kites sailing high above them from the small park between the road and the ferry parking lot. “I suppose you like this apartment, huh, Mac?”

“I like it,” he said, keeping his focus fastened to the view outside.

Meara turned to Otis. “Before I get too excited, I’d better hear what he’s asking for rent.”

“We didn’t discuss that, fully.” Otis pinched his lip. “He said the place has been sittin’ empty for so long that five dollars would be more than he was gettin’ before.” He chortled.

“Yes, but I expect it’ll be more than five dollars. I’d have to pay a fortune anywhere else.”

“I think two hundred a month should do it.”

Meara gaped. “Two hundred. No. You mean four hundred.”

“Cat’s whiskers,” Otis said with a grin. “Two hundred is about right.”

“Oh, I feel—”

“You feel like you’ll say, ‘It’s a deal,’” he said.

She nodded and smiled. “Mac, you think we should move in here?”

Mac giggled. “Cat’s whiskers,” he said.

Otis stepped back. “Oops! There I go again.”

“Otis Manning,” Nettie said, shaking her finger at him. “I’d better wash both your mouths out with soap.”

Bubbling with giggles, Mac hurried to Otis’s side and wrapped his arm around him. “Both get our mouths washed out, don’t we?”

“Looks like it, son,” Otis said, rumpling Mac’s hair.

* * *

With her spirits lifted, Meara drove down the lane to their cabin. Soon they'd be in a more comfortable setting, but first she had work to do and so much to buy. Supplies and linens, dishes and pans, and beds. The Mannings had taken her list and had said they would gather up what they had, and Nettie had said the church was having a rummage sale the next day. She could pick up a few things there, perhaps.

She parked, and Mac flung open the door, anxious to get outside. He'd been in the shop and apartment much of the afternoon, and his energy was straining for release.

As she unlocked the cabin, a new thought struck like a hammer. She would be five miles away from Jordan. From what she could tell, he went into town for groceries and supplies, but little else. And she had no reason to come here anymore.

Her thoughts clogged like a bad drain. Why did she care about Jordan? He'd been kind to Mac...and to her. Picturing herself sprawled on the sand by Dooley's exuberance, she smiled. Life in the cabin had offered her fresh air. Sunshine. A new beginning. Forget Jordan. She and Mac would create a new life in town.

Meara tossed her purse on the sofa, locked the door and dropped the keys into her pocket. She would thank Jordan for the apartment. This time she had a reason to speak with him. She and Mac followed the pine-shaded path to the sunny beach. The glimmering lake rolled in like blue corrugated paper sprinkled with gold dust.

She drew in a deep, refreshing breath. Her life was about to begin, a new adventure. Her life before... She stopped herself. Memories rushed in like a river, washing away the joy that she had gathered on the banks. She did not need self-pity. Her new adventure had opened doors she'd never known before. Hope and happiness flooded her.

Mac toddled along beside her while she reviewed her plans for the coming days. Tomorrow morning she would go to the church, and then she could shop for the other things she needed. Perhaps she'd go into Cheboygan. The town was larger and had well-stocked shops. But thinking of Mac, her spirits were dampened. She'd kept him bound up in the apartment all morning, and tomorrow would be the same.

As they rounded the tree-lined curve in the shore, a long, disjointed kite drifted in the sky above the water ahead of them, its sections undulating on the lake breeze. Her pulse skipped. Mac saw it, too, and let out a joyful cry. They hurried ahead, and the distant figure of Jordan grew nearer until they were at his side.

"What is that?" Meara asked, gasping for breath.

Mac's face skewed, and a giggle rose. "A kite, Mama!"

She dropped her hand on his shoulder. "Yes, a kite, Mac, but what kind?" She pointed at the sections rising and falling with the air current. "See how it moves on the wind." She looked to Jordan for the answer.

"It's centipede style," he responded. "It's created in sections." He aimed Mac toward the front of the kite and pointed. "See the head, Mac? It's a dragon. When the Chinese fly this kite for their New Year's celebration, they're asking the gods for good luck."

"God?" Mac said. "Ask Jesus for good luck."

Jordan raised an eyebrow. "No, they…well, something like that." His shoulders tensed, and he tightened his rein on the thick string as the kite looped on the billowing wind.

Mac clapped his hands. "Me. Me."

"This one is hard to manage, Mac. I'll let you try a smaller kite another time. Okay?"

Disappointment registered on Mac's face, but he nodded, his focus still glued to the mesmerizing kite.

Jordan tightened his grip and wound the thick string, bringing the lovely creation back to earth. The kite soared and plummeted as he manipulated the cord. Finally, he took backward steps to avoid the water, and Meara shot forward to grasp the kite as it dipped toward the damp, shell-speckled sand.

"A save," she called, smiling over her shoulder at Jordan, then returning her gaze to the amazing centipede. Its body was sectioned, and the colorful green-and-red cloth was connected with some kind of plastic tubing. The dragon's head appeared painted, rather than dyed, in blues and greens with blazing red eyes.

"It's wonderful," Meara said, lugging the cumbersome kite toward him. "It must have taken you forever to make this."

In awe, Mac clung to the centipede's red-rimmed tail. "I helped," he said, settling his section of the kite in Jordan's outstretched hand.

"You're a big help, Mac. Thank you."

The fluttering wind tugged at the taut fabric, and Meara struggled to keep it close to her side until she could place the burden in Jordan's arms. He gathered the cloth-covered frame and headed toward the house.

Mac followed but Meara remained behind until Jordan's voice reached her ears. "Come up to the house, Mac, and I'll show you what I'm working on now."

The child glanced over his shoulder, beckoning her to

follow. Wisdom told her to hightail it back to the safety of the cabin. In Jordan's company, life brightened as brilliantly as his kites. But she saw no future in it, only a deeper loneliness for having known him. Yet Mac's eager face loomed before her, and she pushed back her fears and hurried up the path.

With Mac manning the door, Jordan wrestled the large, jointed kite onto the porch. Managing his heart was as difficult. Each time he saw the boy he ached and yearned to be the father he could never be. And when he gazed at the delicate, fiery-haired woman, he felt a longing he couldn't explain. If he had a brain, he would discourage their entrance into his house and into his life.

Hearing the ruckus, Dooley bounded to the porch from inside the house. In a flash of fear, Mac stepped backward as Meara drifted through the doorway. In a heartbeat, Mac's chin jutted forward, and with renewed courage, he stood his ground while Dooley's wet tongue drenched his cheek.

"More kisses," Mac said, his voice a mixture of fear and laughter.

"Dooley, down," Jordan commanded. "Let the boy be." He grasped the dog's collar and pulled him away as the setter strained to give Mac one final slurp.

Jordan gave a decisive tug on his collar, and Dooley obeyed, coiling himself on the porch rug and panting as his eyes focused on Mac.

The boy kept himself aimed at the dog. "Good dog," Mac said with a noticeable lack of confidence.

With amusement brightening her face, Meara covered her curving mouth, obviously hiding a chuckle, and wrapped a protective arm around Mac's shoulder. "Dooley likes you, Mac. He thinks you're pretty special."

"Yeah," Mac said. But his positive comment didn't disguise his real attitude as he backed against Meara's leg.

Jordan's mind and emotions raced as he watched them. "Have a seat." He motioned to the cushioned wicker furniture. "How about something cold to drink? I have lemonade. Anyone interested?"

"Me," Mac said. "I like...lemonade."

"And how about you?" His gaze drifted to Meara, who sank into the wicker seat with his question.

"Lemonade's fine, if it's not too much trouble."

"No trouble," he said, turning away and heading into the house. The lemonade was no trouble, but she was. She tugged at his emotions as powerfully as a kite on an escalating wind. The truth rose in his thoughts. He had to reel in his heartstrings before they broke or knotted in his rising panic. He'd had too much heartache. He couldn't bear any more. And love? It had been buried with his family. He had no more to give. Jordan knotted his heart to stop his thoughts, poured glasses of the tangy liquid and carried them back to the porch.

Dooley had edged forward, but now, relaxed and smiling, Mac leaned forward and petted the dog's back. Jordan shook his head. The dog didn't mind him any better than he minded his cautious inner voice.

"Here you go," Jordan said, handing a glass to Meara and one to Mac. He settled into a wicker chair and stared out through the rust-pocked screen to gain control of himself. Meara's musical voice wrenched him back.

"I came down for a reason, by the way. I wanted to thank

you for letting us rent the apartment. It's perfect for now, until we decide what we're going to do. But I wonder if..."

Her eyes widened, and she seemed to struggle for the right words. "If Otis didn't make a mistake. I don't think he quoted me the correct rent, and I wondered...what you had in mind."

Jordan dragged his index finger through the condensation that had formed on his glass. With control, he lifted his gaze to hers. "What did Otis tell you?"

"But...I want you to tell me."

"You can't remember?"

She blinked. "No, I remember. He said two hundred dollars, but I don't think—"

"Yes, two hundred. That's what I told him. Is that too much?" He kept his voice steady to cover his falsehood.

A flush rose on her fair skin. "Too much? No, it's not enough."

Jordan studied the pinkish blush that colored her cheeks. The summer sun had tugged a smattering of freckles from hiding and the faint brown flecks spattered her nose and forehead. He studied the pattern, thinking of the dot-to-dot pictures he had drawn as a child.

Meara nailed him with her steady gaze. "Why are you smiling?" Her soft lilt sharpened as her shoulders tensed, and she pulled them erect. "You think I'm foolish for asking. I don't want charity. I can pay my own way."

Her words jolted him from his reverie.

"Charity has nothing to do with it! That apartment has been sitting empty since I bought the shop. The rent is pure profit."

"But you have to consider the utilities—the electricity and water and gas."

He ran his fingers through his hair. "I suppose, then, I'm only making one hundred and fifty a month profit. Really, don't worry about it. You're doing me a favor." His mouth tugged toward a grin. He focused on Mac, who had shifted his petting to the dog's head. "I have someone else to pet Dooley instead of me all the time. Mac's a great dog-sitter."

Mac let out a widemouthed laugh. "Dog-sitter," he repeated.

Dooley rose and plopped his head in Mac's lap, and the child leaned down and pressed a loud smacking kiss on his brow.

Meara opened her mouth to speak, then closed it. She shifted her gaze and stared through the screen. "Well, thanks, then, if you're sure." She heaved a great sigh. "I have so much to do. Nettie told me about a church sale tomorrow, and what I can't pick up there, I'll have to buy in Cheboygan, I suppose."

"That's probably the best place to shop," Jordan agreed, thinking of the stores in Mackinaw. "Most stores in town are for tourists. But if you're looking for a seashell ashtray, you can probably get one next door to the kite shop."

Meara's tense face shifted to a smile. "I'll keep that in mind, though I have little use for an ashtray."

Feeling more relaxed, he grinned back. Thinking about her lone car and no trailer full of furnishings, his curiosity was aroused. "You don't have anything from your old home?"

"No, nothing except our clothing. And a couple of Mac's toys. The furniture wasn't mine."

Nothing was hers? She rented, then? Maybe those two husbands Mac had mentioned were wastrels or gamblers. Sadness caught in his chest. What a depressing life she and Mac must have had.

Her face brightened. "Otis said they had a few pieces of furniture stored in their basement. He'll let me know tomorrow what he has that I can use."

"So tomorrow begins your furniture hunt. What will you do with Mac?" His stomach churned. Why had he asked?

Her gaze drifted toward the child, then to him. "He'll have to go with me, I suppose. I dragged him around today and he did okay. He'll manage."

"A boy needs to play. Bring him down in the morning and I'll keep an eye on him." He swallowed the knot that rose to his throat. Why couldn't he control his mouth? "Would you like to help me build a kite tomorrow, Mac?"

"Sure. Build a kite." With enthusiasm, Mac flung his head forward and back.

"Don't knock yourself out, Mac," Meara said, shifting her gaze to Jordan. "Are you sure? He'll be fine with me."

"I'm sure." Fool. "Mac'll have more fun making a kite than shopping. Trust me."

"I do trust you. And thanks. To be honest, I hated to make him spend the day in captivity again."

She set her empty glass on the nicked side table, and before he could offer her a refill, she glanced at her wristwatch and stood.

"I'd better get back. It's getting late, and I'm sure you have lots to do."

He rose and looked at Mac. "I'll show you the new kite tomorrow. Okay, Mac?"

"Okay. Tomorrow," the boy said, slipping from the chair.

Dooley rose and stretched his legs, the muzzle of his nose pressing against Mac's leg. The boy eyed the dog and wiped the damp spot with his hand. "Down, Dooley," he said in a commanding voice that mimicked Jordan's. The dog peered at him and, in slow motion, lowered himself to the floor.

"Good job, Mac," Jordan said. "First time I've known Dooley to listen to anyone but me."

Mac grinned. "I'm a dog-sitter."

"And I'm a Mac-sitter." Strangely warmed, he tousled the child's hair and followed them to the door. "See you in the morning, then."

"Thanks," Meara repeated, and taking Mac's hand, she headed down the path to the beach. With a final wave, she turned toward the cabin.

Jordan watched them until they rounded the bend, still wondering why he'd agreed to watch Mac. "Just curiosity," he said aloud. He wanted to know more about them. Where had they lived? What kind of men were Mac's two fathers? Tomorrow he could garner some information from the child.

Chapter Five

Meara surveyed the cozy apartment. In only a week, she'd gathered bits and pieces of other people's lives and now called it "home." The Mannings surprised her with much of what she needed, and the church rummage sale filled in the rest. In Cheboygan, she bought bedding and bath linens, a few odds and ends, and that was it.

Footsteps sounded on the outside landing, and Nettie called out a greeting. Meara swung the door open wide, pleased to see the elderly woman who had become, in the past days, an important figure in her life.

Nettie, her plump cheeks glowing from her climb up the stairs, beamed at Meara. Her generous arms were burdened with a large cardboard box.

"My word, Nettie, what do you have there?" Meara reached out and lifted the cumbersome carton from her grasp.

"Another little treasure I found in the basement. Just look."

Meara eased the carton onto the table and pulled open the lid. Inside, special protective wrapping hid the contents.

With care, she lifted an item and pulled off the thin foam covering. Her breath caught in her throat. “China cups,” she whispered, eyeing Nettie’s instigating grin. She picked up the translucent cup spattered with delicate shamrocks and turned it over. “*Real* Belleek. From Ireland. Oh, Nettie, you shouldn’t.”

“Don’t ‘you shouldn’t’ me. I should and I wanted to. Keep looking, dear.” The older woman pulled the box lid back as Meara laid the lovely pieces on the table.

“And the matching teapot,” Meara cried as she lifted it from the box. “But don’t you want to keep this yourself?”

“I have an old teapot I’ve used for years. This one seemed too lovely for just Otis and me. You have years of entertaining ahead of you.”

“But—”

Nettie shushed her. “And since I’ve been listening to that Irish brogue of yours, I knew the charming set belonged to you. No one would love it more.”

Meara cradled the pot against her chest. “I do, Nettie. It takes me back home. Thank you.” She lifted a finger and wiped away the pooling tears that escaped her lashes. “Sit, please. I’ll make us a pot of tea.”

Meara turned on the burner and rinsed the kettle with hot water. “Is Mac behaving himself downstairs?” she asked over her shoulder.

“He’s as good as gold. Don’t you worry about him.”

“I don’t want him to drive Otis crazy, that’s all.” She filled a tea ball with leaves.

Nettie chuckled. “Too late for that. Otis has been crazy for years.”

Her description of Otis caused Meara to smile. She had grown to love the man.

"Really, Otis loves children," Nettie said. "He'll find all kinds of ways to keep the boy busy."

"You're both so kind." The kettle whistled, and Meara poured the hot water into the pot. "I have so many things on my mind, sometimes I don't know which way to turn."

"Something bothering you?"

"Not really." The truth prodded her. "Yes, I suppose it has. I've been thinking about work. Finding a job."

"You'd like a job?"

"*Need* a job," Meara responded as she carried a small tray into the living room and set it on a side table. She sank into an overstuffed flower-print chair. "I'm trying to get by on a small inheritance." She cringed when the words left her mouth. A payoff is what it was. She could hear them. *"We'll pay you to leave our home and our lives."* She had rights as Dunstan's wife, but she could no longer bring herself to live under their scornful eye. She accepted the money, but heated shame shot through her. She'd cheated Mac of his rightful legacy. How could she explain it to anyone? She couldn't.

"A job," Nettie repeated. "That shouldn't be too hard. What about the kite shop? Otis needs another clerk. The woman he has now is leaving. And soon. Look how handy it would be for you."

"I saw the sign in the window, but I wasn't sure what I would do with Mac." A sinking sensation weighted her. "And I'm scared, Nettie. To tell the truth, I haven't worked since I left County Kerry." Images of the small shop floated through her mind, its shelves filled with souvenirs and gift items covered with symbols of Ireland: shamrocks, claddagh, Celtic knots and crosses, leprechauns, and rainbows. "I worked in a small gift emporium."

"Well, a kite shop can't be much different. The hardest work is the tourist season, but you'd be surprised how many interior decorators drop by to look at the kites, even in winter."

"Interior decorators? You mean they use kites in their decor?"

"Surprised me, too. They buy them for business offices and lobbies, restaurants, and even some private homes."

"I'd never have thought of that."

"No. But they do. So how about getting downstairs and talking to Otis. I'm sure he'd be relieved to know he has a good worker. Especially someone he can count on."

Nettie's words marched through her head. *Someone he can count on.* That's what she needed. She hadn't really had a cherished friend, someone to depend on, since she'd left her homeland. She'd been so naive. So hopeful. Yet what a horrible mistake she had made in marrying Dunstan. A mistake...except for Mac.

"And a pound of lean beef," Jordan said, watching the man wrap his ground round in white butcher paper.

A shopping basket jostled him, and he pulled his cart closer to the counter. The aisles were narrow, and being Friday, all the campers and tourists had crowded into the small IGA store for their groceries. Next time he'd go to Food Town in Cheboygan. Today he'd manage, since his list was short. Dog food, mainly.

"Anything else?"

His mind adrift, he lifted his eyes to the butcher.

"Will this be all?" the man asked again.

"Yes, thanks." He dropped the wrapped beef into the basket and maneuvered down the next aisle. Dog food. He stacked the cans beside the carton of orange juice and six-pack of soda. A loaf of bread and that was it.

The checkout line wound down the aisle and around the magazine rack. He eyed the only other register, but that line was as long. He settled back to wait. Nearing the periodicals, he passed a candy display and, instinctively, grabbed a package of suckers. For Mac. The boy entered his mind too often.

His thoughts drifted back to the day Mac had stayed with him while Meara shopped. His reasoned incentive had been as successful as Meara's first attempts at kite-flying. He'd learned little about them—only that Mac and Meara had lived in a big house with his grandparents. He grimaced inwardly, recalling his attempt to pry information from the child.

The customers inched forward, and finally, he paid for the items and pushed his empty cart against the wall. When he veered toward the doorway, his stomach dipped to his shoes. "Hello," he said, gazing into Meara's surprised eyes. "Terrible day to shop."

"I was thinking the same thing." She stepped away from the other checkout counter with two large, unwieldy bags clutched in her arms. One appeared to be escaping her grasp, inching downward toward her legs.

"Let me help you," he said. He slid his arm around the bulkiest sack of groceries, then opened the door and held it with his back.

Meara wrapped both arms around her lone paper bag and

stepped outside, her hair ablaze in the sunshine. "Thanks, but I could have managed."

"I know you could have, but why should you, when I can help?"

The tiny freckles on her nose had darkened in the past week, and he fought the desire to linger on her lovely face, clean and natural without makeup, as always.

She gestured toward her car, and he followed, his pulse skipping as he viewed her trim figure from behind. Petite. Delicate.

When she opened her trunk, she tucked the bag into a corner. He followed her example and propped the larger paper sack beside it. "There you go."

She stood with her hand on the trunk lid, gazing up at him. When her hand swung down, dropping the lid, he winced at the unexpected slam.

Delicate. He nearly chuckled aloud at the paradox. She was strong and capable. He had to remember that. "So, how's the apartment? And Mac?" he asked. And *you,* he said to himself.

She searched his face before answering. "Fine. Everything's fine."

"Good." He wanted to say more, but what? His tongue tied itself in a knot. Get yourself away from here, he thought.

"Otis hired me to work in the shop. Did he tell you?"

"No. No, he didn't, but that's great." He stared at her again, longing to escape, yet not wanting to leave her side.

"Mac loves looking into the park and watching the kites. He'll never want to move."

"I'm pleased he's so happy." With the suggestion of her staying in the area, his chest restricted. Did that make *him* happy? *Happy?* How long had it been since the word entered his thoughts?

"It's comfortable there. And Nettie has become a good friend."

"She's a nice lady." He could barely speak. Meara glowed in the late-afternoon sun, warm and shining…and beautiful.

Her shy gaze caught his. "Would you like to stop by and see the place? And Mac? He'd love to see you, I know. He talks about you all the time."

The child's image rose in Jordan's mind—his trusting face and beaming smile. The picture rent his heart. "Well, I just stopped by to pick up dinner for Dooley." Surprising himself, a grin pulled on his lips. "Sounds like a play or movie. 'Dinner for Dooley.'"

"*Breakfast at Tiffany's,*" she added. "Or *Guess Who's Coming to Dinner?*" She appeared to relax.

Her eyes glinted with amusement, and they warmed him. "I suppose he can wait a few minutes."

"Wait?" She tilted her head quizzically.

"Dooley. He can wait to eat. I'd like to see Mac."

"Good," she said. "Follow me." A laugh bubbled from her throat, and she looked at him with embarrassed eyes. "I suppose you know where the apartment is."

He grinned and headed for his car. He wished his mind and mouth would work out a deal. Cooperation. Maybe compromise. He said one thing and his heart wavered whether it was what he should have said. Too late now. But he could make it a short visit.

Meara's pulse raced as she headed back to the apartment. Though only a week had passed, it seemed like forever since she'd seen Jordan. She glanced in her rearview mirror, admiring his reflection, handsome with his strong jaw and sculptured nose. She admired the wispy strands of graying hair that graced his temple. Though at first glance he looked distinguished, almost aloof, in time his quiet, gentle nature revealed a different image, gracious and vulnerable.

She pulled into the parking lot behind the shop, and Jordan parked alongside. Mac spied her from the back workroom and rushed outside. Though he headed for her, his rubber-soled shoes skidded to a halt when he eyed Jordan. He veered in his direction and stuck out his hand. "Hi, Jordan. Otis said 'horse's mouth.'"

Jordan faltered at Mac's words while laughter rippled from Meara's chest.

"That will take some explaining, I imagine," she said as she lifted the trunk lid.

Jordan ruffled Mac's hair. "Just a little." He returned his gaze to her and reached for the heaviest bag.

Seeing him with Mac, her heart swelled with tenderness. Mac had been fatherless even with a father. No man had tossed him a ball or pitched him a Frisbee. Or had gone outside on a summer day to fly a kite. Nothing…until Jordan.

And now her son idolized him. She winced, thinking how hurt Mac would be when Jordan lost interest or returned to his college life again.

"Come, see my room," Mac said, pulling Jordan along by his fingers.

"That's why I stopped by. And I wanted to say hello."

"Hello," Mac said. "Come and see." He beckoned him to follow, and the two climbed the staircase.

Meara gathered up the second bag and followed them,

her mind wavering between avoiding this man who tugged at her heart or pursuing him for Mac. For Mac? Who are you kidding? she thought. Yet Jordan was a stranger in so many ways. She knew nothing of his life—only vague references to some tragedy that had taken him from his career. Was it a wife? Divorce, perhaps? Or her death? What would cause a man to run away from his familiar surroundings and comfortable life?

She knew why she had run. But in her case not *from* life, but *to* life. She had been without an existence for so long. Her small world had been confined mainly within the walls of the Hayden mansion. *"No, Meara, you stay home with Mac. The excitement will be too much for him." "People stare at the child when you take him out, Meara. Stay home where you belong."* The horrid, remembered words…

"Okay, Mama?"

Mac's voice jolted her from the frightful memories. "What? I didn't hear you."

"Jor-dan said I can come to his house and help build a kite. Can I?"

"Probably, Mac. Let's see when the time comes."

The answer suited him. He swung through the doorway with Jordan in his wake. When she stepped inside, she heard Mac giving him the "five-dollar" tour of the small apartment—Jordan's apartment, no less. But he listened, and his pleasant, throaty voice drifted from Mac's bedroom.

She stored the groceries, then waited in the living room. Within a minute, Jordan came through the doorway.

"It looks like home," he said. "You did good."

She grinned at his playful bad grammar. "Thanks. I'm surprised the furniture looks as together as it does, coming from so many places."

"I'm sure you feel more settled…with a place to live and a job."

Nodding, she motioned to the love seat. "Sit for a minute. Would you like some iced tea? Or a soda?"

He glanced at his watch. "Sure. Thanks. Iced tea sounds fine."

Meara turned toward the kitchen and spotted Mac lingering in the kitchen doorway, watching.

"Mac, you'd better get back downstairs before Otis thinks you're lost, okay?" Meara said, shooing him toward the door.

"I'm not lost. I'm here." He poked his chest.

"I know that, but Otis doesn't. He'll be sending out a search party."

"Party," Mac said, giving them one last ray of his smile before heading back down the staircase.

Meara grabbed the drinks and returned to the living room. Jordan had settled on the love seat, and she handed him a glass, then sank into the chair.

She took a sip and continued their earlier conversation. "I feel at home here, and I'm relieved about the job. Mac can play nearby, and I won't have to worry about him."

"And I mean it, you know. He's welcome at my place, too. I'll let him build a paper kite. He'll enjoy it."

"Probably mess it up, but thanks."

Jordan shot her a pointed frown. "Why 'mess it up'? He can learn…like anyone."

Cold shame poked her conscience. She shouldn't have said that about Mac. But it was true. She worried about his ability to learn. His education. Her thoughts stirred her latest concern. "I'm not sure what I'm going to do with him this fall."

"This fall?" He lifted an inquisitive gaze to hers.

"School."

"Oh, yes." He sipped the tea and continued. "What did Mac do last year?"

"He's been homeschooled with a tutor. But I want him with other children now. He's been hidden away too long."

Jordan's eyes widened. His mouth moved as if to question, but instead, he clamped his jaw. His perplexed gaze searched hers.

Hidden away. She'd said far more than she had meant to. "Do you know anything about the schools around here? Is there a school for…special children? Disabled children."

His gaze stayed riveted to hers. "This is a small town. If there were, I suppose I'd have heard of one."

"I wonder what they do for children who are…children with special needs." Muscles tightened in her neck, and she raised her hand and kneaded the ache. "I should drop by the school offices and talk to someone." She dreaded the tedious job of finding a proper school for Mac. Not because it wasn't important, but because she'd heard horror stories from the Haydens about those schools.

"What about a regular classroom?"

"No, that's not for Mac. I don't want him treated— I don't want him to feel different. Children can be very cruel."

"Some are, I suppose. But Mac's not really disabled in the serious sense of the word."

"What are you talking about?" she snapped. "He has

Down Syndrome. He's a slow learner. To you, he probably looks younger, but he's eight."

"Yes. You told me, but—"

"I want him to have the best education he can." A ragged sigh shuddered from her throat. "I'm sure I'll find something." She didn't want to defend her belief. She'd seen how people treated Mac. How the Haydens treated Mac. She wouldn't allow her son to be rejected or scorned ever again. He needed love and protection.

Jordan looked away and sipped his tea in silence. Meara hesitated, wondering if she'd offended him. He stared at his tumbler.

"I was rude," she said finally. But he didn't understand. People didn't understand what she'd been through and how her heart cried out to protect her son. "I'm sorry. I—"

"Mac's schooling is none of my business. I shouldn't have said anything." He rose, and with a final swig from the glass, he set it on the table and strode toward the door. "I should probably stop to see Otis while I'm here. When I show up, he thinks I'm a mirage."

Without another word, he vanished through the kitchen door.

Meara sat nailed to the cushion. She'd offended him with her sharp tongue. But he was right, Mac's schooling was none of his business. No one's business but hers.

Chapter Six

Jordan fled down the steps and entered the shop through the back door. Meara's defenses had triggered his memories. Parents protect their children. But what had she meant by "hidden away"? Did she really mean Mac? And from what? His mind churned, trying to make sense of what she had said.

When he stepped from the small workroom into the shop, Otis's head jerked upward and he stared at Jordan with surprised eyes.

"Hold on there. Am I seein' a ghost?" Otis's astounded expression flickered a glint of good humor.

"No ghost," Jordan said. "I ran into Meara at the IGA and she invited me to stop by and see the place. She's fixed it up pretty nice with all your hand-me-downs."

"Yeah, but it takes talent to do that, you know." He laid a hand on Jordan's shoulder. "Well now, what do you think? You haven't seen this place in a while."

"It looks good." He surveyed the walls and displays, then added, "Where's the Edo warrior kite?"

"Someone bought that beauty. For a wall hangin'. Perfect, if you think about it."

"I suppose." The three-hundred-dollar price tag rose in his mind and amazed him. People spent money on anything.

As he focused on Otis, Mac shot around the corner.

"I heard you," the boy said.

"You did?" Jordan grinned at the child's eager face.

Otis chuckled. "Doesn't miss much, does he?" He shifted his gaze toward the boy. "Tell Jordan what you're doin', Mac."

"Me." The child jabbed his index finger into his chest. "Making kites."

Confused, Jordan eyed Otis. "Making kites?"

"Designin' is a better word," Otis said. "Crayons and paper. I told him to draw some pictures."

"Ah." Jordan rested his hand on Mac's shoulder. "When you come over to my place, you'll have to bring along your designs. Maybe I can use one of them."

"A kite for me?" Mac asked, his eyes as wide as silver-dollar pancakes, his grin as sweet.

"Maybe. I'll look at them and see."

"Okay." The final word drifted behind him as he disappeared around the corner.

When Jordan shifted his attention back to Otis, a serious expression had settled on the man's usual jocular face.

"Something wrong?" Jordan asked.

"I'm glad you stopped by. I know you don't like to socialize much, but you might want to drop next door to the gift shop and talk to Dawson. He mentioned the place might be sold soon."

"Hatcher finally made a good offer, I'd guess." What

now? If Hatcher bought the gift store, the others might give way to the pressure. And Otis was correct. Jordan didn't want to see the town dirtied by a topless—or near-topless—saloon. "I'll go over and see what Dawson says."

Otis squeezed his shoulder and dropped his hand. "Good. You might get more out of him than me."

Distracted, Jordan mumbled an agreement and headed for the front door. "I'll talk to you later."

He stepped outside, surprised at the orange and purple trails that cut across the sky. He glanced at his watch. His short visit hadn't been so short, and poor Dooley was probably waiting by the door for his supper. At the thought of food, the scent of baked bread taunted his tastebuds. He eyed the bakery, wondering if the owners were caving in to Hatcher's offer to buy their building. The bakery would be a real loss to Mackinaw. The gift store was another story.

He opened the shop door and stepped inside. Customers wandered down the aisle, fingering the cheap souvenirs and a few worthy gift items. "Junk," thought Jordan. Most of the items were cheap, useless knickknacks.

The manager, Bernard Dawson, stood behind the cash register, and when he noticed Jordan he did a double take. "Do my eyes deceive me?"

Jordan stretched his hand across the counter toward the man. "No, how are you, Bernie?"

Dawson took his hand in a firm shake. "Not bad, Jordan—and you?"

Jordan nodded. "I'm doing fine. But you probably guessed I'm not here to talk about our health. Do you have a place we can speak privately for a few minutes?"

Dawson surveyed the customers and waved over another clerk to handle the cash register. He maneuvered himself from behind the counter, and Jordan followed him toward the back room.

"I'm curious about the rumor that Cliff Scott might sell the place," Jordan said when they were alone.

Whether from surprise at seeing him or amazement at Scott selling the store, Dawson spilled the story quickly, and Jordan did what he was compelled to do. "Tell Scott before he signs any agreement to talk with me. I'll up the price if I must. I'm not willing to see a tacky bar take over this spot, Bernie. How about you?"

The man agreed, and with another quick handshake, Jordan stepped back outside, wondering why in the world he'd offered to spend that kind of money for the gift shop…junk shop, really. Shaking his head, he wandered toward the bakery. The delicious smells emanating from the place lured him. But Otis's face peering from the kite shop window stopped him, and he decided to return and talk to the man.

Quickly he told Otis the results of his conversation, and as the last word left his mouth, Mac appeared at his side, pulling him toward the back of the shop.

"Mama says time for dinner, Jor-dan."

"Time for you, Mac." Jordan was sure Meara was in no mood to include him in a dinner invitation.

"You, too," Mac said, tugging at his leg.

"Time for me to eat, yes, but I have to get home and feed poor old Dooley."

"Poor old Dooley," Mac repeated. But persistently he prodded Jordan toward the back door.

Jordan knew that once outside he could make his escape. His car was parked next to the door. But as he stepped into the fresh air, Meara appeared from the enclosed staircase.

"I thought you left," she said, peering at him. Her curious eyes drifted to Mac.

"I had to take care of some business," Jordan said, "but I'm on my way."

"To eat with us," Mac said, singing the words.

Jordan's lips curved to a grin at the child's simple aria. "I didn't realize we have a Pavarotti here," he said. The word *we* jabbed back at him.

"Mac likes to sing his sentences. I suppose it is like a little opera." She grinned at Mac, then returned her less-friendly gaze to Jordan.

The brilliant green color of her eyes, like gemstones, glinted shards of gold in the setting sun, and Jordan caught his breath at the sight. He raked his fingers through his hair and stepped backward toward the car to make his escape. But Mac still clung to his leg, pushing him forward.

"Eat with us." The child's words sounded like a proclamation, but he looked questioningly at Meara.

"Yes, if he'd like to, Mac. But Jordan said he has to go home."

"After," Mac said. "Dooley eats after."

Jordan squirmed. "I told him I had—"

"Dinner for Dooley," she said, her face softening in the brilliant fireworks of the setting sun.

If she'd been angry before, her displeasure had faded like the vanishing rays.

"You're welcome to eat with us," she added. "I have plenty. Then you can make a quick escape and feed Dooley."

Her eyes locked with his. *Quick escape.* He wondered if she had read his mind.

"You won't have to cook for yourself, at least," she added.

"That's true." He had beef waiting in the car. Garbage, now.

"Come," Mac said with a final prod. He edged toward the wooden staircase and beckoned with his fingers until Jordan yielded to his whim and followed him up.

A delectable aroma wafted through the doorway as Jordan reached the landing. He glanced behind him at Meara, who trailed up the staircase. "Something smells great." He stepped through the doorway.

"Hamburger stroganoff," she said with a grin. "I like beef stroganoff, but that takes time. Hamburger's quicker." She passed by him and pulled out a chair. "Sit. We'll eat in a minute."

In a moment she slid a place mat and table setting in front of him, along with a glass of iced tea. With another sashay, she added a bowl of rich beef in thick sour cream sauce, another of white rice, and a plate of sliced fresh vegetables.

Jordan eyed Mac, who sat patiently in the chair with his hands folded. When Meara joined them, she bowed her head and began to pray.

Discomfort settled over Jordan. He hadn't prayed in so long, not since his wife and Robbie died. He had never totally accepted Lila's strong faith in God and the Savior she had taught Robbie to accept. But he hadn't argued with her. Maybe she had been correct.

He'd read the Bible countless times—each year at least once while teaching a class called "The Bible as Literature." As he'd tried to show the students the Bible's incongruities, those who'd believed fervently justified the discrepancies. His message hadn't swayed them from their faith.

After a while, he began to wonder if what they said had meaning. Sometimes, the individuals who defended the Bible as God's Word made sense. But then came the car accident. And he realized, if God was real, He was not a loving God. And Jordan closed his eyes to the new beliefs that were pressing on his mind…and his heart.

"Amen" echoed as Meara, then Mac, made the final affirmation. Jordan moved his mouth but no sound left his lips. Meara smiled as if he had also validated the prayer, and passed him the rice.

Why had he deceived her? The question lingered in his thoughts through dinner. Why didn't he tell her that the God she depended on was not one whom he could rely or trust on. He wanted no part of a cruel, unloving God.

With the meal nearly finished, Meara leaned back in her chair. "So what kind of business kept you in town today?"

Curiosity rang in her voice, and he told her the story. "It seems Hatcher is willing to pay a hefty sum for the property. And Dawson seems to think that Cliff Scott will take his offer."

"What can be done? Mackinaw doesn't need a place like that. This is a family town. Tourists bring their families here."

"I know." A long blast of air left his lungs as he flopped against the chair back. "So I opened my big mouth and said I'd give him a better offer."

Meara's eyes widened. "A better offer? You mean, you'll buy the building next door?"

"I don't have much choice. If Scott sells, the other shops will be close behind, I'm thinking."

Her face filled with concern, and the reaction surprised

him. She'd only been in town a brief time, yet already showed signs of attachment.

She gasped. "But— But that's a lot of money. How will you get it back?"

He shrugged. He hadn't thought of that. All he cared about was thwarting Hatcher's plan.

"You could expand the kite shop. Add some other items." Her eyes narrowed and she bit her lip. Silence weighed on the air as she stared into space. Jordan could almost hear her mind whirring.

Finally she lifted her eyes, which were sparkling with enthusiasm. "Maybe we can brainstorm some ideas. What do you say?"

Astounded, he admired her eagerness, and her animated expression rattled his pulse. "*We,*" she'd said. "Maybe *we* could brainstorm." He'd used the term himself earlier. Why did the *we* pop up for both of them? What bound them together?

A hymn Lila sang wandered through his thoughts— "Blest Be the Tie That Binds." But Jordan wanted no ties. Especially "ties that bind." Freedom is what he wanted. Never again would he be tied to anything. When heartstrings were tangled around other hearts, life hurt too much.

Chapter Seven

The summer sun sneaked beneath Meara's bedroom shade, and she opened her eyes. The clock's digital numbers surprised her. Eight-thirty. And the quiet also amazed her. The early-morning bustle of tourists usually floated up to her windows, but today she heard nothing but cushioned silence.

Sunday. No wonder. She tossed back the daisy-print sheet and swung her legs to the floor. Sunday. Again the day lifted her thoughts. So long ago, she'd promised Nettie that one weekend she would visit her church. Now, at the end of June, she'd not kept her promise, and with the building only a few blocks away, the location seemed perfect. And the people, too. She'd met so many genial men and women when she attended the congregation's rummage sale back in May.

Rising, Meara stretched her arms above her head and headed for the bathroom. She could take a quick shower and dress before Mac awakened. In the mirror she viewed a relaxed, pleasant face. Joy pricked her senses. Out from under the Haydens' mandates, she could make her own decisions: where she would go, what she would do and what she might say. Independence.

Yet her independence held responsibility. She'd felt abandoned. Perhaps, somehow, she deserved it. She'd made a bad choice marrying Dunstan...but her son deserved none of it. Mac. Her son, the innocent, who needed so much. She'd never allow him to feel abandoned again.

Refreshing water splashed over her as she sudsed and rinsed her hair. After a sweep of the thick terry towel, she slipped into her robe and scurried to the kitchen to fill the coffeemaker.

During her second mug of coffee, Mac ambled sleepy-eyed and yawning into the kitchen. He rested his head on her shoulder and rocked to one of his nondescript tunes.

She petted his cheek and noticed his half-closed eyes. "It's Sunday, Mac. What do you say we go to Nettie's church?"

"Otis's church?" Mac asked.

"I suppose." Nettie was the churchgoer. Otis? She didn't have a clue. "How about some cereal?"

Mac nodded, and she filled a bowl, then grabbed her cup and headed back to her room. By the time Mac had finished, Meara was dressed. Then she helped him find appropriate Sunday clothes.

Later, when they exited the enclosed staircase, the morning breeze carried the familiar scent of the lake, a mixture of seagrass, fish and warm sand. But circling the building, a new aroma greeted them. From the bakery the fragrance of fresh-baked bread and cookies teased her palate. In a couple of hours caramel corn and chocolate fudge would fill the air and blend with the fumes from cars filling the slots in front of the tourist shops.

Ahead, the white church building, rising close to the lake, appeared around the bend in the road. Cars filled the nearby parking lot, and parishioners meandered toward the wide double door, holding their children's hands and smoothing their rumpled clothing. The organ's jubilant chords lifted on the breeze, and the music beckoned Meara.

On the sign outside, Meara read that Sunday school preceded the service, so she led Mac into the sanctuary. Inside, the air felt cool, and the stained-glass windows bathed the aisle and pews and gilded the worshipers' complexions with a wash of color.

An usher greeted them with a smile and a bulletin. Unable to spot Nettie, Meara inquired about her, and the gentleman pointed down the left side toward the front, where the older woman sat, her white hair adorned with shades of pink and gold from the window's reflection.

When Meara slid into the pew, Nettie smiled warmly. Mac crawled over Meara and approached the elderly woman. "Where's Otis?"

She grinned and squeezed his hand. "He's in the shop this morning. This is his Sunday to open."

Mac accepted her response and slid in between the two women, nestling close to Nettie.

The service began, and with enthusiasm Meara joined in the prayers and songs. She had missed attending worship these past weeks. Today she felt wholesome and cleansed.

Mac's attention drifted as the service progressed, and Meara quieted him with a tender shush. Soon Nettie's seasoned hand gave him pats and hard candy until he settled back against her shoulder and drifted off to sleep.

Meara glanced at the two, and a quiver of longing traveled over her, yearning for a real family for her son. Grandparents, aunts and uncles—people to give him attention and affection. Her homeland glided into her thoughts—Erin's lush green landscape with the serenity broken only by a distant bleat or the sweet tinkle of a lamb's bell. In Ireland, loving hands and voices had surrounded her.

The pastor's voice captured her attention. The hair bristled on her arms as his words settled into her consciousness.

"God did not promise us that life would be perfect. He did not guarantee we would walk this earth without feeling pain, hunger, anger or grief. Remember that through it all God is with us. Listen to what God tells us in First Peter, chapter four— 'However, if you suffer as a Christian, do not be ashamed, but praise God that you bear that name.'"

Suffered? Yes. Tears pooled in her eyes, and she blinked to stem the rising flood. She had tried so hard to keep her faith. And she had. Yes, she had. Despite her frustration, she knew Christ was her Savior, but...

The pastor's words rose again and invaded her thoughts. "So, then, those who suffer according to God's will should commit themselves to their faithful Creator and continue to do good."

That was her problem. She had often repeated the words "my life is God's will." But did she really believe it? The Bible told her to be faithful to God and do good. Had she been faithful? And what good had she done?

Unconsciously, her hand shifted to Mac's soft arm. She

brushed his cool skin, and the soothing motion calmed her thoughts. Despite Mac's problems…and despite her own, God was giving her another chance for a full and happy life. Be faithful and do good—she repeated the words in her head.

The congregation rose for the final hymn, and Mac stood, lazy-lidded, and clung to the pew in front of him, maintaining his balance. He yawned and grinned at her. She returned his smile. As voices lifted in song, she joined in the well-loved hymn: "My faith looks up to Thee, Thou Lamb of Calvary, Savior divine…"

Be faithful? She would.

With the resounding last note, she closed the hymnbook and greeted Nettie. "I promised I'd come, and here I am."

"Bless you. And little Mac, too," she said, holding him against her side. "Sunday school is before service. Mac would probably like that better."

"I know, but we came on short notice. When I woke this morning, I just wanted to be here."

"Now, won't the Lord be happy to hear that."

As they moved down the aisle, familiar faces from the rummage sale day nodded in welcome, and Meara returned their greeting. A woman beckoned to her, and she guided Mac away from the flow of traffic toward the lady.

"Remember me?" the woman asked. "Sara Burns. We met at the rummage sale."

"Yes, I do," Meara said.

"I see you have your boy with you today." She eyed Mac, but her friendly smile hid any curiosity.

Mac stuck his hand toward her. "I'm Mac."

She took his hand. "What a polite fellow you are. It's

nice to meet you." She raised her eyes to Meara's, then returned her attention to Mac. "I hope you bring your daddy next time."

Meara's pulse skipped, anticipating Mac's response. Her mouth opened to cover the woman's blunder, but Mac was quicker.

"I have two fathers in heaven," Mac said, gazing in earnest at the woman.

Sara's uneasiness was clear in her eyes. She peered first at Mac, then at Meara, and finally at Nettie. "Oh, I'm sorry. I didn't—"

Meara touched her arm. "One father is the Heavenly Father." She hoped she'd soothed the woman's misery.

"Heavenly Fa— Uh, yes." She looked again at Mac, then at Meara. "Then, I hope the two of you worship with us again. We love seeing new faces."

"Thank you."

Sara smiled and backed away. *Escaped* was more like it.

Nettie caught up with them, and they stepped outside. Heavy traffic moved along the city street. Mac stuck close to Nettie's side, holding her hand, and Meara sensed he was struggling with a thought.

Finally he halted. "Where's my grandma?"

The question jarred Meara's perplexed thoughts. He'd not mentioned his grandmother since they moved. Meara supposed the "father" reference had been the catalyst. Usually when he asked, Meara had dismissed his queries with a description of their adventurous journey. But he could no longer be put off.

"She's in Petoskey, Mac."

Nettie's face grew curious.

"I want to see her," Mac said.

Meara forced her expression to remain stoic. What had brought about this sudden interest in Dunstan's mother? Her gaze shifted from Mac to Nettie's inquisitive face and her neatly curled crown of white hair, and Meara had her answer.

"Later, Mac. We'll discuss it when we get home."

"I—"

"Later," Meara repeated, pinning him with her eyes.

He dropped his gaze.

They walked without conversation until the bakery's aroma captured their senses.

"Smells tempting," Meara said, easing their disquiet.

"Cookies," Mac said, his eager steps guiding him ahead to the bakery window.

Nettie paused at the kite shop door, and Meara hesitated, knowing she'd flustered the woman.

"Let me buy us a treat," Meara offered. "I'll make tea. In the lovely pot you gave me," she added, hoping the reference would ease the strain. "I'll make a cup for Otis, too."

Nettie rested her hand on the shop door. "I'm sure he'd enjoy that. I'll wait inside." She pushed a stray, windblown curl from her cheek and opened the kite shop door.

"Come on," Mac called, and Meara followed him into the bakery. At Mac's prodding, she selected a sampling of doughnuts and cookies, then carried the string-tied box into the kite shop.

A few customers meandered through the store while Otis was giving change to a customer. For a fleeting moment she gazed at the well-dressed gentleman, eyeing his neat slacks and tweed sport jacket. Unusual garb for the typical tourist.

As he turned toward the door, their eyes met. Being caught gawking at him, Meara flushed. He gave her a friendly grin and slid passed her. Chancing another curious look as he opened the door, Meara saw him give her another look. Did she know him? She followed his exit, watching until he reached his automobile. Nothing registered.

With a broom in her hand, Nettie bustled in from the rear of the store, sweeping the aisle beside the workroom. Wasn't that just like her.

"I'll bring you down a treat in a few minutes," she said to Otis as she passed.

With an acknowledging wave, he returned his attention to a customer.

"I'll be up in a minute," Nettie said, pushing dirt into a dustpan.

Agreeing, Meara headed for the kitchen. As the teakettle whistled, Nettie tapped on the door, and Meara beckoned her inside.

"Now that's done," Nettie said between small puffs of breath resulting from her trip up the stairs.

"You work too hard," Meara said, pouring the water into the teapot. "Go inside and sit. I'll fix the tray and be in shortly."

Nettie ambled into the living room, where Mac sat with his nose pressed against the window, watching the kites in the park. Meara heard their quiet conversation and Nettie's gentle chuckle. As she carried the tray into the room, Mac gave Nettie a hearty hug.

"You're such a loving young man," the elderly woman said, patting his shoulder. As if they were conspirators, they quieted and followed Meara with their eyes.

"So what's all of this?" Meara asked with a curious frown.

Mac giggled and shook his head, his lips pinched together.

Meara eyed him, then Nettie. "Here's some juice, Mac. Nettie, help yourself, and I'll run a cup of tea and doughnuts downstairs for Otis. I'll be right back."

Mac had already grabbed a cookie in each hand.

"One at a time," she said to him. "Nettie, you're in charge while I'm gone."

Before she descended the stairs, Nettie's voice echoed behind her. "Did you hear your mother? I'm in charge," Nettie teased.

"Uh-huh. You're in charge, Grandma," Mac answered with a conspiring giggle.

Grandma. Meara stood on the second step, waiting for her aching heart to quiet.

A rap on the back door brought Jordan to attention. Dooley tangled under his feet as he opened the porch screen and let the dog out the front. When he reached the back door, Blair Dunham stood on the other side of the screen, his gaze focused on the ground.

Jordan's pulse shifted into second gear, like a semi climbing a twenty-percent grade. His friend's presence confounded him. He forced his legs forward and dragged a pleasant expression to his strained face.

"Blair, my word, what are you doing here?" He pushed open the screen door, and his old friend from the university, dressed in slacks and a tweed jacket, crossed the threshold. He extended his hand in greeting.

"I was in town and thought I'd look you up. It's been too long, Jordan." He wrapped a firm hand around their clasped palms in a lengthy handshake. "I miss you, man."

Jordan extracted his hand and ran his fingers through his hair, contemplating the situation. "Well, thanks. How about a cola? Or I could make some coffee."

"Cola's fine." Jordan surveyed the room, then peered through the archway toward the lake.

"Let's sit on the porch," Jordan said, motioning him ahead. "There's a nice breeze out there." On the way, he pulled two sodas from the refrigerator and grabbed the tumblers from the cupboard.

Blair passed him and continued to the porch, and when Jordan entered, the man stood at the screen, peering out at the water.

"Here you are," Jordan said, setting the bottle and glass on the end table and slumping into a chair.

Blair glanced at him over his shoulder, then turned back to the lake. "You're right about the breeze. Real nice and great view. But quiet." He jammed his hands in his pockets and pivoted on his heel, facing Jordan. "Too quiet. Too lonely. Doesn't this eventually get to you?"

A prickling of irritation rose up Jordan's arms to the nape of his neck. What right did Blair have to arrive out of his past and challenge his choice? "I like it, Blair. I like quiet."

"And lonely?"

"No, I have Dooley." Jordan glanced out to where the setter lay coiled on the beach, his eyes directed toward the lake.

"Who's Dooley?"

"An Irish setter who's lying in wait down by the lake. Probably longing to chase some unsuspecting ducks."

Blair followed his gaze and peered out the screen. "I see him." He walked to the chair beside the end table and took a swig from the bottle. "So, Dooley keeps you company."

"In part." Jordan shifted, covering a ragged sigh that stole from his throat. "I'm okay."

Blair sank into the chair. "I stopped at the kite shop in town. I knew building those things was your hobby, but I never thought you'd make a living that way."

Jordan studied his drink and chuckled. "Well, that and a good investment portfolio."

Blair stared at the bottle, running his finger around the rim. "Ah, I see."

"So, what did you think of the kites?"

"Wonderful. Unique. I have one in the car. Thought it'd brighten my office. Something needs to brighten the place. Certainly not those dull student conferences."

"Still complaining about those, huh?" Jordan relaxed against the seat cushion, eyeing his ex-colleague. "What really brings you here, Blair? I know you didn't come to Mackinaw to buy a kite."

Blair cocked his head with a chuckle. "Never could hide anything from you, could I."

"Not really. I remember when you did some double-dealing and finagled away my favorite lit class. I'm surprised I forgave you for that."

Blair nodded and gave a wry grin. "I was a rat. But I did that before we became friends."

"In a pig's eye!"

Blair let out a boisterous laugh. "Take you out of the classroom and you turn into a farmer."

"I could have done worse."

A heavy silence fell like a bag of dried bones. Blair inched his gaze to Jordan's. "You could have. And I'm glad you didn't."

Jordan closed his eyes for a moment, thinking of options he'd considered. Thinking of where he'd been and where he was now. Life. Death. He looked directly into Blair's concerned eyes.

"So?"

"So." He released a lengthy breath. "I'm doing the old man a favor. Brighton asked me to talk to you. The doc wants you back. He sent me to convince you."

"I see. And why?"

"Well, you're one of the best professors the college had. Besides, Gillenfelt is retiring next year, and Brighton's looking for a top-notch replacement to pick up the load." He squirmed against the chair back. "Besides, we all miss you."

Jordan didn't speak. His life three years earlier flashed through his head: classes; conferences; correcting dull, tedious essays; reading an occasional brilliant one; and always, at the end of the day, rushing home to Lila's arms and Robbie's eager face. Yes, he missed it, too. Terribly.

"But it will never be the same. I'm a different man than I was three years ago."

"Different, maybe, but you'll always be a great teacher. The students idolized you."

Yes, they had, he supposed, but that hadn't made life worth living. His family had. A smiling eight-year-old flashed through his mind. Gooseflesh wavered up his arm. Unlike Robbie, this boy wore thick glasses and had a shock of red hair. Jordan clutched the tumbler in his hand to hide the tremors. Was Robbie's face fading from his memory?

"Something wrong?" Blair asked, leaning forward with a disconcerted stare.

Jordan pressed his tense spine against the seat cushion. "No, I'm okay. Just a flashback, I guess."

"Listen, man, I didn't come here to stir up memories. Brighton wanted you to know there'll be an opening, and I volunteered to drive up. I'd like you to think about it."

"Sure," he said, "I'll think about it." At times, he thought about nothing else...until lately. Mac distracted him.

Who am I fooling? he thought. *The boy's mother distracts me, too.*

He pushed away his thoughts. "So, tell me what's up with you and the family?"

Blair turned the conversation to his wife and three children. They talked about curriculum, co-workers, and even Dooley. Finally, Blair looked at his wristwatch and rose. Jordan followed him to the door with another promise to give the proposition some thought.

"You have a telephone?" Blair asked.

Jordan laughed. "That and running water, electricity—all those modern conveniences."

"How about giving me your number? I'd like to keep in touch."

Jordan jotted the number on a scratch pad and slipped it into Blair's hand.

As they moved to the door, a car pulled in next to Blair's. Jordan's stomach tightened as he sighted the familiar freckled face crowned by flaming red hair exiting the car. Her hair hung wild and full around her shoulders.

Blair looked at him with narrowed eyes, then peered out the door again. "Whew! I saw that beauty at the kite shop. I assume you know her?"

"I sure do. She's renting my apartment."

"Your apartment? Wish I had an apartment." He chuckled and pushed the screen door open, stepping outside.

Jordan followed him and buzzed in his ear, "You have a wife, my friend. That's all you need."

Blair gave him a wink. "But I can dream, can't I?"

"No" resounded in Jordan's mind, but he only grinned.

Meara hesitated by her car, and Mac slid into the driver's seat and out the same door, clinging to his mother's dress. Jordan had never seen her in a dress. She looked lovely. Enhancing her emerald eyes, the soft green fabric fell in gentle folds around her trim hips and stopped below the knees of her long slender legs. A brush of color tinged her fine cheekbones and a soft coral highlight brightened her natural pink lips. Gold earrings glinted through the wisps of her untamed hair.

"I didn't mean to intrude. I hadn't expected you to have company," Meara said, still clinging to the open car door, her gaze darting from Jordan to Blair.

"No problem," Jordan said, stepping forward. "Meara Hayden, this is Blair Dunham. We were co-workers a few years ago."

Blair extended his hand. "I believe we almost met earlier today. At the kite shop."

"Ah, yes. I thought you looked familiar."

"And who's this young man?" Blair asked, eyeing Mac.

Jordan moved forward and wrapped a protective arm around the boy's shoulders. "This young man is Mac. He has quite a handle for a lad."

Mac gave him an inquisitive look.

Blair extended his hand. "And what's the rest of that name, son? Mac what?"

Mac took his hand. "Dunstan MacAuley Hayden," he said, giving three firm pumps of his hand with each part of his name. He turned and squinted into Jordan's eyes. "Where's my handle?"

Unexpectedly, a warm, full laugh exited his throat. "'Handle' means your long, distinguished name. My handle is Jordan Evan Baird."

"Does Mama have a handle?"

But Blair didn't wait for the answer. He grasped Jordan's arm in a firm shake. "Listen, man, I have to get going. And you obviously have some business to take care of here." His eyes sparkled with mischief. He pivoted toward Meara. "Nice to meet you."

"My pleasure," Meara said.

"Nice to meet you," Mac parroted.

Blair tousled Mac's hair and leaned into Jordan's frame. "Good to see you, man. Give the offer thought." He eyed him slyly. "And I'll take you at your word."

Jordan's brow furrowed. "My word?"

Blair glanced over his shoulder at the new arrivals. "I think you *are* okay."

Jordan caught his drift and shook his head. Blair never had viewed women as Jordan did.

With a wink, Blair got into his car, waved and backed down the driveway.

"I hope I didn't interrupt anything important," Meara said again. "Funny. I did see him in the kite shop. He stood out in his sport coat."

"I suppose he would." Jordan moved back to the door. "Would you like to come in?"

"I really came by for just a minute. We're having dinner nearby, and I thought I'd stop to ask if tomorrow might be all right to bring Mac over." She searched his face. "For the kite, remember?"

"I remember." Her eyes took his breath away—deep, glinting green.

"I thought if he were occupied, I might have time to run

to the school and talk to an administrator about his schooling this fall."

"Tomorrow works for me."

"Works for me," Mac echoed.

She took a hesitant step backward. "Thanks. I'll be going, then."

Jordan longed to wrap his arms around her lovely shoulders, to rub his fingers along her elegant cheekbone, to press his lips… He dragged his fingers through his hair, wanting to erase the images that stirred inside his mind. "You're sure you won't stay?"

"Yes. But thanks for the invitation. Mac's hungry." Her shapely, full lips rose to a smile. "And so is his mother."

"Then," Jordan said, extending his hand, "I'll see you tomorrow."

She placed her delicate, cool palm against his broad, firm hand. "Tomorrow."

Meara nuzzled Mac's shoulder, and he climbed over the driver's seat. When he'd fastened his seat belt securely, she slid into the car and closed the door.

Jordan watched, mesmerized, as she turned the car around and drove down the leafy lane to the highway.

"Tomorrow," he said, swallowing a lump of emotion. He'd lost control.

The self-built dam crumbled. The world flooded in, and he could do nothing to stop it.

Chapter Eight

"You're doing a wonderful job, Mac." Jordan stood above the boy, guiding him as he twisted the cord that tied the two dowels together. "Your mom will be proud of you."

"She'll be proud." Mac gazed lovingly at the paper kite he'd formed from colored tissue.

Jordan had done the best he could to model this kite after one of Mac's hasty drawings. The boy had remembered to bring the pictures along from the day Otis had diverted him in the shop. Mac might be slow, but he didn't seem to forget a thing.

A light breeze rustled the birch leaves near the house, and Jordan eyed the lake. Small ripples glazed the water, nothing Mac's kite couldn't handle. He had hoped to wait for Meara's return to show her the grand performance, but something was keeping her. He checked his wristwatch. Three hours had passed since she'd delivered Mac to his doorstep.

"Needs a tail," Mac said, fingering the end of the kite. "Blue tail. And red."

"Blue and red?" Jordan eyed the box of cloth strips nearby. "Let me see." He rose and selected Mac's choices.

"Blue and red," Mac repeated, a glowing smile coloring his cheeks.

"Want to give it a try?"

Mac's head shot up. "Fly the kite?" His eyes widened.

"I think we can. Maybe your mom will come soon and she'll see you."

"Where's Mama?" He glanced over his shoulder through the screen. "With...Grandma Nettie?" A grin curled his lips.

Jordan's ears tuned to the boy's question. "Grandma Nettie? Is that what you call her?"

He nodded vehemently. "Said I could." His eyes glowed.

"That's nice."

"My...grandma..."

Jordan watched him search for the words. "Your real grandma?" he prodded.

"My real grandma is..." After a lengthy silence, he shook his head with a look of disappointment. "Somewhere."

A car door sounded, and he and Mac turned toward the driveway and waited.

"Hello," Meara called from the back door.

Jordan rose, heading toward her. "You're just in time for the big event. Come in."

She pulled the handle and entered, her face strained and unsmiling.

"Something wrong?" he asked. "Not what you wanted to hear, I expect."

Seeing him, Meara crumbled. Frustration filled her at each turn. She had had little success at the administration office, and her talk with the special education director had been as unsatisfactory. The day had been a failure. "Yes, you're right. No program for Mac."

"Nothing?" He tilted his head.

"Certainly, they have a learning resource room of some kind. A special-ed teacher working with all kinds of special-needs students. But they're only in her classroom one or two hours a day."

"Then what? Sent to other teachers?"

"Yes, mainstreamed. Pushed into difficult situations with normal-needs children. Children who... Never mind—I need to think this through. Getting discouraged won't help."

"True."

He gazed back at Mac, who stood in the doorway, holding his colorful, new kite. "We have a treat for you," Jordan said.

She eyed Jordan, then peered at Mac. The kite. He must have made it. "What do you have?" she asked her son.

"Kite. I built it." He poked his chest with his free hand.

"And we're just going out to give it a test run," Jordan added. "Care to join us?"

"Sure," Meara said, following him to the porch. She dropped her purse on the chair and stepped out the front door.

The sun-baked sand glistened as if with diamonds, and a gentle breeze rippled the lake and played against her skin. Jordan grabbed two beach chairs along the path and carried them to the sand. She sat and watched Jordan create the illusion that Mac was flying the kite. With both sets of hands on the string, they pulled and tightened until the strange-shaped structure floated over the water.

Curious, she approached Jordan. "An unusual design," she said. "And you say that's Mac's creation?"

A gentle grin curved his mouth, and he tilted his head toward Mac. "He drew a picture of it with Otis. I promised we'd try to make one he designed himself."

"Oh, that's wonderful."

She returned to the chair, admiring Jordan's kindness. With tenderness he talked to Mac, complimenting and correcting, teasing and delighting.

Eventually the kite returned to earth, and Mac leaned against her shoulder, listening to her praise while Jordan took the kite to the porch and returned with some sodas.

Mac settled on the beach with Dooley curled at his side. With an old coffee can and a large rusted spoon he found lying on the grass, he dug in the sand.

Swigging from the bottle, Jordan gazed out at the water.

Meara pondered his silence. What secret thoughts tensed his jaw? Who was his friend and why had he visited yesterday? And what offer had he asked Jordan to consider? A wave of loneliness rippled through her. Greater desolation than she had felt at the Haydens'. *That* solitude she'd accepted.

"You're quiet," Jordan said, shifting his eyes from the lake view to her.

"Thinking. Like you." She averted her gaze and focused on Mac. "Thanks for being such a nice friend to Mac. And to me. My life has been unsettled, and you've given me...a lift. And some hope."

"You're welcome. I sense you've had a hard time. But things seem to be pulling together."

"They have. You, the Mannings, the apartment, the job—everything, except for Mac's schooling. And I can solve that, too."

Jordan gave her a puzzled look but didn't ask how she'd solve the problem.

She wasn't sure herself, but she would.

"The Mannings are a wonderful couple. I don't know what I'd do without them either." Jordan paused, then added, "Mac called Nettie 'Grandma' today."

Meara faced him. "They seemed to have conspired. He misses things as they used to be."

"And you?"

Tongue-tied, she struggled momentarily for the right words. "Not really. I miss security. But I love my freedom. Away from the watchful eyes of...Dunstan's family."

"Is that the real grandmother Mac mentioned today?"

She swallowed. "He did? Again? He asked me yesterday where his grandmother is."

Jordan faltered. "You've only been married once?"

"Why...yes." She studied his face, wondering why he'd asked. "What made you think—?"

"Mac mentioned two fathers."

Meara closed her eyes, almost hearing the conversation. "He means Dunstan and God."

A look of discomfort spread across Jordan's face, and Meara longed to end the discussion.

"It's all so complicated," she said, feeling her shoulders rise on a sigh.

His words were so soft they barely reached her ears: "Some things are difficult to discuss."

"I don't want to burden people with my problems. They finally work themselves out." Yet, she hadn't worked out the pain.

"Memories, experiences hurt sometimes," he said.

His words squeezed against her heart. His tragedy. He knew what she meant. Would he ever tell her? Her own unwillingness to share goaded her. How would he ever relate to her if she continued to hide her own pain?

"When Dunstan died, we left his family home. Not with the best of feelings. To me, it meant freedom. To Mac, it meant a new, frightening world. Dunstan's home was all he'd ever known."

"You were uncomfortable staying in the house after your husband's death?"

The answer stuck in her throat. The horrible truth choked her, plundered her emotions. "Yes. It was his parents' home…though the only life I'd known in America. But that wasn't my motivation." She looked away a moment before gaining the courage to tell him the truth.

"They asked me to leave."

There, she'd said it. A sense of calm had settled in her body. "They paid me off. Paid off their debt to me and their grandson with a small gratuity. Like a charity case."

"Please," Jordan said, his body visually straining at her words, "you don't have to—"

"We were an embarrassment to them." A ragged sigh tore from her throat. "I must say it aloud, Jordan. Now that I've said it, maybe the shame and sorrow will go away. I should have fought for my son's rightful inheritance."

"Fought?" Jordan's voice rose on the wind, and Mac turned toward him, surprise on his face.

"Sorry," he said, lowering his voice. "Fought? With what? You had no knowledge of the law. You had no support."

"I know, but I had God…and I should have turned to

Him. I didn't. I try to solve everything myself. And some things a person can't handle on his own."

She lifted her gaze to his and saw an expression she'd never seen before. Apprehension? Awareness? Astonishment? "What are you thinking?" she asked.

He stared over the lake. "Just some things I heard long ago. Questions I'd raised to myself. Questions I've never answered."

She shifted in the beach chair, leaning forward, trying to see in his eyes. But he riveted his attention to the distant island.

Finally his lips stirred, moving softly in a near whisper. "Don't chastize yourself, Meara. Look at yourself. Many people wouldn't have survived." He shifted to face her. "You've done well."

"On the outside, maybe." She longed to know what hidden meaning clung to his knowing words.

She leaned back against the canvas chair, hoping to give him time, time to tell her what suffering he'd endured.

"The water's calm today," Jordan murmured. "Only a faint breeze rippling its surface."

He turned to her as if they were old friends, chatting, their previous conversation forgotten.

"Do you miss the cabin?"

His disjointed discourse confused her. But she didn't draw him back. "Not the cabin, but my closeness to the water. I miss swimming."

"You're welcome to swim here. Anytime."

"Thank you. That would be nice. At the apartment, I can look out at the marina and see the pleasure boats and the ferries heading for the island, but it's not the same as a sandy beach."

"Nothing is as quiet and as soul-stirring as the beach, is it." He lifted his eyes again to the lake. His gaze swept the vista, from the awesome suspension bridge, past the quaint island, to a distant ship on the horizon probably making its long trek from the St. Lawrence Seaway to Chicago.

Meara left him in his solitude, pondering her own thoughts. But she jolted to awareness when he smacked his hands together, revitalized.

"Hungry?" He spoke to Mac. "I'm starving."

"Starving," Mac answered, and rose from his preoccupation with the mounds of sand, seashells and, of course, Dooley. He wandered toward them, sand clinging to his denim pants and sprinkled on his glasses.

Meara rose. "We'd better get going, then," she said.

"Going? No," Jordan said, "you're welcome to eat here. You fed me dinner once. Now it's my turn."

She flopped back into her chair. "But—"

Mac put his finger against her lips. "No but, Mama," he said.

They laughed at his serious expression, and he repeated his words, his finger lingering on her mouth.

"I can't say no to that, can I?"

"I don't think so." Jordan rose. Dooley joined them, charging up the path, and they followed in his sandy paw prints.

Inside, Mac had the job of filling Dooley's dish with four large scoops of dry food, and Jordan stared into the refrigerator, locating the fresh Italian sausage and a variety of greens for a tossed salad.

Meara worked on the salad while Jordan prepared the meat, and sauteed peppers and onions. After eating the meat and vegetables on a bun and a large helping of salad, they were filled. A bag of store-bought cookies brought a smile to Mac's face, along with a dish of ice cream for dessert.

Sitting over coffee, Meara thanked him. "You certainly know how to come up with an impromptu dinner. Peanut butter and jelly might have been my offering."

"You were in luck. I went to the grocery store before you arrived this morning. Thinking ahead."

Mac scraped his spoon against the ice-cream dish.

"If you keep that up, you'll eat glass chips, Mac," Meara said.

"I like ice cream." He grinned and licked the bowl.

"Mac, shame on you. That's not at all polite."

Jordan lost the battle against hiding his amusement and released a hearty chuckle. "But it's honest and natural." He ruffled Mac's shoulder. "I like ice cream myself, pal. But when you're my age, you're not allowed to lick the bowl."

"Not allowed," Mac repeated, setting the dish on the table. He rose and headed toward the living room, nuzzling Dooley.

"You're so good with him." She warmed at his tenderness. "Like a father. Mac thinks so much of you. He's done more with you than he ever did with Dunstan. Much more."

"I'm not his father, Meara." His eyes flashed with fire. His jaw tightened and he spoke between clenched teeth. "I don't have a son."

Ashamed of her blatant comment, her face flamed with embarrassment. She had put him in a defensive position. Why hadn't she thought? Any man would feel trapped by her "like a father" comment.

"I'm getting too close to him," he said. "Maybe I need to distance myself. For Mac's sake."

As much as she hated his words, he was right. If Mac got

any more attached to him, it could only cause her son more hurt. "I understand."

He rose and carried dishes to the sink. She joined him, her mind whirring in consternation and humiliation. She'd over-stepped every social rule she'd ever learned. She had pushed him into a corner.

"Mac, we need to go. Jordan has more things to do than entertain us." She faced her host, forcing her eyes to hold his at full attention. "Thanks so much for amusing Mac and for the nice day. And dinner. It was wonderful."

"You're welcome."

Rattled, she held her hand out, and he took it, holding her palm against his, her pulse pounding against his flesh. With a gentle squeeze, he released her fingers. She reached out to Mac and moved to the door in one sweep.

"Good night, Jordan." She hesitated for one shivering moment.

"Goodbye," he answered. "So long, Mac."

With tears blurring her path, she pushed her son through the doorway, closed the screen and climbed into the car. Her last sight was Jordan silhouetted in the doorway, his words ringing in her ears.

Goodbye.

Chapter Nine

The telephone's ring brought Jordan in from outdoors. For some reason, he'd been motivated to plant some flowers in the empty beds along the front of the house. For the past two years the grass and weeds had infringed upon the original plot, but today, he'd pulled them and covered the area with a bright mixture of impatiens.

He pulled off his work gloves, leaving them on the porch, and answered the phone. Otis's voice greeted him.

"Problems?" Jordan asked.

"You know how the grapevine works. I heard from Dawson, next door, that Hatcher is miffed. He knows you offered Cliff Scott a better price for the shop than he's willing to pay, and from what I've heard, he's trying to stir up trouble for you."

"Trouble? What kind?"

"I'm not sure. Dawson said he'd heard that he's going to the zoning board. What do you think he's after?"

Jordan rubbed his jaw. "We checked on the church's distance from his proposed saloon, and we can't stop him that way. He can't be worried about that."

"Right. So, what do you think he's looking for?"

"Can't imagine. Let me think about it. And thanks, Otis, for the warning. If you talked to Dawson, then you're aware that Cliff Scott is selling me the store. We just signed the agreement yesterday."

"Yep. I guess Cliff told Hatcher you gave him the better offer and he'd rather stick with someone he knows."

"I can see why Hatcher's upset. He likes to be the winner." Jordan's mind churned, trying to fathom Hatcher's line of thinking. "But I can't imagine what kind of trouble he's stirring up. I'll get back to you, Otis, and thanks again for the warning."

After he hung up, he grabbed a soda and returned to the flower bed. The last few flowers sat in the plastic cartons, waiting to be planted, and he slipped on the gloves and kneeled to finish the job.

Life seemed to be tugging him out into the world again. But no longer did he feel the strong urge to resist as he'd done months ago. Hatcher's plan to buy the property and his fight to save it prodded him as he went into town—especially now that he had a building to handle. Meara and Mac sparked his yearnings for a family and his need to let the past rest in a quieter grave.

Of late, he handled the memories of Lila and Robbie with less pain, with less longing to hold them in his arms. The God Lila trusted had a different plan than Jordan had had for his life. His choice was nil. Now it was over, done, complete, final. A man couldn't conjure his loved ones back to life. And

Lila would want him to stop grieving and move on. If any woman loved life, it was she.

But perhaps his son's death was the hardest pain to bear. Eight years old, his life still ahead of him, turned to ashes before he experienced one glowing moment. No tears, but a fleeting sensation of anger rose in Jordan. Yet even anger was useless.

The last crimson flower rested in its new home, and Jordan pressed the rich, moist soil around its tender roots. The earthy aroma of new growth filled his senses. Tender roots, new life—like a child ready to grow and blossom. Like Mac. And maybe like his own stilted, interrupted life.

After he gathered everything and picked up the trowel, Jordan carried the empty containers to the garage and tossed them in. He slid off the work gloves. In the gloomy shadows something tugged at him, and he surveyed the boxes and cartons stored against the wall.

Books and lecture notes—his college textbooks caught his interest. Blair's visit had stimulated his memories. He pulled open the top carton, reached inside and pulled out the first book he touched. *The Complete Works of Shakespeare.* No, not the Bard. He stared into the box, reading the next title: *The Bible as Literature.* He folded the box lid and carried the thick book into the house.

Placing the textbook on the kitchen table, he viewed the title and wondered why he'd brought it inside. Perhaps Meara's interest in God had stirred his curiosity. He poured a mug of thick, ripe coffee, his stomach balking at the acrid odor, and slid onto a chair.

His fingers tapped against the blue hardcover as he sipped the aged brew, his mind swinging from Hatcher's scheme to Meara's God. On a whim, he drew his finger through the dog-eared leaves and flipped the book open. The New Testament.

Jordan stared at the page and focused on a verse. First Corinthians 13:1. Why? Had chance prompted him to turn to the Bible's most beautiful, complete description of love? He had no need to read the verses. He knew them by heart. His students loved this section of the Bible, whether viewed as literature or God's Word. It spoke of basic human values, basic human need.

Skimming the lines, he faltered at verse twelve. Like the string of a kite, the words strained his thoughts, tugging his heart and brain. "Now we see but a poor reflection as in a mirror, then we shall see face to face. Now I know in part, then I shall know fully, even as I am fully known."

Was this his life? Pieces of a puzzle spilled out on a table, pushed into place section by section. The picture offered only a brief glimpse of abstract reality, unclear and incomplete. But in time the image merged and grew into a total picture, a whole, full existence. Perhaps someday he would understand.

He was spurred into action. He would take a ride to town to find out what he could, maybe talk to other store managers. If Hatcher was riled, who knew what new ploy he might be generating?

Customers wandered through the shop, intrigued with the unique kites. Jordan's creations were expensive, and families looking for ways to amuse their children had no intention of spending that kind of money for a kite.

Meara wanted to encourage Jordan to add the less-expensive tissue-paper ones she remembered from her childhood—like the ones she had bought Mac—at least something more affordable. But she hadn't seen Jordan for a couple of weeks, not since she had bungled with her "like a father" reference. Over and over she questioned why she had ruined their friendship by unnerving him with her comment.

Too late. She'd messed things up good. Perhaps Otis would talk to him about the toy kites. They would be good for business. But then, why did she care? It had nothing to do with her.

But it did. The shop had to do with Jordan…and Jordan, well, he touched her heart whether she wanted him to or not.

The bell jangled on the shop door, catching her attention, and she stepped away from the counter where she was sorting the dowels and dyes that Jordan carried in the store for would-be kite-makers. She headed toward the portly gentleman who paused at the counter, his attention sweeping the walls and ceiling displays. In passing, she adjusted two soft-cover books on the art of simple kite-making that stood among a small assortment.

"May I help you?" Meara asked as she approached the gentleman.

His attention stayed with the wall hangings. "You sure have a lot of kites."

She didn't like his tone, and her inner voice retorted, *This is a kite shop. What did you expect?* But instead she smiled and responded with a pleasant "Yes."

"Is Baird here?" His gaze darted around the shop again, but this time as if searching for Jordan.

"No, Mr. Baird isn't usually in the shop. Can I help you?"

"He has an apartment rented upstairs, right?"

His cocky look annoyed her. And she sure wasn't planning to tell him she lived there. "Yes. The apartment is already rented, in case you were interested in it."

He let out a snort. "I'm interested, all right. You can tell Baird he's breaking the zoning law by renting that apartment...just in case he's interested."

Meara swallowed a gasp that rose in her throat. "Zoning law? What do you mean?"

"This strip is zoned for business only. Nonresidential. Just tell him Don Hatcher dropped by, okay? And he'd better clear out that apartment or he'll find himself in real trouble."

Before Meara could respond, he spun on his heel with a nasty chuckle and swaggered through the doorway.

She closed her gaping mouth, yanked her sinking heart back into her chest. What would she do now? This situation had worked so well. A home, a job close by, Mac safe and happy here. Was God punishing her for her contentment? For her newfound freedom? Had she not grieved enough for her dead husband who, other than her son and her name, had given her little else?

By her own stupidity, Jordan seemed to be rejecting her. And now God. What was left?

Jordan pulled in behind the kite shop and eyed the enclosed staircase. How would Meara react if he knocked on her door without a phone call—but with an apology? He hadn't seen her for nearly two weeks. After they parted company on a tense note, he had done nothing to ease the situation or explain it. He'd reacted from fear. Not only fear for Mac, but truly fear for himself. These two people had needs that he didn't know he could handle. They needed security, contentment and love. Security, he could offer anyone. But the others? Probably not.

To offer contentment and love, the giver had to be contented and lovable. He wasn't and might never be. Only time would give him the answer. And in their wake, he could easily drown in the love Meara and Mac had to offer before he knew if he could give any in return.

Jordan turned off the engine and climbed from the car. He had to see Meara about Hatcher's visit. And he couldn't let things go on this way, no matter what rational thinking told him.

He climbed the staircase and rapped on the door.

When Meara answered, her face paled as their eyes met. Then she flushed. "Jordan." His name was a whisper.

"May I come in? I need to talk to you." He managed restraint. "But first I want to say I'm sorry—"

She closed her eyes for a moment and shook her head. "Please, don't apologize. The blunder was mine. I put you on the spot, and that was wrong." Her jaw tensed. In the silence, her eyes searched his. "I wanted to phone you. I should have."

"No, it was my place to call. I'm the one who overreacted."

"I'm glad you came. I've miss—" She clamped her lips together, and her sentence hung in the air.

She didn't need to complete it. Jordan filled in her words. And he'd missed her and the boy. But he knew better than to say it aloud.

Meara opened the door wider. "Come in. Please. Mac's downstairs. He's missed you terribly. If he notices your car, he'll be up in a heartbeat."

He stepped inside with her words sending a prophetic shiver through him. Despite logic's warning flares, he responded with his heart. "If he doesn't notice, I'll say 'hi' on my way out."

Yes, the boy missed him. Mac was filled with love and happiness at his attention. The child had needs. And that was Jordan's concern. Could he protect himself from hurt without hurting the child?

"Have a seat. I'll get you some iced tea." Her words were amiable but distant.

He wandered into the living room, familiar and cozy, and sank into the chair.

Meara followed close on his heels and slid a filled tumbler on the table at his side.

"You said you had to talk to me?"

"Right." He wanted to talk about so many things, but wisdom said to get down to business. "Otis told me you had an unpleasant visit from Hatcher yesterday."

At the mention of the man's name, her face paled. "Yes, I wasn't sure what he meant. He said something about the zoning laws." She ran her hand across her ashen cheek and pressed two fingers against her untinted lips. "Do you think you've really broken the law, letting us rent the apartment?"

Anger flooded him. Anger and irritation at the presumptuous, inappropriate action of Hatcher. What business was it of his? And what right did he have to cause Meara unnecessary fear?

"Please don't worry, Meara. I'm on my way to the clerk's office, and I'll check the zoning laws. I know this apartment was rented before I bought it. In fact, I stayed here a brief time before I got the house on the beach."

"I don't want to cause you any problem. We can find another place—"

"Those were Hatcher's words and threat, not mine. Let me take care of it, please. Don't worry. I'll check it out."

Her voice softened. "All right."

"I should have expected something like this from him," Jordan said. "Otis mentioned a while back that he'd heard the man was out to get me in some way." He rubbed the cords of his neck, wondering if he really was breaking some kind of law. "I didn't pay much attention. Next time I'll listen."

"I'll be anxious to hear what you learn."

He sipped the tea, watching her sit quietly across from him, her delicate hands clutched in her lap. "Are you working tomorrow?"

"Only in the morning."

"It's supposed to be hot tomorrow. Why not come by in the afternoon? You and Mac can take a swim."

"Mac's afraid of water. We have to be so careful. He gets infections easily."

"Then, you can swim, and I'll keep an eye on Mac for you. We can talk then."

"Swim. That sounds nice." Her face brightened. "We'll take turns."

"No, I'm not much of a swimmer. But I know you like the water." He was a good swimmer. But he had to hide the truth.

"I'd like to—if it's really okay with you."

He ached to hold her in his arms, to calm her uncertainty. "It's really okay." Why couldn't he admit to her and to himself that he was falling in love with her? And with Mac. "It's more than okay."

* * *

The next afternoon Meara climbed from the car. While Mac scrambled across her seat, she grabbed her towel and duffel bag from the rear seat. Mac hurried ahead and rang the doorbell.

"Come in," Jordan said, stepping aside for them to enter. "I began to wonder if you were coming."

"Hi, Jor-dan," Mac said.

"How are you, pal?" Tenderly, Jordan kneaded the boy's shoulder.

Meara winced at her son's obvious admiration. "We ate lunch first, and I had a couple of errands to run. But wild dogs wouldn't keep me away. I'm so anxious to find out what happened."

He beckoned them toward the living room, speaking as he went. "I would have called you last night, but I didn't get a firm answer from my lawyer until this morning."

"Lawyer? What happened? Is there a—"

"Don't worry yourself to death, Meara—"

"To death?" Mac's voice registered a tremor of fear.

Meara caught his hand. "It's an expression, Mac. It means, don't worry your silly head. Jordan's only teasing."

"Don't worry your silly head," Mac parroted with a playful giggle.

Jordan's face buckled and his downcast eyes spoke his apology. "Sorry," he whispered.

"It's okay."

"Have a seat." He motioned to the sofa.

She sank into the soft cushion. "So tell me."

Dooley darted in from the porch, his tail wagging like a flag, and Mac wrapped the setter in his arms.

"Dooley's ball is on the porch, Mac," Jordan said. "He likes to play fetch."

"Okay! Come, Dooley." Mac toddled off with Dooley tethered to his leg.

Jordan sat across from her. "After I left you yesterday, I went to the county planning commission and checked out the zoning laws. The shop's property is designated as a business district and nonresidential. But I read further and found some lingo about nonconforming status."

"What's that?"

"A 'grandfather clause.' The law says that an individual shouldn't be deprived of his property value through subsequent zoning laws."

Hearing the information, Meara felt her pulse ease. "Then, they can't stop you from renting the apartment."

"Yes and no. As always, there's a hook."

"A hook?" Her stomach tightened.

"The underlying principle presumes the property should eventually meet the law. There's usually a time limit connected. For example, if a restaurant sits on land that's rezoned for residential, the restaurant can continue its business. But—and here's the problem—if the business is closed for two years, then it has to meet the compliance of the new zoning law."

Her heart slumped to her churning stomach. "So that means, we have to move."

"Not necessarily. That's why I checked with my lawyer. I wondered if my thinking made sense. The county zoning law says that after two years or more of disuse, the building must conform. But I lived in the place for a couple of weeks not quite two years ago. And before that, the tenants had moved out only about a year before I bought the place. Nonconforming status runs with the property, not with the landlord."

"Then, it's okay?" Her emotions bounced like a yo-yo from fear to relief and back.

"The lawyer thinks so, but I'll have to request a special review from the County Appeals Board."

"No, Jordan, please. We'll find another place to live. That's too much trouble for you. I wouldn't think of asking you to go through that."

"You're not asking me, Meara. It's what I want to do. My lawyer says I have a sure case. Hatcher stirred up the hornet's nest, but I'll shoo them back without a sting."

"But—"

"But nothing." He rose and motioned for her to follow. "I think it's time for you to take a swim. Nothing like a brisk splash in the lake to wash away your troubles."

She grabbed her towel and joined him outside. Mac and Dooley trailed behind them down the path. Two beach chairs sat in the sand, and Jordan eased into one, holding back Dooley as Mac climbed into the other.

Meara dropped her towel on Mac's chair back, slipped off her sandals and dug her feet into the warm sand. The sun heated her body, but she knew the water would feel like ice. She slipped off her knit jogging shorts and top, then took a deep breath. Charging forward, with her feet prodded by the rocks, she dove deeply into the aqua lake.

Her spine tightened in the freezing temperature, and she plunged her hands through the water, gaining speed. As she approached the sandbar, the lake warmed to a tepid bath.

Her body relaxed, and she surged through the rolling

waves like a fish after bait—excited and anticipating. She sought the shoreline where Mac leaned on Jordan's chair as if discussing the world's problems. She hoped he was not a bother, but she tossed her worries aside and dove again into the rejuvenating water.

Jordan eyed Meara's lean, firm form as she dashed across the sand and dove into the frothy green-blue current. Deep, even waves rolled in as she glided toward the sandbar. If only he could close his eyes from the lasting reminder of his family's horrid death, he would don his swimsuit and skim the lake like a seal, joining her in the heated water of the sandbar.

"You don't like the water, Mac?" He turned his attention to the boy. Dooley's sandy nose rested in the child's lap, and, preoccupied, Mac petted it.

"Water makes me…sick." His blithe eyes became serious. "I go to…the hospital."

"Then, you're a smart boy to stay away from it. You don't want to be sick."

"I don't want to, Jor-dan." He nodded his head with firm conviction.

"That's right." Jordan quieted, his mind drawn to Meara's plight with Mac. Alone, she had her hands full. In many ways, the child was a delight. Gentle. Lovable. Too lovable.

But the child was a responsibility. He needed attention and guidance. Special care in many ways, and Meara had to do it alone. Yet, he'd never heard her complain. Only the opposite. She was so defensive when it came to Mac. Maybe more than was good for the boy. And more than was good for her, too.

Guilt assailed him as he thought of the boy's fondness for him. And his for Mac.

"Do you love me?"

Mac's voice flew through the air like a dart and pinned Jordan to his chair. How could he answer the child's question?

"I love you, Jor-dan." Mac leaned on the chair arm, gazing into his face.

Jordan's pulse pushed against his temple and sweat broke out on the nape of his neck. "You're my favorite pal, Mac." He swallowed the bile that rose in his throat. Hurt. That's all he could offer the child.

"Fav'rite pal." He poked his chest. "Me, too. You're my fav'rite pal." Mac rose and leaned his cheek on Jordan's shoulder.

It was all he could do to keep from clutching the child in his arms and weeping. His body shook with longing to repeat Mac's words, "I love you." But those words were a promise. A commitment. Never again would he love anyone like he had loved Robbie…and Lila. Love meant worry and hurt and loneliness. He could bear no more scars.

"I didn't see you…for a long time," Mac added, rocking his cheek against Jordan's shoulder. "I miss you."

"I know." Jordan closed his eyes, stemming the flood that pushed against his eyes and heart. "Grown-ups are busy people. We have to work and take care of business. Just like your mom. She has to work."

"Mama works. I'll work when I grow up. Okay, Jor-dan?"

"Okay, Mac. I pray you will." Like the passenger in a plummeting elevator, his breath left him.

Pray. Where had the word come from?

"We'll pray," Mac said, grasping Jordan's two hands in his and closing his eyes.

Aching deep in his being, Jordan shut his eyes and silently paraphrased Mac's words. *Mac will work and live a full life when he grows up.* If Meara's God was truly looking down on them, Jordan wanted Him to know he meant every word he said.

Chapter Ten

Tourists paraded through the streets in droves on the Fourth of July weekend. Meara and the other clerk scurried through the shop, answering questions and ringing up sales. Meara checked her wristwatch. Otis would be in at six, only a few minutes away. She took a calming breath and helped the next customer.

When Otis arrived, Meara left through the front door and headed for the bakery. As her hand touched the door handle, a voice brought her up short.

"Meara! My word, we had no idea where you were."

Meara swung around and faltered, both surprised and distressed to see her cousin. "Alison, what are you doing here?"

She wrapped Meara in a fleeting embrace. "Why, vacationing, silly. Doesn't everyone come to Mackinaw on the Fourth of July?"

Remembering the busy kite shop, Meara agreed. "I'm just surprised to see you, that's all. Where's Roger?"

She heaved a sigh. "I left him in the leather shop across

the way. You'd think he's never seen one before." She waved her hand in front of her nose. "The smell was too pungent on such a hot day. I thought I'd be sick."

Meara nodded in understanding. The sun's heat burned against her skin even in the late afternoon. She stepped aside to allow a customer to enter the bakery.

"Anyway," Alison said, lifting her eyebrows, "I wanted a treat. You know, a cookie or something. Roger's so watchful about my weight."

"You're as thin as a rail. I wouldn't think he'd be concerned." Meara eyed her cousin.

"But not for long." Her eyes brightened, and she covered a giggle.

A second passed before Meara understood. "A baby! Congratulations, Alison. I'm so happy for you." Meara knew they'd waited so long to have a child, as if afraid Meara's destiny would be theirs. So many cruel thoughts boiled over in Meara's mind. Would she disown her child if he or she wasn't perfect? How could Meara forget her cousin's snubbing after Mac was born? "And I pray God is good to you," she added.

Alison's face paled, and she pressed her hand on Meara's arm. "How can I ask you to forgive me for my neglect? I'm so sorry, Meara. We just didn't know how to handle things when Mac was born."

Meara had no desire to discuss this on the street. "Forget it, Alison. That was long ago."

"But I can't forget. I'm so ashamed. And when you left so quickly after Dunstan's death, I was shocked. Why did you leave?"

The truth? No, it would serve no purpose. "I felt we had

to leave eventually. Quickly seemed the best." Another customer darted past them to enter the bakery.

"Oh, you poor dear. I can't imagine why you would leave that lovely home for…well, for the unknown. And with no word to any of us. They have no idea where you've gone."

"Yes, that's true." Wisdom told her to say goodbye to Alison and let the past fade. Why try to explain now? But Meara longed for family and connections to her lovely green Erin.

"Would you like to come up? Mac and I live above the kite shop." She motioned upward toward the windows.

"Above this little shop?" Alison's widened eyes peered over the doorway to the two windows.

"Yes. Why not find Roger and come?"

Alison flung her arms around Meara's neck. "Oh, I'd love to see your home. Thank you."

"I'm taking Mac to the park for the fireworks tonight. You're welcome to join us. Or just come up for a moment, if you'd prefer."

"Thanks, Meara." She took two steps backward. "I'll find Roger right away." With a wave, she scurried across the street and down the sidewalk.

Alison's face told the tale. Clearly, she had been shocked at the less-than-affluent life Meara had accepted without a backward glance. Did she want to see the apartment to gape, or was she really happy? Meara didn't have an inkling.

She hurried inside the bakery for her desserts and dashed through the kite shop to the back staircase. When Meara stepped outside, she waved at Nettie in the marina's meager park. Nettie had agreed to keep an eye on Mac while he watched the tourists fly their kites.

Nettie signaled her, and soon she and Mac crossed the ferry parking lot and reached the stairs.

"I met my cousin outside the bakery a few minutes ago. I haven't seen her since Dunstan's funeral." She held her hand against her pounding heart.

"Such a nice surprise." She eyed Meara. "Or is it?"

"Oh, we had words...well, not words exactly. Silence, really. She didn't know how to handle..." She hesitated, indicating Mac with her eyes.

Nettie nodded. "I understand. Many people can't handle life's unusual blessings." She patted Meara's arm. "But don't worry. Today you have a chance to heal those wounds. Say a little prayer. God can mend the biggest schism."

"Thanks. I need a reminder from time to time."

She had so often neglected God's promised guidance. "I always try to fix things on my own, Nettie. Will I ever learn?"

"If you open your eyes and your heart."

She gave the woman a quick peck on the cheek. "You're a dear. Will you join us at the park? We'll save you a corner of the blanket."

"We'll see. Otis isn't one to fight crowds after a busy day in the store, but I'm going in to give him a hand."

"Hope to see you later."

Meara shooed Mac up the stairs and hurried behind him. She put the kettle on for tea, then rushed into the bathroom to run a comb through her hair. With a swipe of her lipstick, she colored her mouth with a pale coral hue.

"Mac," she called from the bathroom. "Come wash your hands, and let me look at you. We're having company."

Mac came around the corner. "Jor-dan?" His face glowed with anticipation.

Her pulse lurched at the name. "No. It's family I haven't seen for a while."

"Grandma?"

Again the child wrenched her heart. "No, a cousin. Just get ready, Mac."

Hurrying into the kitchen at the sound of the whistling kettle, Meara brushed errant tears from her eyes. Neglecting the Haydens was hurting Mac, and she didn't know how to solve the problem. She poured the boiling water into the teapot to steep, then studied the kitchen for her next project.

The picnic basket sat on the table, and Meara checked inside. She'd already tossed in extra dinnerware, anticipating the Mannings would join them—and there was the vague hope of running into Jordan.

Then she opened the bakery box and laid out a selection of cookies and pastries for the company. With her tray filled, she headed for the living room.

A rap on the door signaled their arrival. She set the tray on the coffee table and answered. "Come in," she said, maintaining a pleasant smile with her greeting.

"Meara, it's good to see you," Roger said, pressing a kiss on her cheek and embarrassing her.

"Alison tells me congratulations are in order."

"Yes. Yes," he said, his gaze darting toward Alison.

"When's the baby due? He or she—do you know?" She gestured them toward the living room.

"A little before Christmas," Alison said, "and no, we decided to be surprised."

"That's more fun, I think." Meara guessed they'd had every test in the book completed to avoid having a disabled child. "Have a seat, please. I have some tea steeping for you."

They sat on the sofa, and Meara headed for the bedroom. "Let me check on Mac, first."

Tonight, she felt terribly protective, and he'd taken far longer than she had expected to get ready. Peeking into Mac's room, she chuckled. He had pulled on a clean shirt, combed his hair, and was wrestling with his shoelaces.

"Can I help you?"

"No. Jor-dan showed me. Bunny ears, see."

He looped the strings on each side and folded them into a knot. She should have taught him a simpler way, like Jordan had. Mac struggled so often to make a secure knot.

"That's wonderful. Come out when you're ready. I want you to meet my cousin."

When Meara returned to the living room, she sat for a moment, then rose to prepare the tea. After she filled their cups and offered her guests the sweets, she sank into the chair across from them.

When Alison's gaze drifted over Meara's shoulder, Meara turned around. "Come here, Mac. Let me introduce you."

Unsure of the guests, he edged forward and stood beside her chair.

"Mac, this is Alison and Roger Garrison. They're our cousins."

Bravely, Mac stepped forward and extended his hand to Roger. "Hi. I'm Dunstan MacAuley Hayden. Nice...to meet you."

Roger's gaping mouth curved to a smile. "Hi there, Mac. I'm glad to meet you."

Alison leaned forward with a whisper. "He's so polite, Meara."

"Say thank you, Mac." Meara swallowed her initial response: *My son isn't deaf.*

Mac followed her direction with a "Thank you."

"How sweet," Alison gushed.

Meara bit her tongue, again. She wanted to heal wounds, not deepen the scars. She strained for conversation, and after refilling their teacups, she looked at the time. "As I mentioned, we're going to the park for a picnic and then to watch the fireworks. Can you join us?"

Alison's head swiveled, her eyes searching Roger's.

Roger and Alison obviously made a decision with their eyes. "Why…uh, we don't want to put you out, Meara," Roger said.

"I have plenty of food. I thought perhaps other friends would meet us there, so I've prepared extra."

Alison shifted her gaze again. "Why, that would be nice. We've heard the fireworks are wonderful."

"Wonderful," Meara agreed, "and unique. You can see three separate displays. One in the park, another in St. Ignace across the bridge, and another on Mackinaw Island. I suppose there aren't too many places that can boast that."

They chuckled politely, but despite their attempts, Meara sensed their discomfort.

"While you finish your tea, let me get the basket ready. If we want a table, we need to get going."

Within minutes, Meara and her guests descended the stairs and trekked the fifteen-minute walk to the park. A few revelers had gathered, but Meara found a table beneath a shade tree and spread out the picnic: cold fried chicken, salad and a loaf of crusty bakery bread, along with fruit and sweets from the bakery.

"This is wonderful," Roger said, gazing at the array of food.

"May we pray first?" Meara asked.

"Certainly," he said, quickly bowing his head. The others followed.

"Heavenly Father," Meara began, "we thank you for the lovely day, for food to fill our stomachs and for family to share our meal. We ask that whatever sorrow or pain lives in our hearts, You heal it quickly. In Jesus' name we pray. Amen."

When she opened her eyes, Alison and Roger looked at her with knowing eyes, but said nothing, except to repeat the "Amen" and dig into the fare.

Mac held out his plate, and Meara forked a piece of chicken, but before it hit the plate, Mac let out a yell. "Jor-dan!" The child crawled from the bench and headed across the grass.

Jordan wheeled around and met Mac, whose outstretched hand beckoned him toward the picnic table.

Meara rose as they neared and made swift introductions. "Join us, please. There's plenty."

"Come!" Mac directed, slapping his palm against the bench next to him.

A silly grin stretched across Jordan's face, and he caught Meara's eye. "It works for Dooley." He slid next to Mac at the table.

Meara handed him the utensils, and Jordan filled his plate. The conversation moved from babies to kites to the pesky seagulls, and, to Meara's relief, no more mention was made of the Haydens.

Jordan pushed his plate back and sipped the iced tea while Mac sang one of his senseless songs in his ear. As

Meara opened her mouth to suggest he give up the tune for a while, Jordan tousled Mac's hair.

"You've been patient enough, pal," Jordan said. "Let's go down by the water and take some crusts of bread. Maybe we can distract these irritating birds for a while."

He rose, and Mac scampered from the bench and trailed after him.

Alison followed him with her eyes. "He's a handsome man, Meara. Where did you find him?" Her eyebrows lifted as she spoke.

"Mac found him on the beach." The image of Jordan lollygagging among the shells and driftwood made her chuckle. She controlled herself and continued. "Jordan owns the kite shop, and he designs and builds all of the wonderful kites in the store. He's also my landlord."

"Landlord. That's all?" Alison's face shifted to disbelief. "No teeny bit of romance?"

"No. Sorry to disappoint you." Meara didn't admit to the emotions that wrought her heart, nor confess her dreams.

"Too bad," she mewled. "He looks like a great catch."

"Alison," Roger said, resting his hand on her arm, "the man's not a fish, and I don't think this is our business."

"All I mean is, he's wonderful with the boy," she said to Roger, then turned to Meara. "Wonderful with Mac. He seems kind. And sincere. And he's so handsome."

"I'll give him that," Meara said, hoping she sounded casual. "Jordan's kind and sincere." And much more than that, she thought. So much more her heart hurt. "But it's too soon, Alison. I've only been on my own for a few months."

"But that can't be much fun."

"Not fun, but I'm learning a lot about myself. I like that."

"You see, Alison," Roger said, "once you have this child, life will be different, too. Everything doesn't have to be entertaining."

Her lower lip protruded like a pouting child's. "I know, but I… Never mind, Roger."

Roger turned from his wife and focused on Meara. "Did Alison tell you about Dunstan's father?"

Meara's stomach dipped and rose. "No." His expression looked serious. "Is something wrong?"

Alison's hand shot forward and grasped Meara's. "Oh, I'm sorry. I was so busy talking about the baby I completely forgot."

"What is it?" Meara's eyes shifted from Alison to Roger.

"He had a severe stroke—just terrible," Roger said. "He's quite feeble."

Meara wanted to say that he got what he deserved, but compassion shuffled her negative feelings aside. "I'm sorry. And Mother Hayden? How is she?"

"As well as can be expected," Alison said. "Mr. Hayden ruled the home. She's had to take over now, and it's not easy for her."

"No, I suppose it isn't." Meara envisioned the meek, silent woman. "Send her my regards if you see her, please." Shame nudged her as she intentionally neglected reference to Dunstan Sr.

Then guilt surfaced. In Christian love, she should do something. But what? She'd lived unhappily in the home for years. Yet Edna Hayden was not the thorn that prickled Meara's life. She and Meara were in all essence roses between two thorns: Dunstan and his father. Two men made from the same mold, she'd sadly learned.

The conversation shifted to the crowd, water crafts, and how expertly Jordan played with Mac. Finally she caught sight of Jordan heading back, with Mac a few feet ahead. When Jordan's attention veered and he waved, Meara followed the direction and saw the Mannings coming across the lawn, weaving their way through the crowd.

"Hello," Meara called, motioning them to the table. She unfolded a blanket and spread it out in front of the table. She offered Nettie and Otis the bench and slid to the blanket with Mac leaning against her side.

Following the new introductions the conversation was filled with Nettie's chatter and Otis's witty tales, and Meara peered across the water, her heart lifting with the rising colors against the evening sky and the closeness of her son and Jordan. Peace. For once in her life, for this fleeting moment, she was filled with peace. The sunset spread across the horizon in swatches of gold and coral, blending to purple and blue like Joseph's coat—a message from God that everything happens for a purpose and good can come from evil. This time felt perfect.

Darkness lowered, and they sipped tea between their chatter and moments of lovely silence. Others lit lanterns or camping lights, but they remained in the shadows of the gaining half-moon in a cloudless sky.

"It's about that time," Jordan said, slipping from the bench beside Meara. He glanced down at the heavy-eyed Mac. "How's my pal doing?"

Mac gave him a lazy grin and rested his cheek on Meara's leg.

Jordan leaned toward her ear. "I have a feeling he'll miss his first big fireworks display."

She grinned and ran her hand along her son's hairline, wishing she could run her fingers through Jordan's graying, breeze-blown locks that lay in soft waves against his ears.

Jordan curled his legs, Indian-fashion, and she shifted to make herself more comfortable. The table conversation droned like a distant bee, but her thoughts tuned to the soft sound of Jordan's breath so close to her ear.

"Would you be more comfortable if you lean against me a little?" He shifted his shoulder and braced it with his arm behind her.

In breathless delight, she rested against his firm, muscular body. No words acknowledged the action. She couldn't speak for fear of weeping in sheer contentment. So often she blamed God for her hardships. Today she sent a hushed *thank you* for the glorious evening.

As the silent prayer rose to heaven, the first brilliant display shot into the darkened sky. Mac jerked in his sleep and opened his heavy eyes.

"Sparkles," the boy exclaimed, pushing himself up with his arm.

"Beautiful, isn't it?" she whispered.

"Beautiful," Jordan murmured.

His voice drew her gaze from the spangled sky to his eyes. Fireworks shimmered through her body. His tender face spoke to her—words she would never believe if she heard them aloud.

"Pretty," Mac called, as the sky filled with multiple swirls and sprinkles of color.

The crowd oohed and applauded with each fiery blast, and Meara's heart thundered as loudly as the missiles that soared like dazzling flowers into the sky.

Jordan caught his breath, gazing at Meara's profile in the glowing light. Her slender back pressed against his shoulder, and he could smell the delicate scent of flowers in her hair.

With a subtle shift of his body, he nuzzled closer and he felt the rise and fall of her breathing against his arm. A shiver pulsed through her. Was she chilled on such a warm night? But her face shone with contentment.

In sudden awareness, his stomach twitched. What was he doing? In the cover of darkness, he'd lifted the gate of his fortress—a fortress already crumbling from Meara's presence. Once, he was safe behind those walls. But he'd opened the door, and the hinges grated in his ears, determined to remain ajar.

A reverberating tumult boomed in the evening sky, shapes and colors bombarding overhead with glorious showers of swirling fairy dust. Cheers and applause blended with the fireworks thunder, and when the last glowing ash fell to the dark water, hushed silence settled over the crowd.

Shifting his weight, Jordan rose and gave Meara a hand, then helped a sleepy Mac to his feet. The others spoke their goodbyes, each heading in a different direction. Jordan lifted Mac in his arms as Meara gathered the blanket and empty basket.

He wanted to offer them a ride—his car was nearby—but he couldn't, and he couldn't explain. Instead, he cowered under avoidance. "I'll carry Mac home for you."

"Please, Jordan, no. He can walk." She tilted her face close to Mac, nestled in his arms. "You can walk, can't you, Mac."

Mac's sleeping eyes stayed closed, and she didn't insist. "Thanks. I suppose it's foolish to wake him."

The boy was light in his arms, and he ached, carrying the

child so close to his heart. Robbie had been larger, more solid, but the memory rose like a dark cloud. He forced it away.

They walked in silence, only occasionally commenting on the evening. He wondered about the cousin. He hadn't known Meara had family nearby, but tonight he wouldn't ask. Perhaps the question would stir memories, and the evening was too tender to ruin with inquiries.

At the apartment, he laid Mac in his bed, wished Meara a quick good-night, and hurried down the stairs. He was wracked with confusion. He'd allowed too much to happen. And he had his dark secret that would send Meara scampering away from him.

He rounded the strip of shops and turned toward the park. His car was a block from the silhouetted lighthouse, and he was glad that they hadn't passed it on the way to the apartment. What would he have told Meara if she had recognized it nearby?

Chapter Eleven

Meara combed her flyaway hair and caught it in a scarf at the back of her neck. She needed a haircut, but Jordan had mentioned how pretty her hair looked long, and she hesitated to make a change. Foolishly, she hung on to every word he said, savoring it like a rare fruit.

Tonight she was curious. Along with Otis, Jordan had invited her and Mac to his house. Business, he'd said. Praying nothing was wrong, she hurried Mac out of the apartment and they climbed into the car. In the afternoon, the sky had been overcast and the temperature cooler than usual for August. Clouds had billowed on the horizon and moved across the lake in dark brooding masses.

Now they hung over the area, heavy with rain. Flashes of slithering light darted across the horizon. Meara glanced in the back for her umbrella. The brightly colored fabric lay folded on the seat.

Before they'd gone a mile, large drops splattered on her dusty hood and blurred in rivulets down her windshield. The wipers splashed back and forth across the glass in a steady rhythm, their music only muffled by the occasional rumble and clap that rolled through the sky.

Through the curtain of trees, the sky ignited like a raging forest fire followed by a deafening roll of thunder. Mac ducked and clutched her arm.

"Careful, Mac, I'm driving. We don't want an accident."

He placed his hands over his ears. "Stop the noise, Mama."

"I can't. We'll listen to the music." She snapped on the radio and searched amid the crackle and fizz of static until she found some pounding rock music. She hiked up the volume, hoping it would drown out the frightening storm.

The dark road hazed in the pelting rain, and oncoming lights blurred her vision. She gripped the steering wheel with white knuckles and swung into Jordan's driveway, parking next to Otis's sedan. As she reached into the back seat, the house's back door opened, and Jordan darted outside, flinging open a wide umbrella. In two strides he was at the door, and then he sheltered them as they hurried inside..

As they dashed through the doorway, another jagged bolt ripped through the sky, and Mac slammed his hands over his ears. "Stop it," he ordered.

Jordan wrapped a protective arm around his shoulder. "You're inside, pal. Nothing can hurt you now. I turned the TV on for you." He addressed Meara. "It's an African safari program about animals. Is that okay?"

"He'll like that."

After being greeted by Dooley, Mac headed for the living room entertainment.

Meara hesitated for a moment, wishing things were different. Once again she and Jordan weren't alone. Lately their meetings were business or casual conversation with others around and no time to talk privately. They hadn't talked about their Fourth of July evening, and since that night, a twinge of discomfort crept through Meara when they were together. Besides, she was still curious about Jordan's friend Blair. What offer had he made?

"We'll talk at the kitchen table. The TV noise won't bother us that way." He glanced through the window. "It's bad out there. How was the driving?"

"Terrible. Really hard to see the road between oncoming traffic and the lightning. Look at my hands."

Trembling, she held them side by side, and he pressed them together with his palms.

"How about some coffee? That will, at least, give you a different reason to have the shakes."

She grinned and followed him into the kitchen.

"Bad driving?" Otis asked.

She nodded and repeated her tale.

"I'll want to get moving as soon as we're done here. Nettie is not a brave soldier in thunderstorms. She'll be on her knees, pleading with the Lord for protection. So I need to get home to give God's ears a break."

Meara laughed at Otis's accurate description of Nettie. She was a strong believer, faithful in prayer and an avid talker. Jordan motioned her to a chair and slid a steamy mug of coffee in front of her.

After refreshing the other two cups, Jordan joined them and shared his news: the gift shop deed was in his pocket, and he needed to decide what to do with the building.

"I'd like to hear your thoughts. Right now, I've been thinking I'll just close the place. See if I can sell the junk to another souvenir shop. Maybe rent the space out or use it for storage for the time being."

"Seems like a waste of money to me," Otis said, leaning back in the chair.

"Before I do too much, I'd like to see what else Hatcher has up his sleeve," Jordan said. "I go to the board of appeals on the zoning law early next week. At least I'll know where I stand on that issue."

"Next week?" Meara asked.

"No worries, remember?"

She nodded and swallowed the other comments vying to be released.

"S'pose you could get a little for the trinkets if you sell them in a lot. Maybe the Bargain Hut," Otis said with a chuckle. "But some of those thingamabobs would bring in more money if you sold them yourself in the shop."

"I know, but it's a hassle. That means hiring more help. I can't ask you to run the gift shop, too, Otis."

Otis leaned on his elbows and peered at Jordan. "You blind? How about this lovely lady sittin' with us here. She's got a head on her shoulders. And good ideas, too." He gave Meara a merry wink.

On Jordan's serious face, a grin flickered. "So tell me about these good ideas."

His gaze nabbed Meara's darting eyes, and she steadied herself. Here goes, she said to herself. "You know how some of your kites sell as wall hangings for restaurants and other businesses. Homes, too. Otis mentioned it when I was hired, but now I've seen it with my own eyes. I'm surprised at how many are bought to be used as home accessories." She hesitated, overwhelmed suddenly by a sense of incompetence. "Maybe I don't know what I'm talking about."

Otis gave her a playful nudge. "Go 'head. I've had to listen to your ramblin'. Tell the horse's mou—" He stopped abruptly, then breathed a sigh. "The big ears is in the living room. Gotta keep a leash on my tongue. Nettie's soap tastes horrible."

His silliness made Meara harness her courage. "Maybe we could add other decorative items to the inventory. Little by little. You could do what you said, and sell the souvenirs to other shops."

"Or toss them in the trash bin in the back," Jordan said.

"That, too." He made her smile. "But some of the bric-a-brac is quality porcelain and china."

Otis chuckled. "You can tell she's been scoutin' the place out ever since she knew you were buying the shop."

"Is that right?" Jordan ask, touching her arm with a gentle pat.

Heat rose to her cheeks. She hated her fair skin. Every emotion lit up her face. "Guilty as charged." She lifted her gaze to his smiling eyes. "Anyway, as I was saying before Otis tattled, we could add wall accents, pillows, vases, scatter rugs, candles, dried flowers. The kite shop could become a mecca for professional home decorators. Or just tourists wanting to buy pretty things."

"My idea seems easier," Jordan said. He stared into space.

They waited, neither saying a word.

"Let me think on it," he said finally. "I suppose I could hire a couple more clerks and move you into the new shop." His eyes pinned Meara. "What do you say? That means full-time work. At least, full-time responsibility."

She hadn't considered that. If Mac attended school, her days would be free. But she'd balked at sending him to public school. Yet so far, that was her only choice...or homeschooling again. "Might be taxing at first with Mac around, but I'd like to give it a try. And I'm still determined to find a school for him this September."

"I'd really thought of storage or renting the place, but I suppose that could be a hassle, too."

"You ain't a-kiddin'. This town has had some pretty cheesy shops," Otis said. "Yours could be a breath of fresh air."

"You're right." Jordan grinned at his "pretty cheesy" phrase. "Let me think on it. I don't want to rush—"

Before the sentence left his mouth, a piercing blue light shot across the sky, filling the air with an acrid stench of sulphur. A clap of thunder that shook the house followed on its heels.

"Now, that was close," Jordan said as the lights flickered and died.

The outdoor pandemonium was trailed by Mac's hoot, sailing into the kitchen from the living room.

Meara bolted from her chair, but in the darkness, she faltered. "It's okay, Mac. I'll be there in a minute."

"I'll get him," Jordan said, rising and edging his way from the table. "Hang on, Mac," he called. "I have a flashlight right here, and some candles if we need them. Usually the lights are off only a couple of minutes."

In one moment, a beam of light shot from across the kitchen, then bobbed past as Jordan headed into the living room for Mac.

After Jordan guided him back to Meara, Mac clung to her side. She patted his cheeks and felt a few stray tears rolling from his eyes.

"Well, I imagine Nettie's under the table, talking to the Lord a mile a minute, so I'd better get."

"Let me light a candle, Otis." The flashlight swayed through the room, and in a second, Jordan returned with a candlestick. Meara took the matches from his hand and lit the broad taper. A warm glow brightened the room.

Jordan led Otis to the door with the flashlight, and Meara sank back into her chair with Mac fastened to her lap.

"I suppose we should go, too," she said when Jordan returned.

"No way. You're not going out in this weather. And who knows if the lights are on in town? Grab that candle and let's go to the living room where it's comfortable."

Meara lifted the candle and moved slowly in the dim light, Mac at her side. Jordan lit two more thick, sturdy candles, and a warm glimmer flickered around the room.

The thunder rolled in the distance, and in minutes, the lightning had softened to a faraway flash zigzagging over the lake. With the ebbing storm, Mac relaxed and stretched out on the sofa.

Jordan punched the TV "off" switch, then sat in the chair across from her. "The storm's quieting. At least for now."

Sitting in silence, Meara soothed Mac with her hand until his breathing became slow and even.

"He's asleep," she whispered. "I figured that would happen."

"It's late, too." He leaned toward the light. "Nine-thirty."

"I wonder if the lights will come on tonight? I can't stay here forever."

"I suppose not," he said.

In the cover of shadows, Meara gathered her courage,

longing for the answers to questions she'd been wondering about. "Remember the day your co-worker was here? Blair somebody?"

"Yes, Blair Dunham."

"Well, he mentioned...making an offer to you. Is it too personal to ask what that's about? I've wondered."

Jordan chuckled. "Not as long as you don't mind my probing, too. Blair's from the university where I taught. There'll be an opening sometime next year, and he told the dean he'd let me know about it."

"You're going back?" She suspended breathing, waiting for his answer.

"I'm not sure. I'm thinking."

"Oh." Like the distant thunder, anxious thoughts rumbled within her. Would he leave? In the silence, she waited for his "probing" question. An uneasy feeling settled over her until he finally spoke.

"I didn't know you had relatives nearby."

"Alison? She lives over on Lake Michigan. I just happened to run into her. We were close once, but things happened, and, well, it was sad really." She hesitated, wondering if she wanted to tell the story.

"I didn't mean to pry. I was just surprised."

"You're not prying. It just hurts a little yet." The story rolled from her tongue—Alison's coldness after Mac was born, the hurt, the loneliness for family. "And I didn't really have family with Dunstan. He changed after we were married and was terribly distant after Mac was born. And Dunstan Senior was the same. Worse, maybe."

"You said you'd been unhappy." His voice sounded weighted.

"Alison told me Dunstan's father had a bad stroke. When I first heard, I had such mixed feelings. Do you know what I thought?"

The candlelight flickered across his serious face. So tender, the look in his eyes. And kind.

"No, what did you think?"

"I was glad. That was my first reaction. The old man got what he deserved. God punished him for his unkindness. But...then I felt horribly guilty. God doesn't punish people like that."

"What makes you believe that, Meara? Maybe God does use His power to chasten. To get even."

"How can you say that? We're His children." Her hands trembled as she clutched them to her breast. "Parents aren't vindictive. They don't intentionally hurt their children. Discipline them maybe, but not hurt them."

"Have you heard of child abuse?"

Her chest tightened. This was not a side of Jordan she knew at all. Wasn't he a Christian? He bowed his head when they blessed the food. He... She stopped. He did little else. But he was filled with gifts of the Spirit—compassion, kindness, humility. She leaned forward to look in his eyes, amazed she'd never asked him.

"Are you a Christian, Jordan?"

Are you a Christian? Jordan's stomach twisted like a hangman's knot, and his thoughts whirled out of control. How could he answer her? If he told her where his convictions had been for the past three years, she'd walk out the door and never look back.

But things had changed. Since he'd met her, Meara had caused him to face a decisive fact. Two women that touched his life in the most amazing way believed in God. Were they God's catalyst that would stir his faith?

"Jordan?" Meara leaned forward into the candlelight, her lovely face marked by deep, strained furrows. "Are you a Christian?"

Words jumbled on his lips, and he prayed his first prayer. *God, if You are real, give me the right words.* A rush of anxiety swept through him. He lowered his eyelids, waiting for something to happen. But not knowing what. When he opened them, Meara's anguished eyes locked with his.

"I can't answer your question, Meara."

"You what?" She fell back against the cushion. Her face a shadow.

"I don't have a clear answer for you. I'm like a student who stares at a true-and-false question and sees both sides as the answer."

"How could I have known you this long and not realize that you aren't a Christian?"

"I didn't let you. I've read the Bible so many times. I've taught it in a class. But I was the teacher. I was supposed to have the answers. How could I ask my students to explain their faith?"

"Then your heart was open? You were asking yourself questions?" Her tone brightened.

"Yes, Lila believed, and I had begun to listen and learn from her. But I was like a pendulum, swinging from one side to the other. I had opened my heart to understand, but—"

"But what, Jordan? What would close the door to the Spirit's prodding?"

He wasn't ready to open the wound again, to spill out the

details of that horrible night. But she deserved an answer. "A tragedy. A horrifying tragedy."

"What happened?"

"My wife..." The words seared his throat. "My wife and son were killed." Hot sorrow pressed against his eyes, and he turned his face away from her. In the dim light, he hoped she didn't see his tears.

"I'm so sorry, Jordan." Her voice was a whisper. "I can't imagine your grief. How did it happen?"

"Car accident." *Accident.* The word jabbed his memory.

"Oh, how horrible. Your wife and son." She rose and knelt at his feet. "But you can't turn against God. You can't."

"And why not? If God is Almighty, why not? He could have prevented it. But I was punished for my wavering faith."

She grasped his hands and pressed her forehead against their entwined fingers. "If you've read God's Word, you know that evil forces work night and day to undermine our faith, to destroy our trust in God and in each other, to twist love from our hearts, to replace forgiveness with doubt and fear. God doesn't do that."

Tears flowed from her eyes, washing his icy fingers. He longed to hold her against him, to comfort her, but he had little to offer except hope. "Meara, please, I—"

"Read the Bible again, Jordan. You said you've read it many times, but this time open your heart and mind. Read it again. God planned for our salvation long before the earth was made. Sin, death, evil—God knew we would need His saving grace."

He felt drained. "I have moments when I know God is real, but I don't trust my judgment anymore." A sudden, icy awareness shivered through him. “Maybe I don’t have faith in myself.”

“But you’re intelligent. With the seed of faith you already have, study the Bible. I’ll help you find answers if I can.”

He responded with a nod.

In the hushed silence, Mac’s deep, even breaths confirmed his sleep. Jordan slid his hands from Meara’s and rested them against her concerned face. Her cheeks were warm, and he brushed his fingers along the graceful contour to her lips, tracing her perfectly shaped mouth.

Her eyes widened, yet she remained silent and unmoving, except for a breath that shivered into the darkness.

His failing defenses rearmed, and he shrunk back, killing his powerful longing to kiss her.

“The storm’s passed.” Meara’s whisper broke the stillness, and her questioning eyes remained locked with his. “We’d better go.”

Jordan stood, overwhelmed by the emotion that tangled in his heart. “I’ll follow you home.”

“No. That’s not necessary.”

“Not necessary, but I want to. Just to make sure you’re home safe. Might be a tree down or something along the way. I’d never forgive myself if anything happened to you.” The words seared like a flaming arrow, and his past, like a mound of ashes, rose in his mind.

Chapter Twelve

In the quiet of the new store, dust rose from the display shelves as Meara boxed trinkets and cheap souvenirs. The Bargain Hut had offered a fair price for the lot.

After much scrutiny, they had agreed upon what to sell and what to keep for The New Curiosity Shop. Jordan had laughed when she'd suggested the name—with a twist—that she had borrowed from Charles Dickens. Jordan had *laughed.* When they'd first met, he'd never laughed. Rarely grinned, for that matter.

She closed the lid on a box, shoving it aside, and pulled another forward. She wrestled with her thoughts, trying to stay focused on the seemingly eternal task, but the mundane activity allowed her mind to wander. For the fourth time that afternoon, tears filled her eyes and sneaked a lazy trail down her cheeks. Pulling her hand across her face, she erased signs of her frustration.

"Looks like the job may take a lifetime."

She jumped at the voice and swung around. "Jordan, you scared me."

"Sorry, I didn't mean to."

"I know. It's not you, it's me."

"I stopped to see how you're doing." He stood at the storeroom entrance, gazing at the wall to his left. "I think I'll put an opening between the two shops." He returned his focus to her. "Makes sense, doesn't it?"

"A lot of sense. Customers can't help but wander through an open doorway." She tried to form a grin but her muscles struggled against her effort.

Jordan closed the distance between them. "Something's wrong. Can I help?"

"Not unless you can build a school for special students." Her attempt at being lighthearted was failing.

"Ah, I forgot. You went to school this morning."

She nodded. "IEPC meeting. That's the individualized educational planning committee." The sentence faded and her tears won the battle again. "It was terrible."

He lay his hand on her shoulder. "How?"

"They tried to be nice but they don't understand Mac. He's the first Down child they've had." She brushed away a stray hair glued to her cheek by a tear. "The special education teacher talked so loudly to Mac—right in his face—he covered his ears. I almost threw my hand over Mac's mouth to keep him from telling her to be quiet."

A grin brightened Jordan's face.

She shrugged. "You know Mac."

He nodded.

"He'll be in the learning center for four hours a day with other special students, then mainstreamed for the rest."

"Is that bad?"

"I don't know. He'll have classes with regular kids in art, music and physical education. I can't believe I'm even considering this. Mac needs attention and special training…not being jumbled up with regular students. Being with those children might be horrible."

"And might not be, Meara." He grasped her shoulders and caught her gaze. "Give the school a chance. And give Mac a chance."

A sob rose from her throat, and she pushed her face against his chest to mask her rising emotion. His hands slid from her shoulder to her back, and he drew her close, soothing her with quiet, comforting words. A sense of wholeness…of warmth spread through her, feeling at this moment protected and… And what?

She captured the reins of self-control and lifted her head. "I'm sorry. I didn't mean to fall apart."

He tilted her chin upward with his thumb and finger. "And what about faith? And prayer? You're the lady that drills all that into my head. Should I assume that God can't help you?"

"Remind me what the Scriptures say, Jordan?" She studied his face, wondering if he were actually reading the Bible.

"'Ask and you shall receive.'" In thought, he lifted his face heavenward. "And how about 'Then you call upon Me and come and pray to Me, and I will listen to you.'"

Jordan had made his point. Once again she hadn't leaned on God for support. Hiding both her chagrin and delight, she lowered her eyes. "I'll try to do better."

Yet, hearing his testimony, her heart skipped and her gaze drifted to his. "And you've been reading, haven't you."

"Rereading, you mean. Yes." For a moment, his hand caressed her back, then he shifted it upward to her shoulder. "But this time, I'm listening."

"I'm glad." She sighed. "And I'll listen, too."

Their gazes locked, and a discomforting awareness of their close proximity awakened in Meara. She broke from his eyes, stepped back and grasped a handful of plastic tomahawks. "The Bargain Hut's getting a real deal here."

Jordan nodded and followed her example, scooping a huge handful of the plastic Indian souvenirs into the carton.

Clasping another load, Meara stopped in midair. "So to what do I owe this unusual visit? Did you stop by to make sure I'm earning my keep?" With a grin she released the novelties from her grasp.

"I met with the board of appeals this morning."

Her grin faded and her hand flew to her chest. "And?"

"I thought we would have the answer, but we have to wait."

"But why? I thought your lawyer said it looked good."

"I think they're getting static from Hatcher. I only hope that's all they're getting."

Her mind whirred. "You mean…like a payoff."

He drew his hand across his face. "Ignore me, Meara. That was wrong. They're an honest bunch. But Hatcher is stirring up the water."

"How long must we wait?"

"In two weeks I should have their answer."

Her heart yo-yoed to her stomach and back. "Two weeks. If Mac and I have to move, I'd rather do it now before the store opens and—"

"You won't have to move." He gazed into her eyes and tilted her chin. "Remember, 'Ask and you—'"

"'Shall receive.' See how easily I forget." He amazed her. Jordan quoting the Bible, and better yet, sounding like he believed it. "I won't say another word. Promise."

"Hearing is believing." He squeezed her arm and headed toward the storeroom.

When Dooley let out a welcoming bark, Jordan looked toward the house, where Otis gave him a wave. Jordan whistled, and Dooley darted from the lake and joined him with an energetic shake of his wet fur.

Startled, Jordan jumped back, but it was too late.

Otis's chuckle floated on the breeze, and Jordan shrugged with an embarrassed laugh and climbed the hill, wiping the sandy water from his face.

"What's up?" Jordan asked when he reached the top.

"Had some errands to run and thought I'd drop by with some gossip."

Jordan opened the screen and waved Otis inside. "What gossip is that?" He motioned for Otis to sit.

Otis sank into the chair. "I got wind that the T-shirt shop and the restaurant are considering Hatcher's offer."

Folding onto the wicker settee, Jordan rested his cheek on his thumb and rubbed his forehead with his fingers.

"They won't move until the tourist season ends. There's a line of shops going up on the south side of Main. That location gets a lot of traffic, and word has it they might move there." Otis rested his elbows on his knees and folded his hands, staring at the floor. "It's only scuttlebutt."

"Scuttlebutt, but something we need to think about. We can't win the battle by ourselves, Otis."

"That's what I was thinkin'."

"Maybe we're the only ones who care about the saloon."

Otis shook his head. "I don't think so, Jordan. Ya know, I think people jus' aren't realizin' it could be a problem. Some don't even know."

"That could be our solution. Make the community aware of Hatcher's plan. If people don't care about the saloon, then we're already defeated. We can stop fighting."

"But what about the kite shop? And what—"

"I know, Otis. I know." What about Meara? The college job opportunity came to mind. Perhaps he should pull himself together and go back to Kalamazoo. Go back to his world of books, theses and examinations. But it was Meara's face he saw. Then Mac's. He wanted them to be secure and happy first. Then maybe…

"So what, then?" Otis asked, giving him a questioning stare.

"Sorry, I was thinking. Who in the community cares about the city's family image? Motels? Some of the shop owners, perhaps?" He paused, his mind racing for ideas.

"The churches. We have four in town. That's a lot of people."

"Great suggestion. If they don't care, then it's over. A letter, maybe, or a flyer?"

"And we could contact the clergy. Once the people talk it up, word should spread all over town."

A car door slammed. Jordan rose and peered from the porch doorway through the house. "Sounds like someone's here." He walked to the back door and saw Meara's car, but no Meara.

"I'm here," she called from the front.

He grinned and headed back to the porch, his pulse stumbling along with him.

She was standing beside the door when he returned. "I saw Otis's car and figured you two were on the porch." She glanced through the screen. "You're getting a wonderful breeze from the lake."

"We're getting June weather in September. Have a seat." Jordan motioned to a chair. "Something to drink?" His stomach tightened as he gazed at her, her hair in flyaway fashion and her freckles dark from the summer sun.

"No, I can only stay a minute. I just had a couple of things to talk to you about."

"Problems at the store?"

"No, business in the new shop has been wonderful. The end-of-the-season rush has the two new clerks flying. In fact, I've had a hard time keeping merchandise on the shelves."

"We apparently made one right decision."

Frowning, she tilted her head.

"I mean, keeping the gift shop open and getting rid of the junk."

"Now that school's begun, it'll quiet down. We might need to think about some advertising then."

The *we* in her conversation had become familiar, and he liked the sound.

Otis rose. "I'd better git on the road. We've hashed our ideas around enough. If you hop on the letter, I'll be happy to talk to the clergy."

Jordan rose and extended his hand. "Thanks, Otis. Maybe we can lick this thing yet."

Otis grasped his hand in a friendly shake and, with a wave, left through the porch door.

"I didn't mean to interrupt," Meara said, eyeing Otis's exit.

"We were finished. Otis stopped by, worried about some of the latest Hatcher gossip."

"Gossip?" There was concern in her eyes. "Is it serious?"

He recounted Otis's scuttlebutt.

"Sometimes it seems like we're fighting a losing battle. I should say *my* battle." Her voice sank. She glanced toward him. "Sorry. I'm just discouraged."

"What's up?"

"It's Mac. I'm not happy with the school situation. I wish they hadn't started early this year. The new shop's been so busy I haven't had time to monitor what's going on there."

"Is something wrong?"

"First day of school someone stole his notebooks. The next day he told me a group of boys laughed at him."

"Laughed?" His chest tightened, thinking of Mac surrounded by bullies. "What did he do?"

She shook her head. "He told them it wasn't nice to laugh at people."

Jordan fell back against the cushion. "That was it?" Mac was amazing.

"Yes. And he said they walked away."

"Okay, Mac!" His arms flew upward in an exuberant cheer while a grin yanked at his mouth.

"It's not funny. Next time they could hurt him—"

"Meara, be proud of your son. He handled the situation with tact and decorum. What more could you ask of any child?"

She sighed, her shoulders drooping as she caved into the chair cushion. "I don't know what I expect. I just don't want him hurt. Physically or otherwise."

"But we're all hurt at one time or another. It's part of

life." He saw her downhearted expression. "Haven't you been hurt?"

"Yes." She lifted her disparaged face to his. "You know I have."

"So cheer up. Mac is learning to handle himself. Be proud of him."

"You're right, I suppose, but...I can't help it. I—" She stared at her hands twisting in her lap. "And besides, I'm so filled with guilt I can't bear it."

"Guilt? Why?" He held his breath, waiting for her revelation.

"I've avoided my in-laws far too long. I know I should contact them." Her eyes shrouded with frustration. "A telephone call seems...shoddy under the circumstances. I should visit."

"And take Mac?"

Her face blanched. "No. No, not Mac. I'd go myself."

"But he's asked to see his grandmother. He'd be disappointed. And wouldn't they be upset, too?"

"I'll go during the day and tell them he's in school. They should understand."

"Meara, you're clinging to those old wounds too long. Why not bury the past?" The words kicked him in the gut and, looking at Meara's expression, he realized he'd overstepped his bounds. He softened his voice. "Take Mac with you."

This time it was her eyebrows that arched, and his stomach took a bungee dive. Who was he to criticize anyone about hanging on to the past?

She validated his thought. "Don't make me respond to that."

"I know, I have no right to talk."

"I need to go." She rose. "Mac'll be home from school soon." She stepped forward, then faltered. "Actually I stopped by to ask you something. The church is having a father-and-son ice-cream social next week, you know, instead of a banquet. And it happens to be Mac's birthday. I wondered if you'd be willing to take him. He thinks so much of you."

Her voice faded, and she closed her eyes. "I'm sorry. I shouldn't put you on the spot like that."

"It's okay, Meara. Really. I just—" He cringed at the thought of taking someone else's child to a father-and-son activity. Even Mac. The hurt was a pressure against his chest.

"No, I understand. I just feel bad that Mac doesn't have a real father. I'm his mother, but I can't be both. He needs a man in his life." She lowered her eyes. "I'm ashamed of myself. Please forgive me. Mac has so many needs, and I—"

"Mac will survive, Meara. He'll more than survive." With a gentle motion he turned her face and tilted her head upward. "Give him time."

He lifted his finger to her cheek, tracing its delicate line to her full, pink lips. A longing to press his mouth against hers surged through him, but fear and wisdom shackled him.

Her wide-eyed, expectant stare tugged at his awareness. Tenderly he brushed her full bottom lip with the tip of his unsteady finger. "Please. Give us both time."

In The New Curiosity Shop, Meara bent down to pick up a fallen toss pillow and jammed it back onto the stack. The action jarred another one and it toppled to the floor. She closed her eyes, fighting her frustration. She reached down for the pillow and shoved it onto the stack as two more slipped to the tile.

Unbidden tears came to her eyes while her frustration wavered between anger and fear. She pushed a knuckle below her lashes and wiped away the moisture, then kept her hand there, her head bent forward, to gain control.

"Meara, what's wrong?"

She took another swipe at her tears and spun around to face Nettie. "Nothing. I'm fine."

"Fine?" Nettie's kindly eyes filled with worry.

"Almost fine," Meara corrected, knowing she couldn't keep much from Nettie.

The older woman moved closer, bending as she came to gather up the two disturbed pillows. She lifted them, and they settled on the pile as if afraid to move or face Nettie's famous bar of soap.

"You're not fine at all from the looks of it," Nettie said, patting Meara's arm.

"I need a break, that's all."

"Fine. Then we can talk."

Meara didn't want to talk. What could she say that hadn't already gone through her mind a thousand times. She'd allowed herself to have hopes she couldn't have. Yet, looking at Nettie's determined face, Meara knew she would never win a refusal.

She signaled the new clerk she'd hired a week ago and followed Nettie through the door to the kite shop.

"We can go upstairs," Meara said, realizing she had no other quiet place to convince Nettie she was fine.

"Good, and I'll make you some tea," Nettie said.

Meara stepped out into the late-August sunshine, letting

the chill of her worries seep into the summer air. Nettie followed behind her up the covered stairs, and at the top, Meara opened the door and motioned Nettie inside.

Nettie headed for the kettle, snapped it on and pulled two mugs from the cabinet. "You go in there and put up your feet. I'll take care of this."

Having little choice, Meara followed her instructions, pleased for a moment that she didn't have to think or make a decision on her own.

She flopped onto the sofa and slid her legs onto the cushion. Sunlight slipped through the curtains and sprinkled the upholstery with flickering shadows, the movement distracting her from her stress. Soon the scent of lemony tea drifted into the room along with Nettie, her face set with purpose.

"Here you are," Nettie said, handing her the mug, then settled across from her. "Now…what's this all about? Mac's school? I know you've been worried."

Meara shrugged. Mac's schooling hadn't rested easy in her mind, but the problem was much more than that.

Nettie's wise eyes narrowed in thought. "Could it be Jordan?" She nodded her head as if she'd answered her own question.

"It's a lot of things, Nettie. Too many to talk about."

"Never. Start with the first one. It'll get easier." The older woman took a sip of tea and settled the mug against her palm resting in her lap. Her gaze didn't waver.

Meara squirmed beneath the woman's intense look until she finally nodded. "It's Mac…and Jordan."

"Two big problems, then."

Meara didn't understand. Puzzled, she waited to hear

what else Nettie would say but she remained silent. "What do you mean, two big problems?"

"It's like Otis. I have more worries over him than anyone else. The people we love cause us the most concern."

Love. The word rocked her. Meara didn't want to love Jordan. She'd done everything to keep herself from it, but she'd lost the struggle. Even Nettie knew the truth.

"You do love him, dear," Nettie said. "I see it in your face."

The truth charged through her. "I can't. It's impossible."

"Why?"

Nettie's simple question hung before her. What was the truth? She did love him, but she didn't want to. "Because. Because I can't trust him. I trusted once, Nettie. Foolish. Naive. How can I trust a man who has his own problems so bottled up inside him he's ready to burst. One day he'll walk away. I've dealt with rejection before. I can't let it happen again."

Nettie concentrated on her tea in silence—the rare moment made Meara certain she agreed. Finally Nettie shifted and leaned forward.

"Jordan has problems. Deep ones. I can't deny that. Maybe I'm an old woman talking through my hat, but I don't think Jordan has it in his heart to walk away from you and Mac. If any man can be trusted, it's Jordan. Look what you've done for him...and he for you."

Meara had relied on Jordan too much. She knew that. And he had done so much for her and Mac. In comparison, she'd done so little. She'd tried to open doors for him. Especially to his faith. She'd failed.

"He's not a believer, Nettie. How can I have *faith* in a man who doesn't know the meaning of the word?"

Nettie's eyes misted and she pressed her hand against her

chest near her heart. "He needs time. Jordan has a good heart…and a soul. He's had a deep loss, and now that he's regained the world, he'll find his faith again."

The depth of her words touched Meara's mind and heart. Still, her doubt, her fear pierced the brighter picture Nettie had painted.

"Maybe in time. But I can't take the chance. I can't love anyone, Nettie. Mac needs all the love and attention I have. I don't have room for anyone else."

Nettie tsked and shook her head. "My, oh my. Do you think love has a limit? The Lord has given us the capacity to love as He loves, Meara. It's limitless. You're a young woman, and the Almighty certainly wants you to find a partner to fill your days. Mac keeps you busy…but he's a boy now. He'll grow up and—"

"Will he, Nettie? We don't know that for sure. Neither you nor I have any idea how long Mac will be on this earth, and while he's here, I'll protect him. I want—" Her voice caught in her throat and she felt the quaver of emotion taking control.

"Aah, Meara." Nettie set her mug on the side table. "We can't second-guess God. Neither one of us knows if we might walk outside and die on the street. Life is a gift and we have it as long as the good Lord allows. But you can't spend your life wondering about things like that. Life is meant to be lived."

Meara lost the battle with her tears as they rolled from her eyes and chose a path down her cheeks. Concern and compassion filled Nettie's face while Meara struggled to make sense of her emotion. Finally she swallowed back the disquiet that raked through her and drew in a calming breath.

"You're right, Nettie, but I don't know if I have the capacity to live. I was bound for so long in my in-laws' world, and when I left, I felt forsaken by everyone. My husband's family, my cousin, my homeland. I had nowhere to turn. Then…I came here and began a new life, but I'm depending too much on Jordan…and my need—our need—frightens him."

"First remember one thing, Meara. You're never forsaken. I think you've forgotten that the Lord holds you in His heart. When things look blackest, God is there and can lift you up." Nettie rose, her gaze directed at the curtains along the front windows. "But you have to ask God. Then you have to listen."

Her words settled over Meara like sackcloth, making her uncomfortable. "I'll try" was all she could say.

Nettie ambled across the room and pushed back the curtain, running her hand across the fabric. "Cobweb," she said, sending Meara a tender grin. She brushed the dust from her hand, then turned back. "It's not easy. We all struggle with giving our problems to the Lord. Jordan still suffers over the loss of his family. He hangs on to his pain as if it's a gift. But you can trust that God won't give up…and you could help Jordan let go."

"Me?" Meara felt a spark of offense. "But that's unfair, Nettie. The closer I get to him, the more he pushes me away. He even pushes God away." She rolled her neck and pressed her fingers against the tense cords of her shoulders.

"You're afraid to trust the Lord?"

"Trust the Lord? What do you mean? We're talking about Jordan."

"We're talking about both. God works in His own time.

You've only known Jordan for a few months. You don't realize what you've done for him. He's come out of his shell. He's beginning to live again because of you and Mac. The Lord needs time to work His way. Jordan needs time to accept it."

Meara had heard this before. *Please...give us both time.* Nettie's words settled in Meara's heart. She needed to let God move mountains. With guilt she recalled how she'd backed Jordan into a corner. "I asked Jordan to take Mac to the father-son social at church."

Nettie settled in the chair again and lifted her teacup, her eyes thoughtful. "What did he say?"

A sheepish grin pulled at her cheek. "He said he needed time."

"And he does, Meara. So does the Lord."

Chapter Thirteen

Jordan had driven past the church at least three times, fighting to keep from turning into the parking lot and surprising Mac in the fellowship hall. He winced at the thought of Mac missing the ice-cream social because of his personal cowardice. But good old Otis had escorted the boy.

Now Jordan inched down the street and around the block for a second time, hoping to catch them leaving the social. In his slow-moving car, he felt like a stalker watching for them. A package sat on the seat beside him. A gift for Mac's birthday. He could miss the church function, but not the birthday. He didn't want to show up at Meara's without Mac there. She might toss him out on his ear.

Though a part of him yearned to attend the gathering, his brain led him away. His personal pain dominated his thoughts, and he could do nothing but hurt the boy. The child was already too fond of him. The fact was clear. And Meara? Was she fond of him, too, or was her interest more for her son?

He pulled to the side of the road and waited. Too early,

he finally realized. He pulled away from the church and drove to the waterfront park near the lighthouse. The setting brought back warm memories of the Fourth of July, when Meara had leaned her back against him. And he had carried Mac home in his arms.

Jordan parked his car, then strolled toward the beach and rested on a bench to enjoy the early-September sun. Squalling seagulls soared overhead, dipping down to snatch leftovers dropped by a picnicker. Cars streamed across the arching bridge, returning from the upper peninsula or heading farther north on vacation.

Children scampered along the water's edge, gathering shells and driftwood, tended by mothers with watchful eyes. Jordan's attention drifted farther out, across the water to the island and off to the horizon. Drifting in and out of reveries and confusion, his mind flagged behind his gaze.

Time ticked away as he thought. What was happening with his life? What hid behind that dark glass the Bible referred to? What picture might rise from his shadowed imaginings? Meara and Mac filled his mind so often. His incomplete life seemed whole in their presence.

The sun lowered in the sky, sprinkling shimmering silver sequins on the rippling water. In the late-afternoon glow, bright sails, minuscule colorful triangles, skimmed across the dusky blue lake. Jordan glanced at his wristwatch. Mac must be home by now. He rose from the bench and returned to the car.

When he parked behind the shop, he grabbed the gift and climbed the staircase, wondering if Meara would be pleased to see him.

The door flew open, and her face flickered with a series

of unnamed emotions. "Jordan, what are you doing here?" She didn't widen the door or invite him in.

He stood, clutching the gift in his hand, his tongue tangled in his response.

Finally she drew back and opened the door. "I'm sorry. Come in."

When he stepped inside, another voice greeted him with a rush of excitement.

"Jor-dan!" Mac propelled toward him as fast as his stubby legs would carry him. "Jor-dan," he repeated, and his arms wrapped around Jordan's trousers.

"Happy birthday, Mac."

"Me," he said, jabbing his chest. "My birthday."

"Yes, I know. I have a present for you. See." He lifted the gift toward the child.

"For me?"

"Sure enough."

Meara closed the door. "Let's invite Jordan to have a seat, Mac."

Jordan sat on the sofa, and Mac, at his side, stared at the unopened gift. Meara remained silent, seated across from him. As subtly as possible, he glanced at her. Filled with discomfiture, Jordan wondered what she was thinking.

"Jor-dan?" Mac said, watching him with curiosity.

His gaze flew to the child. "You're nine today, huh?"

"Yep."

"You can open the gift, Mac. At least if—" he searched Meara's face "—if your mother doesn't mind."

"Yes, go ahead."

The child tore the paper from the gift and pulled out a large book. A colorful kite radiated from the cover.

"Kites," Mac said, flipping through the pages filled with kites of all descriptions.

"I thought you might like the book," Jordan said. "In one more year, you'll be ready to fly one of your own."

"I'm ready," Mac said, his mouth open in a beaming smile.

Meara's gentle laugh swept across the room. Jordan lifted his eyes to her smiling face.

"You'll learn to make very cautious statements around my son," she said. "He's like an elephant. He doesn't—"

Mac giggled. "Not an elephant."

"No, your memory is like an elephant's. They never forget one thing. And neither do you."

"I don't forget."

"You sure don't," Jordan said, leaning back against the sofa cushion.

"Jordan has a good idea, Mac. The kite book will teach you about kites, and when you're a little bigger you can fly a real one."

Though obviously disappointed he had to wait, Mac wasn't disappointed about the book. He nodded and returned his attention to the colorful pages.

"Would you like some cake?" Meara asked. "We cut it earlier when Otis brought Mac home. Nettie was here, too. But we have lots. I'll make some coffee."

Jordan nodded, and she rose, heading for the kitchen.

"Come here, Mac, and I'll tell you all about the kites." Jordan patted the seat beside him on the sofa.

Mac clutched the book against his chest and carried it to Jordan. He slid in beside him, and Jordan felt the warmth of the child's body leaning against his to gaze at the pictures. Mac's wide eyes and gleeful giggles sent Jordan's heart on a journey of silent pain. He'd grown to love Mac. But he couldn't trust love. Not anymore.

Meara returned and handed Jordan the cake plate. She placed the coffee mug on the table, then returned to the chair.

Mac stayed snuggled to Jordan's side, turning the pages, his conversation a singsong rhyme about the pictures.

Distracted by Mac's closeness, Jordan struggled to stay in control. "None for yourself?" he asked, focusing on everyday things rather than the warm feeling that soared through him.

"No, we just finished ours a while ago. Mac had way too many sweets today, between the cake and the ice cream."

Jordan lifted a forkful of cake to his mouth. The yellow cake was laced with cream and pieces of red cherry. He wiped his mouth with the paper napkin she'd given him. "It's great."

"I bought it next door at the bakery."

"I should have guessed." His lips curved to a grin.

"That was understood, I suppose."

He leaned back, enjoying her tender gaze, her full, naturally pink lips parted in a sweet smile. She wasn't angry—at least, not *that* angry—and he relaxed. "You're smiling at me. It's more than I deserve."

"Look at Mac," she said, tilting her head toward him. "Anyone who makes him that happy deserves a smile."

"Thanks, but I'm really sorry I didn't take Mac today. If you'd seen me earlier, you'd believe me. I drove around in circles outside the church, wishing I'd gone. I'm surprised someone didn't call the cops."

"I'm thankful they didn't. You would've expected me to bail you out."

"You've been bailing me out on a regular basis, Meara. I don't think you know what you've done for me."

She leaned toward him and pressed her finger to his lips. "The feeling is mutual, Jordan."

Her touch sent his mind soaring as high as the kites pictured in Mac's birthday book. He'd said enough for now.

Meara sat at the curb, staring at the sprawling stone mansion she had once called home. Home? No, only her place of residence. Home is where the heart is, and this monstrous house had never captured her heart. And sadly, neither had her husband.

The admission's sin and sorrow weighed on her shoulders. She had been younger then. And eager. America touted a land of fulfilled dreams and promises. She shuddered, ashamed of the reality. When Dunstan stepped into her life, she was swept into a dream, and Alison, unknowingly, encouraged the worst mistake Meara ever made.

Gazing again at the cold stone walls, Meara thawed her frozen heart. The Haydens needed her forgiveness. No, *she* needed to forgive and be forgiven. She lowered her eyelids in silent prayer, then climbed from the car.

Trembling legs carried her up the brick walk and onto the broad cement porch. Before her hand touched the bell, the door swung open, and a gaunt Edna Hayden searched Meara's face with apprehensive eyes.

"How kind of you to come, Meara." Edna stepped back and widened the entrance. "Thank you for calling me. Waiting for your visit has been a bright spot in my difficult days."

Meara couldn't believe that she had been a bright spot in the older woman's life. Previously her presence seemed to have been like a ponderous, unwanted cloud. "Thank you,

Mother Hayden. I'd hesitated calling for far too long." She forced herself to press her lips to the woman's cheek.

Edna motioned her toward the parlor, and Meara slid out of her lightweight jacket and carried it with her. She dropped the garment on a chair inside the door and waited for further direction.

"Please make yourself comfortable." Edna's hand swept toward the seating arrangement around the huge stone fireplace.

Meara selected one of the brocade chairs and sank into its thick cushion. Her gaze rested on a coffee carafe and glass-covered pastry tray that had been arranged on a nearby table. Her stomach churned. Could she swallow even a bite of the offerings?

Edna sat on the settee and studied Meara for an awkward span before speaking. "I'd hoped you might bring MacAuley along with you." She lowered her gaze. "But I understand, I suppose." Her sad eyes rose again to Meara's. "You do look well, Meara. Suntanned and full-cheeked. You were looking so drawn before you left. I worried about you."

Meara's mouth dried, and words jammed against her tongue. Edna's warm greeting was unexpected, and Meara's heart twisted in aching confusion. "We're doing well. Mac is in school. Public school for now, but I'm considering another option."

"Yes, Dunstan preferred tutors, you know, but..." She lifted her eyes to Meara's. "But I suppose that is costly. You wouldn't accept a gift of—"

"No. No, thanks. I may homeschool Mac if things don't improve. I wanted him to be with other children, but..." She paused. "But I may have made a poor judgment."

"We'd heard such terrible things. No, Dunstan—my husband—heard unpleasant details about public schools. I've heard nothing." Her eyes widened, and a spark lit her gaze. "It's time I speak for myself, Meara. I've cowered under my husband's demands too long."

Meara's pulse skipped, then pounded in her temples. "I understand, Mother Hayden." And for once, she did. The picture spilled into her thoughts, remembering her earlier confession. As she had been under Dunstan's thumb, so Edna had been under her husband's. Roses between the thorns.

Edna's hand trembled as she raised it to adjust the high collar of her shirtwaist dress. "I've longed to ask for your forgiveness. You needed a comrade—a friend—and I didn't come to you. I am so sorry."

Tears welled in Edna's eyes, and Meara responded without hesitation. She kneeled at the elderly woman's side, grasping her frail hand. "It's I that needs forgiveness. I saw the pressure you lived under. Just as I did. We were both women afraid to stand up for what we knew was right. I buried my heart in self-pity and my time in Mac's needs."

"But you were the stranger here, Meara. And we offered you no love. No chance to win our stiff, unmoving hearts. And Mac..." Sadness rolled from Edna's eyes in wet tears.

Meara's heart filled with grief for the woman and for the past sorrow that might have been eased if she'd taken the chance to approach her mother-in-law. She had been as guilty as they. Meara lowered her head and pressed her own tears against their clutched hands. Surrounded by sorrowing silence, they wept.

When Meara's mind cleared, she raised her eyes to Edna's

sallow face and touched her cheek. "Let's say no more. Our hearts know and understand. Forgiveness is our gift to each other."

Edna nodded and straightened in the chair. She patted Meara's hands with a lingering gaze and whispered, "Thank you."

Weary and drained, yet more reassured than she'd felt in many months, Meara stood and returned to her chair. She pressed her tense body against the chair back and drew in a calming breath. "Now, I'd love a cup of that coffee."

Her taut face relaxing, Edna poured the dark liquid into the delicate china cups. Preparing it to Meara's liking, she handed her the cup, then offered the plate of pastries.

Meara rested against the cushion and talked about her days since she'd left the Hayden mansion. Though Jordan was not part of the conversation, he rose continually in Meara's thoughts, and she couldn't wait to tell him about the visit.

When the carafe was drained, Meara eyed her wristwatch and suggested what her heart least wanted to hear. "May I see Father Hayden before I leave?"

Edna's face registered surprise. A glow lit her cheeks and thanks filled her eyes. "Certainly. He's a changed man, Meara. In many ways."

They rose, and she followed Edna up the long, curved staircase—the staircase that led to her old chambers, the prison where she had lived in exile. Her cold hands clutched the banister while she garnered courage to face her former father-in-law.

But her efforts were wasted: no courage was needed. As she gazed down at the shriveled overlord who'd made her life miserable, only pity filled her. His twisted face turned toward her with glassy, saddened eyes. A rivulet of drool ran from the corner of his mouth while unintelligible rasping words droned from his throat.

Meara shifted to step aside, and gnarled fingers extended from the bedcovers, capturing her hand. Repressing her instinct to pull away, she controlled her reactions and calmed her thoughts. A mournful look came into her father-in-law's eyes, filling her with deep sorrow. But forgiveness lay like a lump of dry bread in her throat. She could not say the words, though she saw the desperate question in his eyes.

With only a few mumbled amenities, Meara drew back and commented on the time. Edna patted her husband's hand, then led Meara from the room and down the stairs.

At the bottom, Meara gathered her jacket and purse. "You'll be in my prayers, Mother Hayden. And I promise I'll bring Mac for a visit. He's asked about you."

Edna's eyes widened. "Mac has asked about me?" Joy transformed her face.

"Yes, many times." Deep sadness knifed through Meara.

Edna grasped her shoulders and pressed her dry, thin lips against Meara's cheek. "Thank you. Today, you've given me more than I had dreamed of. Thank you."

Meara wrapped the frail woman in her embrace, then turned and fled down the stairs to hide her own tumbling emotions. At her car door she lifted her hand in a final parting, then closed her eyes to the depressing memories as she slid inside. She prayed that the only image that would remain was the glow on Edna's face when she spoke of Mac.

* * *

The flowers drooped in the afternoon sun, and Jordan pulled the garden hose from the side of the house and turned on the spigot. His concentration had waned throughout the day as he wondered how Meara had endured her visit with the Haydens. She had called in the morning to announce her decision to go.

He was proud of her, yet apprehensive. The hurt she felt for herself and Mac had created a deep hole in her compassion. A prayer rose from his thoughts for the outcome. Would God listen to him?

The telephone's ring sounded through the porch screen. Jordan dropped the garden hose and hurried inside, anticipating Meara's call. When her greeting touched his ear, his stomach toppled. He closed his eyes, facing the unwanted truth. Truth he'd stifled and pushed from his mind. But a truth that filled him, despite his attempts to destroy it. She and Mac meant too much to him. His emotions scraped raw against his heart.

Sentences tumbled through the line, a jumble of words and tears. "Meara, wait. I can barely understand you. Slow down, please."

He heard Meara's gasping over the line.

"Can you talk now?" Jordan asked.

A controlled "yes" hit his ear.

"Okay, now tell me. What happened to Mac?"

"They broke his glasses."

"Who?"

"I don't know. I picked him up later than I had expected and the principal met me in the hall with Mac."

"Did you ask for details?"

"Mac cried when he saw me. And I was so upset I didn't listen. I just grabbed the glasses and marched—"

"Meara, there may have been a good explanation." He envisioned her as a staunch warrior, protecting her child. "What did Mac tell you?"

"Something about getting knocked off the slide during recess. I don't know."

"From the top? Someone pushed him?" He climbed into his battle gear as easily as Meara had.

"I don't know. Top or middle, but his glasses were broken."

"Maybe he fell off?"

"Knocked…I think…" Her voice trailed off, then surged. "I've had it, Jordan. I'm taking him out of that school on Monday."

"Don't be rash, Meara. Hold on. I'll come over. We can talk." His thoughts bounded wildly. She needed someone, and he longed to be the one. He wanted her in his arms. In his life. Yet there were so many things that kept her at arm's length. So much she didn't know. Too much guilt to share.

When he replaced the receiver, Jordan locked the house and hurried to the car. Urgency filled him. But why? She would be in the apartment waiting for him, and he would change nothing.

Meara had overprotected Mac for too long. It would take more than his feeble urging to change her mind. Eventually she would learn for herself that Mac needed to grow strong and deal with life in his own way. Yes, he was disabled. Special. But he was also special in some wonderful ways that Meara had yet to understand.

Jordan wished he'd learned his own son's specialness before it was too late. Robbie had been bright and loving. Yes, and maybe too mouthy for his own good, but— Jordan cut off his thoughts. Not now. Other things filled his mind. He'd suffered enough with the memories. Tonight was Meara's.

Calming his thoughts, Jordan followed the two-lane highway, focusing on the road but unable to direct his rambling thoughts. His heart pounded with anticipation. For what? Longings shivered to the surface. Emotions. Feelings he'd covered, smashed, destroyed. Yet they were rousing from their years of sleep.

Trees and isolated buildings flashed past his peripheral vision. He was driven by a surging, aching awareness. He hit his brake at the first stoplight. Motels and shops lined the street ahead of him. He drew in a deep breath, amazed at his rattled emotions—excited, anxious and overwhelmed by the feelings.

Chapter Fourteen

Mac rose from his nap, and Meara calmed herself. He ambled from his bedroom with a dazed squint and shielded his eyes from the late-afternoon sun piercing through the window like a fiery arrow.

He leaned his head against Meara's shoulder, and she ruffled his hair, knowing the frightening event at school had exhausted him. He'd be ready for bed again after dinner. "Guess who's coming to visit us." She tilted her head to smile into his face.

Mac perked up and grinned briefly. "Jor-dan?"

"Uh-huh. I've invited him to have dinner with us." She gave him a bear hug and rose, heading for the fry pan to check on their meal. Glancing over her shoulder, she noticed his renewed scowl. "Does your head ache?"

He nodded.

"Bring Mama your glasses and the tape." She indicated her hodgepodge spot. "Do you know where it is?"

He headed for the junk drawer and hauled out a roll of

white surgical tape. Waving it in the air, he carried it to her side.

Meara leaned the spatula against the spoon holder and took the tape and glasses from his hand. Lowering herself into the chair, she gazed at the jagged, broken plastic, then attempted to fit the earpiece together for a temporary repair. "If I fix this, you'll have to be very careful." She peered at him. "We'll find a doctor tomorrow."

"I'm…not sick." His frown drew into a tighter knot.

Meara chuckled. "No, you're not, but your glasses are. I meant an eye doctor. An optometrist."

"Op…tom…trist," Mac sang, and waddled on stubby legs around her chair. "Op…tom—"

A sound on the landing halted Mac's melody, and he bolted to the door. "Jor-dan," he cried, swinging it open. He wrapped his arms around Jordan's legs and nuzzled his face against his jeans.

"I should be so honored," Jordan said, peeling Mac from his limbs and lifting him into the air.

Jordan had hoisted Mac in his arms only once before. At the Fourth of July picnic when the boy had fallen asleep. The loving picture caught her unaware, and her heart tumbled. Today's emotional events raced through her thoughts. Sorrow. Forgiveness. Comfort. Anger. Love… Heat rose to her cheeks with the thought.

Jordan snuggled Mac against his neck and then plopped him back down to the floor. "I'd say I've been duly welcomed."

"Dooley?" Mac said, craning his neck to look at the doorway.

"It's a different Dooley, Mac," Meara said, smiling up at

Jordan from her tedious repair. Meara could see from Mac's face that he didn't understand, but she didn't take the time to explain. She gestured to the wad of tape. "A mighty poor mending job, I'm afraid."

"Let me," Jordan said. But before he took the glasses from her hand, he looked over his shoulder at the stove. "Something really smells good."

His nearness sent her thoughts spinning. A powerful longing for home and family made her chest tighten. Jordan had become a fixture in her life. "Bubble and squeak."

"Bubble and which?" Jordan's voice lifted in amusement as he confiscated the roll of tape and the eyeglasses.

Mac tugged on his pants leg. "Squeak."

"Squeak? So that's it." He ruffled Mac's hair.

"A good old family recipe," Meara said, tethering her galloping heart and rising.

"Family recipe?" He winked. "I'll have to trust you. Bubble and squeak." Jordan sank into her vacated chair and bent over Mac's glasses.

Meara turned the frying mashed potatoes and cabbage patties, and then checked the oven. She studied the thick ham slices warming in the roasting pan, pleased they looked moist and appetizing.

Catching a delectable scent, Jordan gazed at Meara leaning over the open oven. "Now you're tempting me." The double-meaning message hung on the air.

His stomach gnawed from both the ham's sweet aroma and the vision of Meara, her long wavy tresses glowing in the sun's ebbing rays. *Tempting,* yes. No word was more accurate. He ached to run his fingers through her hair and kiss away the worried frown that so often marred her forehead.

"Not for long," Meara said, giving him a smile. "I have to set the table, and then we're ready." She stepped from the oven and eyed his repair. "Are you finished?"

I've only begun, his thoughts answered. He rose, testing the mended earpiece with his fingers. "I think we got it." He beckoned to Mac. "Here you go. Let's give them a try."

Mac tilted his head upward, and Jordan slid the glasses over his ears.

Jordan inspected the slightly lopsided spectacles. "What do you think, Mac?"

"I think...I can see." The child giggled and grasped Jordan's hand. "Thank you."

"You're totally welcome, pal. And if we scoot away from this table, your mom is going to feed us some of that 'squawking bubbles.'" He gave Mac a teasing wink.

The boy's smile broadened to a widemouthed laugh. "Bubble and squeak, Jor-dan."

"Okay, pal." The child's joy lightened his heart.

In a flash, Meara spread out place mats and handed Jordan the silverware, while she set out the dinner plates. The slices of ham appeared on a platter surrounded by fried patties that looked to him like thick mashed-potato pancakes.

When they were seated, he grasped Mac's hand and reached toward Meara. Her face appeared flushed as she rested her small palm against his. Blood pulsed through him, and he wondered if she could feel the pounding of his heart in their knitted hands.

Mac offered the prayer, and after they joined in the "Amen," Meara dished the food onto their plates.

"The salad," she said, leaping from the table to the refrigerator. "Where's my mind?"

Jordan knew where his mind was. Wound around her heart.

With heavy eyes, Mac finished his dinner and asked to leave the table. Meara sent him on his way, but waited while Jordan cleaned his plate. When finished, Jordan leaned back. "You can feed me that concoction anytime you like. It's really tasty." He was filled with her wonderful "bubble and squeak," but more so with her presence.

Grinning, she rose and cleared the dishes. He lifted the serving platters and slid them onto the counter, and when she turned they faced each other, eye to eye. Surrendering his control, Jordan lifted his hand and drew his fingers through her hair, then cupped her chin in his palm.

"You're as luscious as your potatoes and cabbage."

Hoping humor would control his racing pulse, he stepped away and smiled, but his jaw twitched with tension.

Flashing him a nervous grin, Meara shooed him away and rinsed the dishes. Jordan watched her shoulders rise in a sigh, and he turned his back and wandered into the living room.

Mac had drifted to sleep, his chin resting on his hand against the windowsill. Outside, Jordan scanned the paper kites flapping on the end-of-summer breeze, and his gaze returned to Mac. One day he hoped to find Mac on the end of a kite string, alone, watching his kite soar into the clouds. That was his dream for the child.

"Sleeping?" Meara asked as she wandered in from the kitchen.

"Too much bubble and squeak, I think. Should I carry him to bed?"

"Please." Meara led the way. Jordan hoisted the boy in his arms and followed.

When Jordan returned to the living room, he sat on the sofa and waited for her. He hated to ruin the pleasant evening, but they needed to talk about things. Too many things.

When Meara appeared, she paused in the doorway. "Thanks, Jordan. For helping with Mac and for coming over today. I'm sorry I was a wreck on the phone. When it comes to my son, I don't always have control."

"I know. Come here and sit." He patted the cushion on his left and waited.

She sat beside him. "Please don't lecture me." She raised her eyes to his. "I've made the decision and I'm sticking with it. I'm going to homeschool Mac. For now, I think it's the best."

"But—"

"No, listen. Some time ago before I registered him in public school, I'd contacted Christian Home Educators of Michigan. I studied their material, and I know what I have to do."

Determination glinted in her eyes, and he pulled out his flag of surrender. For now. She wouldn't listen to him or to reason. Later maybe, when she calmed down.

"Do what you must, Meara. I can't tell you what's best for Mac. But in my heart I think he needs to learn to live in the world. And the world isn't you. It's hard and scary and frustrating. But Mac will be better for it."

Tears dropped to Meara's lashes, warning him to ease off. "I understand. He's your son." The white flag was hoisted and waving. He closed his mouth and bit his tongue.

Jordan twisted on the cushion and rested his back against the sofa arm. "So tell me about your visit with the Haydens."

He'd caught her attention and, successfully, changed the

subject. Meara poured out her story—the mixed bag of joy and sorrow. When she finished, she paused and a look of concern filled her eyes.

"And I promised I'd bring Mac to visit next time."

"Is that a problem?"

"Not visiting his grandmother." Her face paled, and she rubbed her fingers against her temples. "I'm not sure I want him to see his grandfather."

Jordan rested his hand on her arm. "Are you afraid Mac will be frightened of what he sees? If you explain his grandfather's illness, he'll probably be fine."

"It's not only that. I can't forgive the man. I pity him, but I can't forgive him. If you knew what he did to me. And to Mac. How he treated us. How he hurt us."

"Meara, have you really looked at Mac? I don't see a hurting child. He's joyful and loving. Whatever went on in that house went over his head."

She studied him as if weighing his words.

"I know they hurt you, but look at you," Jordan said. "You have a job. An apartment. You're making your own way. You're happy. What good is clinging to anger? Let it go. The man is dying."

She closed her eyes and lowered her head. "I know, Jordan, and I'm ashamed of myself. I'm supposed to be a Christian. Where's my compassion?"

He slid his hand to her shoulder, and his fingers tapped her collarbone. "It's in your heart, Meara. A little tug, and you'll find it."

"He is dying." She lifted her gaze. "It's awful."

"And vengeance serves no purpose. It poisons the spirit. Take Mac to see his grandparents."

"You're right, I know. I'll find the courage somehow."

"You don't give yourself enough credit. You have courage. And compassion. You're gentle, yet strong." He tilted her chin upward. "And you're a beautiful person."

As her eyes met his, Jordan's heart rose in his throat, and he shifted closer, resting both hands on her shoulders. "Meara, you deserve better than you've had. I wish I could wash away your sorrow. I can't. But I can tell you that you've eased mine. You've made my life worth living, and..."

Longing toppled the teetering stones of his shattered defense. His heart surrendered, and he could no longer fight his feelings.

Meara's eyes widened as he drew her into his arms. He felt the beating of her heart against his own, and with happiness he brushed his fingers along her cheek, then pressed his lips against her warm, trembling mouth.

He heard her intake of breath, and he reined in the longing to swallow her in his kiss. He lifted his mouth and kissed the end of her nose, her eyelids. The fantasy that lived in his heart became a reality. With abandon, he slid his hands through her hair, fingering her soft, flowing tresses.

For the first time in years his loneliness faded. Holding Meara's delicate, trembling body in his arms, he felt complete and whole.

When he released her, she gazed at him and raised her cool hand to his face. Trust and longing filled her eyes.

Jordan's mind spun. Gently he edged away and cupped her cheeks in his hands. "You're the first woman I've longed for, Meara. The first woman I've kissed since Lila."

She paused, searching his eyes. "And I've dreamed of this moment."

Meara nestled against his shoulder, and they sat in silence as the sun slid below the horizon and shadows filled the room. Finally Meara shifted and rose to turn on the table lamp.

He sought her gaze, wondering, worrying that she had second thoughts, but her flushed smile gave him the answer. He lowered his knotted shoulders in relief.

"I'd better be on my way, I suppose," Jordan said, rising.

She didn't protest. He stepped toward the door. "Did Otis tell you I'll be at church Sunday?"

"Church? No. You mean to the worship service?"

He hated to confess that it would be his first time in church since...his family's funeral. The old ache struggled to rise, but he pressed it down. "Yes, it seemed the best way. I'm talking to the congregation about the petition we're distributing to squelch the saloon."

"They passed out flyers last week," Meara said. "People didn't say much on Sunday. Most of them just glanced at it and tucked the paper in their pockets."

"Otis said a few people stopped by the store during the week. At least no one seemed to disagree. The ones who said anything were willing to sign."

"I'm glad." She peered at him, then chuckled.

The look in her eyes made him nervous. "What's funny?"

"To be honest, I'm glad in *two* ways. For one, happy you're making progress with the petition."

"And?" He studied her sparkling eyes.

"And I'm pleased you'll be in church. God has mysterious ways to bring His children back home."

"Like the Prodigal Son?"

"You said it."

His chest tightened at the sight of her smile.

With most vacationers settled back home now that fall had arrived, the church overflowed with worshipers. Meara sat in her usual pew near the front and waited anxiously for Jordan's arrival. Would he sit with her? She didn't know, and wasn't sure if she wanted him to. He'd distract her, for sure.

Since Friday night, he'd filled her thoughts even more than before. The feel of his powerful yet tender arms holding her close shivered through her thoughts, and her senses recalled the fresh, spicy aroma of his aftershave. She had felt so secure and protected in his presence.

When he appeared in the aisle beside her, her heart lurched. His reassuring smile blanketed her worries, and he sat beside her, giving a special wink to Mac, who blinked both eyes in a return greeting. Jordan chuckled and pressed her arm in shared understanding.

With his graying dark hair and his tall lean frame, how distinguished and handsome he could look—dressed in a dark gray pinstripe suit, accented with a deep-tone tie. He could have passed for a corporate executive...or a college professor.

The thought was humorous, but at the same time made her fearful. Would he go back to his career one of these days and leave her more lonely than she'd been before?

Parishioners cast glances Jordan's way, and if he caught their eye, he gave them a pleasant nod or a simple wave. And when the service ended and his presentation was announced, he rose like a Titan and strode to the front, the image of confidence and determination.

"Good morning," he said. "It's nice to be with you today in worship."

His gaze caught hers, and she wondered if he was telling an open-faced lie in God's house or if he meant what he said. He looked sincere, and she tuned out her own thoughts to listen.

"Last week you received a flyer explaining the purpose of this meeting today. I hope you've had time to read it and give it prayerful thought. Mackinaw is a tourist city, a city that draws families...."

Meara listened to his clear, candid presentation. He offered powerful reasons for his objection to the saloon, and what he hoped the petition could accomplish. The people sat in silence, and she glanced around to note if any were leaving. None that she saw.

"So today we are asking you to take a petition and talk to your friends and neighbors about your concern. If we can overwhelm city council with our opposition, we can win a quiet victory for a wholesome, Christian environment for our own families and the families who vacation here."

Applause accompanied Jordan's return to the pew, and after a final prayer, the congregation rose to leave. Men maneuvered through the aisles, approaching Jordan with questions and concerns, and Meara took Mac's hand and followed Nettie and Otis into the late-September sunshine.

Though she lingered outside, Meara knew Jordan had been captured by the throng. Disappointed not to tell him how well he had done, she headed home. But as she climbed the covered staircase, Jordan called her name from the parking area.

She turned with a smile, and he followed her to the landing.

"How did it go?" she asked, stepping into the kitchen. "Did they seem willing to circulate the petition?"

"I think it went well." He trailed in behind her and closed the door. "A few challenging questions caught me off guard, but hopefully I answered them. About forty or fifty petitions were handed out. Otis has the exact number."

She faced Mac, who had plopped onto the living room carpet. "Mac, take your good clothes off, okay?"

He nodded and headed for his bedroom.

Meara continued. "What I like about this approach is that it's organized and civil. I hope Hatcher doesn't try anything too radical." She gestured toward the kitchen chair. "Would you like to have a seat?"

Jordan slid into a chair and leaned an elbow on the table. "If he does, he'll destroy himself. One thing's for sure, Mackinaw is a family-centered town. People don't want problems. They're looking for legitimate solutions, and I think the petition will provide that."

"Let's pray the other churches are as willing."

He nodded, closing his eyes and rubbing his broad hand across his face. "This social stuff will kill me. I've been away from people for so long I'd forgotten what it's like to be incessantly genial."

Chuckling, she nudged his shoulder. "What do you mean? You've always been friendly." But as the words left her mouth, an image rose in her mind, and Jordan's harsh words echoed in her ear: *"This is private property."*

He eyed her. "You're eating your words, aren't you." His

head teetered in a silent chuckle. "It wasn't that long ago. You remember my Private Property sign?"

"How can I forget?"

"I stumbled over it the other day. I'd forgotten I tucked it beside the house. I cringed. Those days are like a dream to me—my reclusive, lonely existence."

He rose and put his arm around her waist. "How can I thank you and…Hatcher?" He chuckled aloud.

"Hatcher?"

"If it weren't for his saloon, I might still be sitting in my house afraid to face the world again. Naturally, you'd be by my side…no matter what. And I thank you for your patience." He tucked his arm more fully around her and coaxed her nearer.

Meara drew in a ragged breath, longing to lift her lips to his. His love was all the thanks she needed. But she heard a sound and turned.

Mac gazed at them from the doorway, his eyes wide and curious. He edged into the room. "Do you love us, Jor-dan?"

An empty sadness washed over Jordan. Mac had asked a similar question months earlier, and he'd avoided the answer. Today he saw the child and his mother with different eyes, but still he couldn't say the words. His chest tightened as he kneeled beside the boy, resting his hands on the small upper arms. "You and your mom are my best pals, son."

Son. The word soared through the room, echoing in his mind and ricocheting through this heart. *Son.* He'd lost his own. Was God offering him another? A child who needed him and adored him without question.

"Best pals." Mac wrapped his arms around Jordan's neck and planted a loud, wet kiss on his cheek.

Unbidden tears filled Jordan's eyes, and he buried his face in the boy's warm neck to hide his emotion. He had to tell Meara soon what had happened that horrible night—before he cared too much. He couldn't bear to hurt her.

He couldn't bear another loss.

Chapter Fifteen

With Mac at her side, Meara marched into Beaumont Elementary School on Monday morning to withdraw him from classes.

The secretary looked at her with placating eyes. "Mr. Baumgarten will want to speak with you before you remove him from classes."

Meara released a stream of pent-up air. "Fine. May I speak with him, then?" She fumbled with the release forms clutched in her hand.

"But he's not here. Mr. Baumgarten's attending meetings out of town and won't be back until the end of the week. Could you wait?"

"I'm sorry, I've made my decision, and your principal won't change it. Let's just fill out the papers, please."

With a look of frustration, the secretary finally acquiesced.

After collecting Mac's belongings, Meara headed home. Yet something prodded her to change direction and keep her promise to Mother Hayden. After her first visit, Meara had searched the Scriptures for answers, and her conversation with Jordan had prompted her to pray. Between the two, she'd garnered courage and unearthed compassion. Before the opportunity was taken from her, she wanted to face Dunstan Sr. again. And this time with Mac.

But her sense of propriety intervened. She wouldn't feel right visiting without a telephone call first.

When she pulled behind the kite shop, Otis beckoned her from the doorway. She climbed out of the car, gathered Mac's school materials and greeted Otis.

"Wanted to tell you before you go upstairs," he said. "Jordan stopped by to talk to you, but you were out." He eyed Mac and the stack of papers in her arm.

"I withdrew Mac from school today."

"Is that right? Decided to homeschool, then?"

Meara's chest tightened, recalling her reasoning. "I told you what happened. Maybe I'm not giving it time, but I think this is best." Noticing the confused look on Mac's face, she wrapped her free arm around his shoulder. "We'll make out fine, won't we."

Though he looked puzzled, he nodded as if he trusted her opinion.

"I took him to a new eye doctor this morning," Meara added. "He'll have his glasses in a couple of days." She gazed at the lopsided, taped repair job. "I hope these hold out."

Otis gave Mac a wink. "They'd better, huh, lad? Or you'll be bumpin' into everything."

"Me," Mac said, poking his chest. "Bumpin' into everything." His face glowed. He released his hold on Meara's skirt for the first time that morning and ambled to Otis's side.

"Did Jordan say I should call him?" Meara asked.

"Oh, sorry. No, he'll drop by in a bit." Otis motioned to Mac. "Want to help me sweep up in here, lad?"

"Sure," Mac said, and darted behind him into the shop.

Meara gave Otis a wave and climbed the stairs to her apartment. She unloaded Mac's materials on the kitchen table and plopped into the chair, her head in her hands. She'd taken on a huge task, homeschooling Mac. Sending him to classes with other special needs children had been her plan. But it wasn't to be. Mainstream or *no* stream—those were her choices.

She leaned back in the chair and looked around the kitchen. They'd managed so far. And they would continue to manage. The apartment and job had fallen into her lap. And Jordan—he'd flown into her life like one of his lovely, extraordinary kites. God had been good.

God was good. If so, though, why did she feel empty and afraid? She rubbed her hand along the muscles in her neck, pressing against the tense knots under her hairline. What was she waiting for?

Even forgiveness had come—forgiving and being forgiven. She paused, remembering. *Dunstan Hayden Sr.* She had one more act of contrition, and the hurt would be where it belonged—in the past. Penance.

Meara pushed herself up from the table, feeling tired. She would call Mother Hayden and plan the visit. After punching in the numbers on the wall phone, Meara sank into a nearby chair. Two rings. Three. A servant answered.

She waited for Edna Hayden's voice, her stomach tightening in anticipation. When the woman answered, her voice was subdued.

"Is something wrong, Mother Hayden?"

A heavy pause hung in the air. Then she answered. "Dunstan passed this morning, Meara."

A hard lump knotted in Meara's throat, and her voice caught behind it. She forced the words out with a sob. "I'm sorry. I'd called to bring Mac over for a visit." Meara's anticipated restitution tumbled to the ground like a dying leaf and sorrow pierced her heart. For Dunstan Sr. or for the doomed visit? She didn't know.

"Bless you, Meara, for thinking of us. It will be wonderful to see the boy again. I'll have something to look forward to."

"Are you all right? Do you have help?"

"I'm fine. Truly. Dunstan's death was inevitable. I had accepted it weeks before he was taken. Now, it's a matter of lawyers and financial planners. I'll be fine."

"And the funeral?" Should she take Mac?

"Dunstan will be cremated, Meara. I've planned a memorial service for next Friday."

"I'll be there…with Mac." Though she had hesitated, her path was obvious. Edna needed Mac. Now more than ever.

She hung up the telephone and rose. Pressing her chin toward her chest, she ran her hand across the taut cords of her neck. She trudged to the stove and turned on the burner under the teakettle. Then she sat at the table, resting her forehead in her hand, thinking. If only she had finished what she had started. Total forgiveness had been so close.

Tapping sounded at the door. Jordan. "Come in," she said, eyeing the doorway until she saw his face.

Hearing her voice, Jordan sensed something wrong. Meara always answered the door. He hesitated, then turned the knob and entered. Looking at her downhearted expression, he knew he'd been right.

"What is it, Meara?"

She straightened her back. "Dunstan's father died this morning." Closing her eyes, she sighed, then she opened them. "And I withdrew Mac from school today."

"Heavy-duty day." He walked toward her and rested his hand on a chair back.

"I called to tell Mother Hayden I was coming for a visit with Mac. I wanted to make amends with Dunstan's father. And now..." She paused, her eyes filling with unshed tears.

"The forgiveness is complete, Meara. Unspoken, yes, but your heart offered the forgiveness. That's what counts."

Jordan was right. God knew that forgiveness was in her heart. Now all she could do was pray that Dunstan's father had been forgiven by God and was in heaven.

"When's the funeral?"

"Cremation. She's having a memorial service on Friday. I told her I'd bring Mac." She plied her fingers along the back of her neck.

"Are you ready to handle that?"

"I'll talk to God. With Him, everything is possible."

Jordan wandered behind her and rested his thumbs against her shoulders. "I think you need a masseuse...or a good friend." Working his fingers along her hairline to her shoulders, he massaged the knots in her neck.

A pleasant sigh left her, and her shoulders relaxed as the tension vanished. "Thanks. Today's not my day, I guess."

Knowing he had more unpleasant news, Jordan felt his stomach roll. When she leaned back, rested, he swiveled a chair around, moved it close and straddled it. Leaning one hand against the chair back, he reached for her hand with the other. Apprehensive, he studied her troubled face, until she winced as if understanding what was to come.

"Tell me," she said. "I can see it in your eyes."

"You're getting to know me too well." He squeezed her hand. "It's not really that bad." He paused, thinking of how to tell her. "I heard from the zoning board today. They've given me a grace period on the apartment." He stifled a deep sigh struggling to escape his lungs.

"Grace period?" She lifted an eyebrow and waited.

"You can stay in the apartment until school's out for the summer. They know you have a young child." He tried to lighten his voice. "But don't worry, I can…I'm going to fight it. I'll go back again and—"

"No, Jordan, it's not necessary. You've done enough. When spring comes, I'll look for another place. Who knows—my life may be heading in a different direction by then." Her eyelids looked heavy, as if she needed sleep.

Jordan rose and pulled the chair from between his legs, then slid it beneath the table. Grasping Meara's hands, he coaxed her up and wrapped his arms around her. She accepted his invitation and laid her head against his chest, her arms circling his back.

Jordan wished he could erase her fears and discontentment. Moments passed without a word—silent, except for his throbbing, racing pulse.

Finally Meara gazed into his eyes. "Thanks. What would I do without you?"

What would he do without *her?* The question washed him with icy foreboding. He slid his hand up her arm and tilted her chin as he gazed into her eyes. "No thanks needed." He lowered his mouth. Her lips met his kiss while her arms slid shyly upward to his neck, her fingers weaving through his hair. A tremor rolled through her body as he drew his hand in gentle circles across her back until she slowly relaxed against him.

When he eased back, he nuzzled her nose with his. "That was better than any thank-you. And much better than a million bucks."

Warmth rippled over him as the lonely years tumbled away. "Guess I'm not too good at being romantic."

She rested her heated palm against his cheek. "Not at all. You're too good."

He captured her hand, drew it to his mouth and covered it with kisses. Her sweet words seemed ripe with promise. *Hope.* If only he could allow himself to feel the same possibility.

Mac rested his cheek against his fist and stared at the table covered with pennies.

"Mac, you still haven't answered me," Meara said. "How many pennies do you have if you have five cents and four more?" She glanced at him, her patience ready to run out the door. "It's the same as yesterday, Mac."

Grudgingly, he jabbed the pennies into a neat line. "I know."

"What do you know?" Meara asked.

"Like yesterday. Five pennies and six. Three pennies and two."

"But I need the answers." Her shoulders nearly hit her ears with her deep sigh. She closed her eyes for a heartbeat and prayed in silence. *Patience, Lord. Like Job or… You know what I mean, Father. I need patience. In Jesus' name. Amen.*

She slid onto a chair beside him and captured his fisted hand. "Listen to Mama. I took you out of school so things will be better. But that means we must have your lessons here. Counting the pennies is arithmetic."

Meara slid the coins around into groups. "See. Five pennies. Count them with me, Mac." She pointed to each as Mac recited the number. "Now, look. Here are four more. One. Two. Three. Four. Now if I push the two lines together, how many pennies do we have?" She watched him fingering the coins.

"Mama?"

"What, Mac?"

"Why can't I go to the real school?"

Meara blew out a stream of pent-up air. "This *is* real school."

His brows knit and he tilted his head, peering at her. "But I mean the *real* one."

She thumped her index finger in front of the row of pennies. "How many, Mac? Count." Meara might have laughed at his expression if she weren't frustrated. She was failing as a teacher. That was for sure.

Mac touched each coin in the row. "Nine." He lifted his face to hers, his perplexed expression shifting to a grin. "Nine pennies."

Her heart tumbled. "Ah, Mac. Nine is correct. Thank you. And forgive your mama for being so—"

"Crabby."

Meara snatched him into her arms and gave him a hug. "I had a different word in mind. But 'crabby' it is."

She released him and rose from the table. "I think that's enough school for today. You have to change clothes. We're going to see someone special today."

His beaming smile signaled a false assumption.

"Not Jordan. Someone else special. Grandma Hayden."

The new information excited him as much as had thinking it was Jordan. Mac scooted from the chair, poking himself in the chest. "I…can see my grandmother." He took a step and stopped. "Today?"

"Today, but you have to get dressed up like we're going to church."

His nose wrinkled in displeasure.

"Grandfather Hayden died, Mac, and we're going to the funeral."

"Died?" A frown creaked his narrow forehead.

Meara knelt down to give him another hug. "He's in heaven now." She couldn't imagine it, but the merciful Lord could work miracles.

The frown faded from Mac's face. "Three fathers in heaven." He spread out his fingers. "One. Two. Three." Counting as he turned, he headed for his bedroom.

Meara placed the coins in a ceramic jar and put it on the shelf. She had known teaching wouldn't be easy, especially with her work in the gift shop, but the task seemed more frustrating than she had anticipated. As she turned to leave the room, the telephone rang, and she grabbed the receiver.

"Mrs. Hayden, this is Mr. Baumgarten from Beaumont Elementary."

"Oh yes." Meara hesitated, waiting for his attack.

"I'm sorry I wasn't here when you took Mac out of school. My secretary told you I was out of town, I hope."

"Yes, she did. Until today." Her voice sounded breathy, and she felt nervous, like a schoolchild being dragged to the principal's office.

"I wondered if there's anything that I can do to change

your mind. Mac was adjusting well here. His teachers all came to ask what was wrong. Even a couple of our students missed him and stopped to see if he were ill."

Adjusting? Missed? "Thank you, but it didn't seem to me that he was doing well. Someone knocked him off the slide. I've had to replace his glasses."

"I'm sorry about the glasses. The recess teacher said one of the students accidentally stepped on them when Mac fell off the—"

"Fell? I thought he was knocked off."

"Mrs. Hayden, if you'd like, I could have the teacher who was in charge that day give you a call. But what I understood is Mac and another boy decided to come down the slide together. Before the teacher could stop them, they let go and flew down, out of control. Apparently, the boy's foot bumped Mac as he came to the bottom, and instead of Mac catching himself, he flew off and hit the ground."

Humiliated at her misdirected anger, she steadied her voice. "You mean, it was an accident."

"Well, yes. If it hadn't been, we'd have brought the parents in to meet with you. I'm very sorry about Mac's glasses. One of his buddies rushed over to help and—"

Buddy? "I understand, Mr. Baumgarten. I guess I assumed someone pushed him…on purpose."

"No. I'm positive it was an accident. Mac's a great boy. We've never had a Down Syndrome student at Beaumont, but I'll tell you more than one teacher has said they'd prefer your son in their rooms over most of the other children—special or not."

Heat rose in her face. "I'm sorry I misunderstood. I appreciate your calling."

"I'd hoped you might change your mind. He'll easily fit back into his—"

"No, I don't want him to get confused. We'll just continue as we are." It was tempting. How easy it would be to send Mac back to school. Teaching was not her cup of…anything.

"The next marking period begins the third week in October. We'd welcome him then, if you change your mind."

"I'll see, Mr. Baumgarten."

When she hung up, she plopped onto the kitchen chair and stared at the ceiling. She'd had a bad attitude about public school from the beginning. Meara realized she'd judged without giving the situation a fair trial. She'd jumped to conclusions. Rash. Isn't that what Jordan called her?

Not much she could do now. She'd made her bed, and, as her mother always said, now she'd have to lie in it.

Still…he'd said the third week in October. Could she reconsider?

That didn't seem too far away.

Meara stood back, watching Mother Hayden's thin arms wrap around Mac's shoulders. While her son beamed, the woman pressed her powdery cheek against Mac's forehead, her eyes misted with tears—tears Meara had never seen when she'd lived in the family home.

"We live in a new house," Mac said to his grandmother, his voice too loud for the somber occasion.

Meara shushed him, but Mother Hayden didn't seem to notice or care. Her soft voice melded with Mac's louder one until organ music drew them forward. With Mac's hand in Mother Hayden's, Meara followed, as they led the way down the church aisle to the front.

Meara stared ahead at the elegant urn seated on a pedestal—inside, the remains of a man who'd been an unkind and unloving father-in-law. Thinking of her own husband, Meara wondered if like-father-like-son had been the reason for Dunstan Sr.'s behavior. Her husband had learned bitter, thoughtless ways from his father. Had the generations perpetuated such behavior?

If so, she thanked the Lord that Mac had escaped the influence. Yet her heart softened for the angry man whose remains were nothing more than ashes in an urn. He'd left no good memories for her. Nothing but heartache.

Meara's gaze traveled to Mother Hayden, a woman who might have offered love had Meara opened her heart enough to ask for it. Her own bitterness had kept her withdrawn from the family as much as had their insistence that Mac's presence would be scorned and that she should keep him away from company.

Though hurt remained, Meara had a greater understanding. Mac had turned out to be a blessing, and perhaps her child could bring a few moments of happiness to a lonely, aging woman.

Mother Hayden held Mac's hand in hers throughout the ceremony. Mac didn't seem to understand this was not a regular worship service. He sucked on hard candy his grandmother had kindly brought along to amuse him. His wiggles seemed ignored by her, too, and Meara's heart lifted at the sight of them together.

As the service ended, Mother Hayden leaned closer to her, above Mac's head. "I've been thinking. Perhaps next Saturday Mac could come to stay overnight. I'd like that."

"I'd like that," Mac bellowed. "I can come, Grandma."

Meara cringed, fighting the desire to say no. Overnight? Could she bear to be away from Mac for that long? "Speak softly, Mac," she said, covering the anxiety that rose in her chest.

She saw her son's eager face and the look of longing in Mother Hayden's eyes, then swallowed her words. "I—I suppose...if your grandmother wants to put up with you." She managed a playful smile.

Mac giggled and eyed his grandmother.

"I'd love it. We have so much catching up to do."

They rose, and Meara took a final look at the urn. "Forgive me," she whispered, knowing only God could hear.

Mother Hayden and Mac had moved down the aisle, and Meara watched them go, feeling lonelier than she had in a long time.

Chapter Sixteen

Meara eyed Nettie peeking through the doorway between the gift and kite shops. Waving hello, she approached her. "Is Mac getting underfoot in there?"

"Mac? No, that boy's an angel," she said, ambling into the room. "How's the homeschooling? Any easier?"

Meara brushed a few straggling hairs from her cheek. "No easier. Mac's working harder, but he's not happy."

Nettie rested her hand on the pile of handmade toss pillows that Meara had battled with days earlier. "Not happy?"

"He's as persistent about wanting to go to the 'real' school as he was about seeing his grandmother Hayden."

"The boy knows what he wants," Nettie said, shifting the hand-loomed place mats into a neat stack.

"I suppose. I really thought I was doing what was best for him."

Nettie paused from her task and caught Meara's eye. "Maybe you were doing what was best for *you*."

Surprised, she drew back. "For me? This homeschooling hasn't been fun for me."

"Don't misunderstand, Meara." Nettie rested her hand against the display counter. "Sometimes what we think is better for someone else is just coating our own guilt or fears. Could be you're trying to make it up to Mac for not having a father. Or maybe taking him away from the Haydens' home? But all Mac wants is to be like the other kids and go to school."

"But he never wanted…" Meara gave a deep sigh. "Maybe you're right, Nettie. Mac didn't attend school before. He didn't have a friend. How could he in…?" She paused and pulled the tangle of stray hair from her cheek once more, tucking it behind her ear. "I'm sorry. You don't need to hear my gripes. Maybe you're right. Maybe I'm overprotecting Mac."

Nettie rested her hand on Meara's arm. "It's natural for you to want to keep him from harm, Meara."

"I'm thinking about public school. I can register him in October for the second marking period."

Noise in the doorway caused Meara to turn. Jordan stood eyeing her, with Mac clasped against his side.

Smiling, Meara gave him a wave. "What's that clinging to your leg?"

"Me," Mac said with his familiar giggle. He tugged at Jordan's hand, urging him farther into the shop.

"I think it's a rag bag," Jordan said, tousling Mac's hair. He sauntered into the shop and paused beside the two women. "How are you, Nettie?"

"Thinking I should be outside in this lovely Indian summer weather," Nettie answered. "How about it, Mac? Want to go for a walk with me, and I'll buy you an ice-cream cone?"

He caught Nettie's skirt. "Can I, Mama?"

Meara agreed, and Mac let out a noisy laugh and leaned his head against Nettie's hip.

"Come on, young man," Nettie said, heading for the door with Mac.

Meara followed them with her eyes until they passed through the doorway. Then, she turned to Jordan. "And what brings you to town?"

"Errands. And you."

She searched Jordan's eyes.

"I brought a few more flyers to Otis for the final church presentation."

Meara poked his arm. "I mean the part about me."

"Did you forget about my offer?"

"What offer?"

He stepped nearer and leaned against the counter. "I offered to help with one of the school lessons."

She grinned, realizing she had forgotten his generous suggestion. "Which lesson did you have in mind?"

"How about a science project?"

"Science? I'd pay you big money."

"Great. I thought we'd go see sea life. Shells. Fossils. Coral. And maybe another time Mac and I could study minerals and ore samples in the lake rocks."

"That's really kind, Jordan."

He grinned. "How about Saturday?"

Her heart bounced to her throat and back. "Saturday morning I'm taking Mac to visit Mother Hayden. He's spending the night. I'll pick him up Sunday. Can you believe it?" Meara shook her head. "Mac yelled yes he wanted to go before I could stop him."

Jordan scowled. “You shouldn’t stop him. He—”

“The memorial service had just ended. Everything was so hushed. I was embarrassed.”

A guilty-looking grin curved Jordan’s lips. “I thought you meant—”

“I know what you thought. No, I agreed. Though I hope it’s not a mistake. Getting up in the middle of the night to pick him up isn’t my idea of fun.”

“He’ll be fine.” Jordan rested his hand on Meara’s shoulder. “Mac knows what he wants.”

She did a double take. “Nettie said the same thing a few minutes ago...and some other things that got me thinking.”

The front door opened, and Meara turned her head at the sound. “Hi, Julie.” She waved at the afternoon clerk and turned back to Jordan. “Want to come upstairs? Julie’s here to take over.”

Filled with curiosity, Jordan nodded.

“I’ll be just a minute. I have to tell her what needs to be done.”

Jordan watched Meara cross the room and speak to the young woman. His mind whirled, wondering what Nettie had said that made Meara think. Pulse stumbling, Jordan watched her animation as she spoke to the clerk. So much had changed since he’d met Meara and since he’d stopped fighting his feelings.

In a moment Meara returned, and he followed her through the storage room and up the back stairs. Inside the apartment, she motioned him to the living room, and in a second emerged from the kitchen with two sodas.

“Here,” Meara said, handing him a frosty cola can. Before sitting she lowered the front shade enough to block the sharp stream of afternoon sunlight glaring through the window, then plopped onto the sofa.

"Thanks." He took a hearty swig, her earlier cryptic comment on his mind. He wiped his lips with the back of his hand. "Now you've got me curious."

"Curious about what?"

"What you said downstairs about Nettie making you think. Think about what?"

She lowered her eyes as if in thought...or avoidance—he wasn't sure. "About me and how I treat Mac."

"How you treat Mac?"

"Not in a bad way." She lifted her eyes. "Nettie says maybe I make decisions based on what's best for me, not what's really best for Mac. She thinks I feel guilty because Mac doesn't have a father, so I overprotect him to soothe my conscience."

Jordan leaned forward, elbows on his knees. "And what do you think?"

"She could be right. Probably is. I shouldn't fear the future and worry about the way things are. I'm ashamed of myself. God gave me Mac, and I suppose He wouldn't have if I couldn't handle the job."

"That's a good way to look at it, Meara. You're the lifelong Christian and should know that God is in control. Both of us need to remember that things happen for a purpose. And not always a purpose we understand. That's the difficult part—the inability to comprehend the 'why' of every experience—good or bad."

Meara nodded. "Just the other day I was thinking how good God's been to me. And I asked myself that very question. If God is so good, then what do I fear?"

Jordan folded his hands and tapped his index fingers together in thought. "The unknown, I suppose. We all like to be in charge of our lives. To have a handle on the details. But some things don't have a handle."

"I realize that." She took a sip of cola. "Prayer. That's what I need. If I can't know the answer to everything, then I should pray for peace of mind. The ability to trust."

Trust. He'd said that so often. Easy to say. Hard to do. Jordan dug into his pocket and pulled out a torn page from a magazine. "Here." He handed the ragged sheet to Meara. "I thought of you when I read this." He thought of her much of the time, but he didn't say so.

She turned it over in her hand, eyeing the large-print title. Lifting an eyebrow, she gazed at him.

"It's from an education magazine," Jordan said. "I still subscribe to a couple of periodicals." He hoped she'd take the information to heart. As an educator himself, he believed Mac would benefit from contact with regular students. They would learn about disabilities, and he would learn social skills aside from academics.

Meara scanned the article and paused. "I wish I could believe this." She looked again at the beginning. "Do you really think these studies are correct?"

"I'd trust them," Jordan said. "The organizations who did the reports have no stake in the results. They have no reason to distort them. Special-needs children perform better and grow more adjusted when attending school with regular students. And it's not only one study, Meara."

He surveyed her expression as she reread passages of the article.

Her cheeks colored a pastel pink. "Nearly every day Mac asks why he can't go back to his 'real' school."

"He liked it there, even with the broken glasses and the other mishaps."

"I suppose stolen books and broken glasses happen to all children—special needs or not."

"Probably." Awareness. She'd begun to understand on her own. Jordan rose and sat beside Meara on the sofa, resting his hand on her arm. "Sounds to me like you've already made your decision."

Meara placed her hand over his. "How can I argue with you and Mac?"

"You can't. We're too smart for you." He tweaked her chin and unfolded his long legs to stand. "I'd better get. So what about the science lesson? And you can come, too. Maybe you'll learn something."

"Better be careful, I might get smarter than you."

He grinned. "If Saturday's no good, Friday, then?"

"That's great, but early, if that's okay. I have to work in the afternoon." She rose and stood beside him.

"Early's fine." Jordan ran his hand along the edge of her cheek. "I like to see you fresh and bright-eyed." He leaned down and brushed her cheek with his lips. If he followed what his heart directed, he wouldn't leave at all.

Dooley's wet nose nuzzled Jordan's hand as it dangled over the mattress edge. He opened a sleepy eye and stared into the dog's brown, placating orbs, then glanced at the clock.

His heart tripped over itself as he swung his legs off the bed and rubbed his heavy eyes. He hadn't slept this late in years. Then he remembered. Meara and Mac were coming early. He shot up from the bed and darted into the kitchen.

As the coffee seeped into the pot, he filled Dooley's bowl and headed for the bathroom. No shower this morning. He washed and brushed his teeth, then headed toward his bedroom to change from his sleepwear—jogging shorts and T-shirt.

But Dooley interrupted his trip. The dog stood at the porch screen door emitting minute, urgent "boofs," his head pivoting to gaze at Jordan.

The decision was easy. Not wanting an accident, Jordan hurried to the screen door and pushed it open. Dooley beelined for the lake, and Jordan fixed his eyes on the dog's motivation. A flock of ducks lifted from the sand and flew with fiercely flapping wings away from their pursuer.

In the dark, cloudy sky, gusty autumn wind thrashed the water. The waves pounded against the shoreline in thick, foaming waves, leaving a trail of debris as they wrested loose earth back into the dark, pitching depths.

Dooley hesitated on the brink of the wild waves, taking cautious steps toward the quacking birds riding on the undulating water.

Jordan called, but the noise covered his voice, and Dooley dove into the frothing waves, heading for the birds. Jordan froze for a heartbeat, then sprang through the doorway and barreled down the dirt path. Dooley would drown if he headed out too far.

Reaching the water's edge, he bellowed the dog's name, wading into the tugging current and fighting to keep his foothold on the shifting sand. In a moment's silence between the waves' fall and retreat, Jordan cried out again, and Dooley turned around.

Pivoting his head, he shifted his paddling and retreated

from the birds. Jordan's heart hammered against his chest. When the setter neared, he grasped his collar and pulled the animal to his side. "You silly dog," Jordan muttered, clinging to the dog until his feet touched the wet sand. He was amazed at the emotion that stirred in him. He loved the foolish setter.

Above him a voice drifted down to reach his ear. He lifted his gaze and his heart stopped. Mac teetered down the path toward him. Jordan froze, unable to move, and dropped his gaze to his legs below his jogging shorts.

Terror filled Jordan's heart. He lifted his eyes to Meara, standing farther back on the path, obviously paralyzed by the hideous sight. Then she moved forward, heading toward him down the path.

As the boy's smiling eyes widened and filled with horror, Jordan stood transfixed. An anguished cry left Mac's lips. "You hurt, Jor-dan?" the boy asked, his sad eyes lifted upward to Jordan's face.

Hurt? Oh yes, he'd hurt for so long—his tormented, scarred legs, but most of all his twisted, pain-filled heart. "My legs don't hurt anymore, son." And neither did the ache that had filled him for so long. That, too, had eased.

Falling onto the damp sand, Mac wrapped his pudgy arms around Jordan's red, distorted legs and pressed his lips against the aged scars.

Jordan knelt and held the boy in his embrace, kissing his cheek and calming his own thudding emotions. Like he, the child was scarred. Differently perhaps, but the scars were as long-lasting as Jordan's disfigured limbs. They would both survive with love and confidence in God's mercy. The long-awaited thought was still alien, but Jordan believed.

Unmoving, Meara stood above him, her gaze not on his legs but on his arms around Mac. Her gentle eyes spoke silent words that soaked through Jordan's body and warmed his fear to confidence and trust.

"Are you okay, Mac?" Jordan rose, his hand still resting on the child's shoulder.

"Me?" Mac asked, poking his chest. "I'm okay, Jor-dan."

"And I'm fine, too, son." At his words, his eyes searched Meara's. She nodded a simple agreement, and the years of hiding his taut, puckered skin ebbed away like the waves against the shore. "But we need to talk," he said to Meara alone.

Her eyes riveted to his, and she nodded.

Caught in her gaze, the years spun through Jordan's mind: his reclusive life, the loneliness, the scars that daily roused his guilt, the never-ending sorrow. Today his confession could give him freedom.

Dooley's bark brought them to attention. Pulling their gaze toward the sound, Meara's scream alerted Jordan before he saw the awful sight. With his interest in the birds, Dooley had again surged into the rolling waves, and Mac had followed.

"Mac!" Meara cried, frozen with fear.

Jordan sighted the massive crest rising in the distance. A receding wave knocked Mac off his feet and dragged him down into the churning foam. His head disappeared a second time, and before Meara's cry faded into the wind, Jordan bolted across the sand and dove into the angry water. He pulled against the current, snatching the child before he plunged again into the murky depths.

With Mac crushed against his side, Jordan paddled with one arm, using every ounce of strength and adrenaline, until his feet kicked against the sand. He bolstered himself against the current, lifted Mac in his arms, and pulled his legs through the seething water to shore.

Meeting Jordan in the shallows, Meara threw herself against Mac, tears washing her death-gray cheeks. Her eyes searched her son's face until the boy's cough rallied her spirit. "Mac," she cried. "Mac."

The child opened his dazed eyes and a deep, rasping cough tore through him again. Jordan lowered him to the ground and kneeled at his side. "Are you okay, son?"

Looking stunned, Mac peered at his mother, then at Jordan, as if sorting out the details. "The ducks," he said, pointing to the empty water. They had flown off in the confusion, and Mac stared toward the birdless landscape. "Gone." He shrugged his shoulders, releasing another heart-rending cough.

A deep breath spilled in a slow stream from Jordan's lungs. "They're gone, Mac. And you could have been, too. Don't ever go near the water alone. Never, ever. Do you hear me?"

"With Dooley," he responded, his matter-of-fact tone laughable, except for the fear that still clouded Jordan's thoughts.

"Dooley isn't an adult, Mac. You only go near the water with an adult," Jordan said.

Mac looked at his mother. Agreeing, she closed her eyes and nodded.

"An...adult," Mac repeated. "Okay, Jor-dan."

Jordan wrapped his arms around the boy and pressed his cheek against his. Once again his distraction had caused a near tragedy. When would he learn? His fear resurfaced. "We'd better get him to the house and dried off."

Jordan trudged up the path, leaving a dripping trail of wet footprints. Meara hurried behind him, her breath coming in gasps. Giving a good, healthy shake of his soggy fur, Dooley followed.

Inside the house, Jordan waited as Meara pummeled Mac's back to help him hack up the water, then she slipped off his garments and wrapped him in a flannel blanket. Jordan gathered the child's sodden clothes, and, after he changed to dry apparel, tossed Mac's wet clothing in the dryer and hung his dripping sleepwear over the laundry tubs.

When Jordan returned to the living room, Mac was cuddled on the sofa with Meara. Motioning he'd be a minute, Jordan entered the kitchen and turned on the burner under the teakettle.

He prepared a pot of tea and, before heading back to the living room, grabbed a bag of chewy chocolate cookies. Not homemade, but the next-best thing. When he joined Meara, the facts were clear. Their science lesson had lost importance in the confusion, and Mac's deep, steady breathing signaled his exhausted sleep.

"We've lost our student," Jordan said, sliding the tray onto a nearby table. He handed Meara the teacup and grasped his own.

"Better he sleep, I think," Meara said, gazing at the slumbering child. She shifted her gaze to Jordan. "I can't thank you enough for your quick thinking. I couldn't move I was so frightened."

"If you'd been alone, you would have. Never fear. A parent will do anything to save his child." His gaze drifted down to his jeans, now hiding the proof of his statement. He'd failed to save his child. But he'd used every searing breath trying.

“You’ve hidden the terror far too long, Jordan,” said Meara. “I want to know the truth.”

“And I need to tell you,” Jordan whispered. “But I’ve been afraid of what you’d think of a man who caused his family’s death.”

Chapter Seventeen

Jordan's hand trembled as he clutched the cup in his hand.

Meara's eyes widened and fearful confusion filled her eyes.

He drew in a ragged breath, swallowing the bile that rose in his throat. It was now or never. He could offer Meara nothing unless she knew the whole miserable truth of the accident.

"Are you all right?" Meara whispered.

"Yes." He paused, rubbing his temples. "No, I'm miserable." He searched her eyes. "I've wanted to tell you the truth—the whole story—but I always lost courage... The truth is painful."

Apprehension flashed across her face, then shifted to accepting calm. "Don't try to startle me, Jordan, please. I want to know what happened. And in my heart, I think you need to tell me. For your own healing."

He nodded and stared at his sock-clad feet, again avoiding her eyes. "Robbie was eight then. About the same age Mac was when we met. I loved my son more than I can say, but…he'd gotten, like most children at that age, a little smart-alecky and sassy-mouthed." He shifted his eyes upward. "Mac will never be like that, I don't think."

Silently, Meara nodded.

"I'd promised myself the next time he mouthed off, I would show him who was boss. I'd tolerated it all evening. On the way home from eating out, he started up again. He didn't like the restaurant, he didn't like the food, he didn't like much of anything. We hadn't let him order a chocolate sundae for dessert. Typical kid stuff, but grating on a parent's nerves."

"Mac gets me down, too, sometimes," Meara murmured.

"Lila tried to shush him, but for some reason, he was determined to keep it up. I cautioned him. 'One more word,' I said, 'and I'll show you who's in charge.'"

Meara's heart ached, watching his pained expression. If she could only calm him, hold him in her arms. She clamped her jaw, controlling the urge.

Jordan leaned forward, elbows on his knees, his eyes begging for understanding. "I never hit my son, Meara. I don't believe in physical punishment. But that night I wanted to give him a smack."

Meara held her breath, waiting.

Pausing, Jordan raised his hand and kneaded the muscles along his hairline, then he sank back again into the cushion. "I could never strike him…but what I did was worse. I was approaching a curve in the road, and I concentrated on the solid yellow line. But Robbie flung out one last comment, and I took my eyes off the road for a second and swung around, facing the back seat, and glared. When I saw Robbie's startled eyes, I realized I'd lost control of myself and I refocused on the highway."

His voice caught in his throat and he closed his eyes. "Too late," he continued. "It was too late. A fuel tanker had crossed the yellow line. If I'd been watching, I could have veered away, but I'd been looking at Robbie for that fleeting moment.

"The truck tried to brake, but the tank swung sideways and we careened into it. Apparently I was knocked unconscious. When I opened my eyes, the passenger door was crushed and Lila was bleeding. Terribly.

"They were both unconscious, and flames were rising around the passenger door. Lila's seat belt was jammed. My hands were trembling violently. I leaped from the driver's seat, but before I could get to the back door, the tanker exploded. Fire and flames shot into the sky and along the cement. I'll never forget that horrible sight."

Meara covered her mouth, holding back the sobs that raged inside her.

Jordan's voice quaked with grief. Between sobs he described the horrifying event. "I stepped into the flames and pulled on the door handle. Locked! I'd forgotten to release the door locks."

He covered his face with his hands. "Oh, God, I am so sorry. So horribly, terribly sorry. Why did I lose my temper? Why?" He raised his head, his eyes pleading. "He'd be alive today if I—"

Meara rose from the sofa and fell at his feet, wrapping his grieving body in her arms. She said nothing. No words could ease the pain of reliving the horrifying moments.

"People appeared from everywhere," he said. "Someone grabbed my arms and dragged me from the flames. I don't remember much after that."

His body trembled in her arms. She cradled him against her, rocking, caressing, comforting.

In time, he calmed and lifted his tear-red eyes. "I'm sorry, Meara. Sorry I had to tell you…and sorry it happened."

"Don't apologize, Jordan. You've kept this inside too many years. I understand why you haven't been able to tell me. The pain must be unbearable, even though it was an accident. You didn't go over the line, Jordan. It was the truck." She paused, drawing in a breath of courage. "Let God in, Jordan. God promises comfort and healing. But you have to accept Him."

"You know how I turned against God. I'm surprised He's even listened to my feeble prayers these past few months. I'd begun to think, to see sense in the Bible's message, but after the accident, I blocked it all from my mind and heart. I called Him 'Lila's God'—even in my head."

"But God's promised, even when we're stubborn, to give us strength and courage. And love."

Jordan's sorrowful eyes knotted Meara's heart.

"But why?" he asked. "Did I deserve such horrible punishment for losing my temper?"

Meara brushed her fingers along his creased brow and kissed his wet eyes. "God said, 'My power is made perfect in weakness.' When we realize we can't survive without God's strength and comfort, then God is perfected in us, Jordan. When we finally give up our struggles and let Jesus carry our sorrows and burdens, then we are made strong through God's power. Do you understand?"

Jordan drank in a calming breath, releasing it slowly. "I try. I really try."

"Lila and Robbie were Christians." She searched Jordan's eyes for understanding.

"Yes, Christians. Both of them."

"And you, Jordan? Would you have come to know God fully? Completely?"

"I don't know. I tried. Sometimes I think I'm too intelligent to believe something so simple, yet terribly complex. Faith, Meara. It takes faith. I trusted in me. I was intelligent, capable, learned. A college professor. I thought I didn't need God."

"But we all do. And when the tragedy happened—and you'll never know why for sure—remember, 'we see through a glass darkly.' Only God knows the whole reason behind everything. You lost your ability to trust. You felt helpless. But God is there to lift you up if you would only ask."

He took her hands and pulled her onto his lap. "I've been afraid to drive with anyone in the car ever since that night. Did you realize we've never been in a car together?"

Meara's mind flew back to the Fourth of July picnic. "You carried Mac home once, when your car was nearby. I wondered why. I decided you didn't want to wake him, wrestling him into the back seat."

"I worried that you'd notice, and I've lived in fear that you'd ask me. I couldn't explain without telling you the whole story, and—" he hesitated "—I wasn't ready."

Mac shifted on the sofa and released a series of hacking, ragged coughs.

Meara slid from Jordan's arms and crossed to Mac's side. She eased him more securely onto the cushion, caressed his hair and waited. Nothing more. Returning to Jordan, she sat on the edge of his chair. "I'll need to keep an eye on him for a few days."

Then the weekend rose in her thoughts and her hand

flew to her mouth. "What do I do now? Mother Hayden's expecting him tomorrow."

Jordan pressed his hand against hers, resting in her lap. "Wait and see how he is in the morning. If he seems okay, take him for the visit and explain the problem. I'm sure she'll call you if he gets worse."

"Nettie's right," she said, fueled with aggravation. "Another example of the overprotective mother. Will I ever stop worrying?"

"Only if you listen to your own advice. Trust in the Lord. Isn't that what you told me?"

"It is. But it's easier said than done."

Amusement filled Jordan's eyes for the first time that morning. Meara captured his hand in hers and raised it to her lips. "We both need to work at it, I guess."

He clasped his fingers around her hand and drew her back to his lap. She snuggled against his chest and closed her eyes, feeling loved and fully blessed.

With red-rimmed eyes, Meara awakened to Mac's persistent cough. She'd heard it earlier when she brought him home from his grandmother's, but it had worsened. She peered at the clock—1:00 a.m. Her heart thudded as fear ricocheted through her. A respiratory infection for Mac was serious business. She crept to the telephone and punched in the familiar numbers.

Jordan answered, sleepy and confused.

"Jordan," Meara said into the telephone. "I'm sorry to wake you but I'm frightened. Mac's cough is much worse than when I picked him up this afternoon. He's struggling to breathe and—"

"Take him to Emergency, Meara. Cheboygan General is the closest. I'll—I'll come and…I'll—"

"No, please, I understand." She paused, remembering his fear. Her hand trembled against the receiver. "I'll take him myself. The hospital is before the shopping mall, I think." She struggled to locate the hospital in her memory. "Yes, I remember where it is."

"No, Meara, I'll pick you up. It's time I deal with my fear."

"But you'll have to come to town and backtrack. I'll drive to your place, then."

"We're wasting time, Meara. Mac might need you on the way, and if you're driving, you can't help him."

Fear gripped her, and she acquiesced. "We'll be waiting."

Jordan slammed the receiver, threw on his clothes and grabbed his jacket. The car keys jingled in his pocket as he jammed his arms into the sleeves and bolted for the door. In the late-night silence, the humming of his tires on the highway and his thudding heart was all he heard.

Meara was waiting at the top of the staircase when he arrived. He rushed up the steps to meet her, then descended with Mac in his arms. At the car, he rested the child's head on Meara's lap in the back seat.

The dark, empty highway rose before him. His sweaty hands clung to the steering wheel as he rounded each curve, fear jabbing his senses. He longed to glance in the back or catch a glimpse of Meara in the rearview mirror, but was thwarted by his panic. If his focus left the road, God might retaliate again.

He grimaced. Why blame God? He and the truck driver were at fault, not God. They had both erred. A careless, horrible accident. The Lord gave humans the ability to make choices. Jordan had made his. His son's good behavior had been his priority. A well-behaved, perfect child. But the outcome was that he now had no child at all.

Mac's chest-splitting coughs repeated in Jordan's ears. The distressing sound was followed by the child's futile attempts to draw a full, lifesaving breath. Desperation filled Jordan. They had no time to spare. He pushed his foot down on the accelerator.

The car careened past the black, wooded landscape. In the distance, Jordan spied a pale glow spreading across the highway. Streetlights. The city. He forced himself to ease off the accelerator. The car slowed and stopped at the first traffic light. Jordan turned right and followed the empty storefront buildings, security lights glowing like dim votive candles.

Mac's breathing worsened. The child's shallow gasps tightened Jordan's chest. Reaching the hospital, he guided the car to the Emergency entrance. A guard rolled a wheelchair to the passenger door, secured Mac in the seat, and Meara and Mac disappeared through the doorway.

His pulse racing, Jordan followed the man's instructions to the parking area. When he turned off the ignition, Jordan pressed his forehead against his aching arms, propped against the steering wheel. A prayer of thanksgiving stumbled through his thoughts. They'd arrived safely. And Mac was in good hands.

When he entered the waiting room, Meara and Mac were gone. The reception desk was empty, and Jordan slumped into a chair, filled with devastating memories. Years earlier Jordan had been wheeled into Emergency on a stretcher. Though his half-conscious mind had screamed for Lila and Robbie, he knew they were gone. Burned in the horrific inferno.

With the acrid smell of burning metal and fuel lingering in his senses, he tugged his thoughts back to the present. A nurse returned to the desk, and Jordan rose on shaking legs.

"I'm looking for Meara Hayden. She just brought in her son," he said.

Professional eyes met his. "They're with the doctor. You are…?" She hesitated.

"A friend. I drove them here."

Stoically, she motioned to the row of chairs. "Have a seat. When I have more information, I'll call you."

Like a chastened child, he stepped backward and settled into a stiff, comfortless chair. Jordan crushed the painful, distant memories. Instead, he relived the day he met Mac on the beach and the child's attraction to his kite. Cheerful moments, days on the beach and hours in the apartment.

Meara's soft lilting voice filled his mind. Aching, he longed to be at her side to comfort her and ease her fear. Prayer, he thought. He lowered his head, his mind searching for the proper words to plead for Mac's safety. *Like the prodigal son, Lord…more like a bullheaded doubter, I'm here, Father. You've opened Your arms and given me another chance. The chance to be a father and to do it right this time. Lord, protect Mac. Heal him. I can't bear to…*

Frozen with the frightful possibility, Jordan faltered, spitting the words into the dump yard of his mind. He refused to take no for an answer. God had taken his child. Would He dare to take another?

Gooseflesh prickled on his skin, and his heart thudded like a jackhammer against his chest—

"Sir. Sir."

He pulled his gaze upward. The nurse beckoned him. Dazed, he followed her through the doorway, checking above each cubicle for the number she'd mumbled as he passed. *Seven. Eight.*

He paused beside the drawn curtain and peeked through the gap. Meara stood beside Mac's narrow bed. When Jordan pushed the drape aside, her eyes shifted to his face. Tears glistened along her lashes.

"How is he?" Jordan edged into the cubicle and stood beside Meara. Even with the oxygen attached to his broad button nose, Mac's gray-tinged coloring had not improved. Jordan frowned at the rise and fall of his chest as he struggled for breath.

"They're taking him to X-ray," Meara whispered, her eyes directed at Mac. "Looks like an infection. Probably from aspirating lake water." She lifted her saddened eyes to Jordan's. "Better this than drowning."

Jordan slipped his arm around her waist, touched by her attempt to find something positive amid her fears.

The curtain slid aside and a white-coated attendant crept past them. Jordan stepped back and guided Meara to follow.

The attendant peered at the chart and turned to Meara. "We're taking him up to X-ray," he said. "You can relax in the waiting room, and someone will let you know when he's back."

"Relax in the waiting room," Meara repeated, rolling her eyes.

Jordan took her arm and led her from the room, muttering that obviously the man had no concept of being a parent. Except for the seriousness of the situation, Jordan might have grinned.

Time dragged. He located a coffee machine and carried two cups of strong, bitter brew to their seats in the half-empty waiting room.

"How long does an X ray take?" Meara mumbled, checking her wristwatch for the umpteenth time.

Jordan didn't bother to answer. No words would soothe her. Or would they? "Meara, take my hand and let's pray."

Meara's eyes widened, and without a word, she took his hand and uttered aloud a mother's prayer.

Jordan joined in the "Amen," and before he could say any more, a nurse motioned to them from the doorway.

Meara charged from the chair and reached the hallway before Jordan disposed of the paper cups and followed.

Entering the room first, Meara released a cry. Jordan rushed forward and gazed over her shoulder, his stomach twisting to a tight, aching knot. He assayed the cause of her dismay.

A doctor stepped around the bed and placed a hand on Meara's arm. "I'm sorry, Mrs. Hayden. The tracheotomy was an emergency. We would have lost him. His lungs were dangerously congested and needed suctioning."

Meara clung to the bed frame. "But was there no—"

"This was the best way," he continued. "He'll breathe much better now that we suctioned some of the infection from his lungs."

Jordan slid his arm around her, pressing Meara against his shoulder. "He knows best."

She turned her face from Mac and searched Jordan's eyes. "They've never done this before, and I—"

"This is a serious infection, Mrs. Hayden," the doctor said. "I assume your boy's had other respiratory problems. It's a common disorder of Down Syndrome children."

"Yes, he has, but—"

"We'll treat him with the appropriate antibiotics, but he'll have to be admitted until he's out of danger."

"Out of danger?" She swayed, and Jordan bolstered her with his arms.

"Are you okay?" Jordan asked, studying her ashen face.

Meara closed her eyes and nodded. "What do you mean?" she asked the doctor. "What kind of danger?"

"This particular bacterial infection causes viscid, stringy mucus. Unless we clear it from the bronchioles, it can be life-threatening."

"Life-threatening," Meara repeated.

"And we could have complications. You know any respiratory disorder is very stressful on the heart. You indicated your son has some congenital heart defects."

Slowly, Meara nodded, a look of resignation on her face. "I understand."

The doctor attached Mac's chart to the fastener at the end of his bed. "I'd suggest you go home."

"Home. No, I can't go home and leave Mac here. What if he wakes and calls for me?"

Though he spoke to Meara, the doctor's eyes pinned Jordan's. "There's nothing you can do tonight. If things get worse, we'll call you."

Jordan pressed Meara closer to his side. "She's the child's mother. She wants to stay."

The physician shrugged and left the room.

Meara buried her face in Jordan's chest, and tension

caught him between the shoulder blades. He could only imagine how she felt, but he longed to insist she go home. Rest would give her strength for tomorrow.

She lifted her face from his shirt. "I know what you're thinking, Jordan. But I can't leave. I really can't. But I'd like you to go home. I'll be fine."

"Meara, I won't leave you alone here."

"Please, you need to call Otis in the morning and tell him what's happened. I'm supposed to work in the afternoon. You'll help me more by calling him and stopping by the apartment. You can pick up a few things I'll need."

Jordan opened his mouth, then closed it. A helpless, empty feeling charged through him. How could he leave her? But she'd asked, and he had no choice. "I'll go, but come back as soon as I can."

"I'll be fine. Really." She moved away from his arms and stood above Mac's bed. The child's chest rose and fell in uneven tremors.

Red-hot anger flared through Jordan's body. *God, if You take this child...* A threat was absurd. Once again he was God's pitiful pawn. Mentally he beat his fists against heaven.

In the middle of the night, Meara slipped from Mac's room and wandered toward the waiting room. Silence echoed in the wide corridors, and she felt more alone than she had since the spring when she and Mac rented the rustic cabin.

Her body ached with stress and worry. She'd heard Mac's hacking cough before, and had always lived in fear, waiting, wondering if this might be the time God chose to take Mac home.

Home. A deep longing seeped through her. She'd so wanted to give Mac a secure, comfortable home. Not that the apartment didn't meet their needs, but Mac deserved so much more. He'd given her joy. He'd filled her with delight at his unique ways. He was a *special* child in every meaning of the word. Jordan had tried to tell her that.

Jordan. If only... She let the thought die. Why drag up wishes and dreams at a time like this. Her son's life hung on the edge. A respiratory infection meant danger to a boy like Mac. One day she'd have to face it. She couldn't hide. *Life expectancy.* The words tore through her.

She stood in the doorway of the empty waiting room and eyed the leatherlike upholstery. Cold and uncomfortable. Still, she needed rest. Her eyelids drooped with the want of sleep. Just for a minute, she thought.

Meara slipped off her shoes and curled up on the hard sofa. No pillow. No blanket. But at least a chance to rest...

"Mrs. Hayden."

Meara opened her eyes and, in the haze of sleep, saw a woman leaning above her.

"Mrs. Hayden, the doctor needs to see you. Your son's had a setback."

Chapter Eighteen

Her heart thudding, Meara flung her legs over the edge of the hospital waiting room sofa and focused on the nurse. "Setback? Please, don't tell me..." Meara slipped on her shoes and dashed on unsteady legs behind the nurse. "He's not—"

"Oh, no," the woman said, her eyes filled with understanding, "but he's having complications."

Meara's hand flew to her heart and pressed against the pounding, hammering ache there. *Please, God, please.* She didn't complete the prayer. God knew her unspoken words.

Darting through the hospital room doorway, Meara saw a group huddled above Mac. A doctor dressed in surgical garb stepped to her side. "His lung has collapsed, Mrs. Hayden. We need to insert a chest tube to aid his breathing."

Mac's whimpers jarred her attention. She squeezed between the two technicians at the child's side and grasped his hand. "Mama's here, Mac. Don't be afraid. Talk to God, sweetheart. He's right by your side."

She clung to his hand until a nurse guided her out of the

way and they rolled Mac's bed through the doorway. Meara followed them into the hall, but the nurse pressed her arm, holding her back.

"He'll be fine, Mrs. Hayden. We do this procedure often."

"Not to my son," Meara snapped, and was immediately contrite. "I'm sorry—"

"No need," the woman said, patting her shoulder. "All parents feel like you. Have a seat in the waiting room and let me bring you some coffee. I'll let you know as soon as the procedure is completed."

With little recourse, she nodded and pushed her shaking legs along the corridor to the waiting room. She sank into a chair and gazed at the wall clock. Four-thirty. The darkness through the window pane indicated she'd only slept an hour before being wakened. And Jordan? Where was he?

She missed his strong, protective presence. Still amazed at her feelings, Meara recalled their first meeting. Jordan's abrupt, unfriendly manner. Hers not much better. Then she believed she would never trust a man again, let alone give one her heart. But time and God had changed all of that.

She longed for Jordan's company, for his support and for his reminders that Mac was in God's hands. How easily she let the fact slip from her awareness. What kind of a Christian was she?

Cringing at her question, Meara raised her hands and massaged her throbbing temples. Silently, the nurse appeared, slipped the strong, fragrant coffee into her hands and disappeared. Meara settled back and sipped the hot liquid.

Gazing again at the clock, she noted the time—4:42. Only twelve minutes had passed. She checked her wristwatch. The same. Anxious for Jordan to reappear, Meara breathed deeply. She drank from the paper cup and, with no success, urged her body to calm.

Perhaps Jordan wouldn't return until later the next morning. He had wanted to stay, but she'd told him to leave. Forced him, if she were honest. But now Meara needed him.

Setting the cup on a table, then reaching into her purse, Meara withdrew a handful of change. She rose and wandered to the hall, searching for a pay phone. She spied it along the wall and moved her numb legs down the corridor. The coins clicked into the box, and she punched in Jordan's number, praying he was home.

The telephone rang. *Once. Twice.* Her heart pounded against her sternum, then skipped at the familiar *click* of the connection.

"What?" Jordan asked when he heard her quavering voice. "What is it?" Panic invaded him. *Please. No.*

"I was so afraid I wouldn't find you. Are you coming back soon?" Meara's voice charged across the line. "Mac's lung collapsed, and they're putting in a chest tube so he can breathe."

Jordan's voice caught in anguish. "I'll be there as soon as I can." His hand clenched the receiver.

The disconnecting *click* sounded, and fear raged inside him. Was it happening again? Had he opened his heart to this wonderful child, only to lose him? He slammed the receiver and smashed his fist against the kitchen counter. Glass rattled, and dishes shifted with a *thud.*

"No," he thundered. "No! No! I can't bear it again. This child doesn't deserve to die. Punish me. I'm a detestable sinner. Me, not the child."

As if his life were repeating, Jordan sensed the depth of

loss. He rammed his hands against the door frame, and tears fell from his eyes. Scalding, purifying, draining. His life rolled through his mind like a silent movie. Black-and-white. Colorless. Dead.

How long would he cling to his past and miss the joy of love again? The delight of a child? The passion of a woman? He'd waited too long. God had struck him down again.

With trembling fingers, he snatched the open Bible from the table and raised his arm to heaven, shaking the book clutched in his fist. He slumped to his knees, his body quaking, out of control. "Show me the words, Lord. Give me something to hang on to. Something to show me You are loving and merciful."

He bent to the floor, the Bible pressed beneath his head, and his tears poured onto the pages. When he'd calmed, Jordan raised himself at the waist and stared down at the open book. He lifted it from the carpet, closed the cover and rose.

He sank into the chair, the Bible resting in his lap. He wanted to believe God was loving and just. But his own distant sorrow persisted as a reminder that things didn't always happen as he desired. Once again he felt responsible for Mac's life being in jeopardy. Whatever he touched turned to ashes.

Jordan inhaled deep, calming breaths to steel himself. He'd survived heartache before. His wife's and son's deaths had dealt him a despicable blow. He'd survived then. He'd survive now. Bracing himself, he said the words. He could learn to live without Meara and Mac. It would be best for all of them.

He'd rebuild the protective wall so strong that even Mac's joyful laugh and Meara's smiling eyes couldn't cause a chink. He should have known better than to want a new life when his own walled existence was waiting for him.

Waiting for him. Meara was waiting for him. Jordan jumped from the chair, dropped the Bible on the table and bolted to the door. He couldn't abandon her now. Meara needed him.

And shoved back somewhere in his heart, Jordan knew he needed her.

Footsteps on the tile floor tapped in her ear, and she raised her eyes to the doorway. Jordan's tall, angular frame appeared, carrying a shopping bag from the apartment full of her requests. She leaped from the chair into his arms.

"Any word yet?" he asked as she clung to him.

"Nothing. It seems eternal."

He rested a hand on her shoulder, his voice measured and quiet. "There's nothing you can do. It's out of our hands."

She peered at him, noticing his detached expression. "But we can pray, Jordan. God is merciful." She brushed tears from her lashes.

He didn't respond.

Her anxiety mounted. She took Jordan's hand and led him to the sofa. What was wrong? His rigid, controlled manner seemed so different from that of the Jordan she'd come to know. Afraid to ask, they sat in awkward silence.

Jordan spoke, his voice distant and alien. "I called Otis. He and Nettie will be up shortly."

"What about the shop?"

He stared into the distance. "He'll have someone cover for him, I suppose."

The air around them was filled with a charge.

Minutes passed, then Jordan shifted in the chair without lifting his eyes. "Otis said he collected most of the petitions. The city council meeting is next Monday. We're on the agenda."

Meara's interest sparked. "How many signatures did you get? Any idea?"

"Five hundred plus. That's more than half the population of Mackinaw City."

"That's good news. More than five hundred signatures should do it, don't you think?"

He shrugged, raising his eyebrows. "I hope so."

His words sent her hopes plunging. "You only hope?"

"I don't want to get too excited. Things don't always turn out the way we expect."

Meara heard deep sadness in his voice. "I'll keep it in my prayers until the meeting."

"Do that" was all he said.

Meara wrapped her arms over her chest to hold back the sudden chill. Her mind struggled to understand Jordan's cold, calculated responses. Was he remembering Robbie's death? A shudder shot down her spine. That had to be it. Jordan was controlling his fear…so as not to frighten her. That had to be it. But the nagging question lingered.

When the nurse beckoned from the doorway, they rose together and followed her down the corridor.

"He's back in his room," she said over her shoulder, "sleeping soundly. The doctor's waiting for you."

With trepidation, Meara stepped into the room, first eyeing Mac, then peering into the doctor's face. He caught her gaze with a faint smile.

"He'll be fine. Everything's under control. See," he said, gesturing to Mac, "he's resting and getting good healing breaths now. That's what he needs."

She nodded without comment.

With a final check on Mac, the doctor shook Jordan's hand, then hers, before exiting.

Meara moved to Mac's bedside and ran her hand down his motionless arm. Her heart felt heavy…for her child and for Jordan. She glanced at the brooding man over her shoulder.

"He's sleeping. That's good."

"He needs his rest."

She faced Jordan, longing to broach him about his sadness. Instead, she gestured to the two chairs near the bed. "Would you like to sit?"

"No, I—I think I'll get back home. Otis and Nettie should be here soon to keep you company. I need to let Dooley out and—"

"I understand." She was listening to Jordan become a stranger.

Edging toward the door, he lifted his hand. "I'll see you, then. Later."

"Later," she echoed.

He spun on his heel and left the room.

Stunned, Meara stared at the empty doorway, reality creeping through her veins. Tears welled in her eyes. She blinked to stem the flood. *Later.* The empty promise was dashed to the ground as were her hopes.

"Nothing's wrong," Jordan lied into the telephone.

"If you say so," Otis said, his tone dubious. "So if everything's all right, why haven't you been up to see Mac? It's been days."

"You said he was much better."

"Right. But that doesn't answer my question. Be honest,

Jordan. You've been their right arm since they dragged you back into the world. I think you owe her somethin'. At least an explanation."

"I've been busy, man. Tell her I've been busy. It's no big deal." His voice soared in pitch and tone, and he winced at the truth he'd exposed by his reaction. "I'm tired, Otis. Maybe I'm sick."

"Sick in the head is about right. Jordan, think of me as your father. I spotted a spark between you and Meara long ago. A flame's more like it. You can't deny that, my boy."

"It died. Fox fire."

"Fox fire, my eye. Git yer sorry hide up to that hospital, son. That woman needs a friend. A special friend. I know you have a heart, Jordan. You're fightin' this saloon battle for the community and tourist trade. People you don't even know. I'll bet my boots Meara and Mac have a place in that hard heart of yours. And no measly wall you try to build can hold those two out."

"Are you finished?"

"No, but I'll hang up..." he said, followed by a soft chuckle, "before you hang up on me."

A soft *click* and the line went silent. His hand trembling, Jordan pushed the receiver onto the cradle and stood in paralyzed silence.

Otis was right. Jordan had promised himself to ease away from Meara and Mac. Not run. He'd deserted her when she needed him most. Pulling a trembling hand through his hair, Jordan leaned against the wall. Could he go to her without crumbling? Would she even want to see him?

* * *

A sound at the doorway caused Meara to look up from the newspaper. When she spied Jordan, her stomach knotted. The past few days, he'd vanished from their lives. She'd wept tears for herself. Tears for Mac. But she felt helpless. Empty. Today she looked in his eyes and saw tension.

"Jordan?"

He took a hesitant step into the room and paused. "I hear Mac's doing better."

Searching his face for more but seeing nothing, she nodded. "They're going to take out the chest tube today."

"Today? That soon?"

"I'm waiting for them now."

He edged into the room and moved to Mac's bedside. "He's sleeping again." He eased his hand forward and brushed his fingers across Mac's hair.

"The nurse put something in his IV to relax him. But they have to be careful. He can't tolerate strong pain medication. It's too dangerous."

Jordan swung around. "Dangerous? How?"

"His heart. And he needs to cough when they take out the tube. To keep his lungs clear. Otherwise, they'll have to put it back." She ached at the thought. What she wouldn't give to take Mac's place. To be the one suffering instead of her son. "I wish it were me in that bed."

"No, you don't. Think. Mac'd be scared to death. Who'd be with him to calm his fears? Only a mother can do that."

Or a father, she thought. But Jordan was right. "I can't bear seeing him this way. I know you understand, Jordan."

His controlled expression caved to one of excruciating sadness.

Meara paled. "I'm sorry. I shouldn't have—"

"It's true, Meara. No need to be sorry."

A noise from outside captured their attention. Two orderlies came through the doorway, and Meara rose, stepping out of their way. Jordan stood behind her, his breath brushing her cheek. She ached to have him touch her, give her a reassuring pat or tilt her chin and offer a comforting look. But she paused, untouched, until the orderlies rolled the bed through the doorway.

"Do you have time to wait with me?" she asked.

Following a lengthy silence, he nodded. "For a while."

She wanted to tell him to leave, that she didn't need him. But truth was, she did. Not just anybody, but Jordan.

She muttered her thanks, and Jordan followed her through the doorway and down the corridor to the waiting room. There, he stopped at the coffeemaker and brought back two cups of steaming brew.

"It smells fresh for a change," she said, taking the cup from him. "Thanks."

He didn't respond, but sank into the chair next to her.

"So what was the result of the council meeting?" she asked, breaking the silence.

"We were tabled to a special meeting. Sounds like Hatcher has his own contingents. From what I hear, the T-shirt shop owner—not sure of his name—and Lombardi, the owner of the restaurant, have both agreed to sell."

"I'm really sorry, Jordan. You and Otis, even the churches, have put so much effort into the petitions. I'd thought that would be enough."

"I'd hoped so, but, like I said, what you want isn't what you get. Life's tough."

Bitterness filled his voice, and Meara cringed at the brutal sound. Her life certainly hadn't been easy. "Life *is* tough.

Lately, everything seems like a lot of hard work and difficult decisions."

"Decisions about what?"

"Many things. Moving from the apartment this spring... and Mac's schooling."

"You're still struggling with that?"

"Naturally." She flung a stabbing look at him, realizing too late that she'd shown her anger. "Yes. I admit that withdrawing Mac from school was presumptuous. We're doing better with the homeschooling, but..."

"He missed the science lesson. I've thought about that."

That shocked her. "You have?"

"I said I'd help out, and I try to keep my promises, but then, neither of us had a premonition about the accident."

"I appreciate that, Jordan. Maybe when they take the tube out..." She bit her tongue. Begging was not in her. No. If he cared about them, he'd suggest it. "Anyway, up until this, Mac asked nearly every day about going back to the school. I did call a couple of days ago to find out about reregistering him."

"What did they say?"

"It's easy. They'll just add him back on the roll. I heard the music teacher would like him to be in their choir. Somehow they know he likes to sing." She chuckled for the first time in days. "I can guess how they found out."

Jordan grinned, and her heart soared.

"You mean, our...your Pavarotti gave them a little concert."

"If I were a betting woman, I'd wager he did." *Our Pavarotti.* She'd caught it even though he'd tried to cover his slip.

The tension in his arm eased, and instead of holding himself like a corpse, he leaned back and stretched his hard, long legs in front of him.

"So what's holding you back?" he asked. "Remember the article I gave you a while ago? The studies show he'd do well back in school."

"I worry whether they'll expect enough of Mac. He has limitations, but I want him to go as far as he can. He needs to be as perfect as he can be."

Jordan shrank at the word. *Perfect.* His son had died because Jordan had wanted perfection. Mac's "perfection" wasn't the same as another child's. One person's difference was another person's individuality. It had taken him too long to learn that.

"What do you mean you want Mac to be perfect? What are your expectations?"

"I want him to reach his potential. You said it yourself. What will happen to him when I'm not here to take care of him? Who'll watch out for him? Who'll protect him from hurt and ignorance of a world that gawks and stares at disabled people?"

"You're talking in riddles, Meara. What you've said is a paradox. Ambiguous. You can't have both."

His frown sliced her confidence. "I don't understand."

Jordan wasn't sure he did, either, but he loved that boy. Yes, no matter what his mouth said, no matter where his reason led him, his heart knew the truth. He loved Mac. He wanted the best for the child. And Meara needed to face reality.

"Mac is perfect," Jordan said.

"How?" She arched an eyebrow as if waiting for a trick response.

"Through God. You're a believer, Meara. You follow the Bible's teachings. I know those teachings. I taught the Bible for years. As literature, but I taught the philosophy. The beliefs. Mac is perfectly what God wants him to be. The struggle we have is to understand the difference between what God wants and what we want."

"I still don't understand. How is Mac perfect?"

"Name a person who isn't flawed. 'Normal' or disabled. Name one. You?" He struck his chest. "Me? Otis? Mac?"

"I won't mention Nettie." He couldn't stop the grin that reached his lips.

A full smile rose to Meara's face. His heart lifted at the sight.

"You really can't name one unflawed person, can you," he continued. "And why? Because there aren't any. God made us as perfect as He wanted us to be. Each of us has limitations. Still, we're perfect, because God made us according to His will. With all our imperfections."

"Okay, so I admit no one's flawless, but that doesn't mean I'm wrong to want Mac to meet his potential."

"Nothing's wrong with that. But we have another challenge to face—to recognize the opportunities life gives us. To accept our purpose."

Confusion crossed her face. "You think I'm talking in riddles? *You* are, Jordan."

"Look, I know I've struggled accepting God's Word, but I know what the Bible says...whether I believe it or not. Our purpose is to align ourselves with God and totally give ourselves to Him. This means, to let our own will go by the wayside and accept God's."

She fell back against the chair. "Are you saying that I'm trying to push my will over God's?"

"I'm not your judge, Meara. But when we manipulate situations to our needs, when you influence Mac's learning by your own fears—"

"You're saying what Nettie said. I'm an overprotective

mother." Her eyes narrowed and she knifed him with her stare.

"I guess that's what I'm saying. Mac won't always have you around. We've both said it. So how will he meet challenges and survive if you shield him from it while you are with him?"

Meara seemed to crumble. "I don't know."

She closed her eyes, and Jordan's heart raced; he feared he'd made her cry. But finally, she opened her eyes filled with stinging confusion, but no tears.

"I'm sorry if I hurt you, Meara."

"I needed to hear it. I keep pulling my mind back to the eight years of Mac's life when he was scorned by the exact people who should have loved him. I can't wash that from my mind."

"But look at him. He's okay, Meara. Remember, we talked about this before. He's happy, loving, gentle. A child without his problems couldn't be any more perfect."

Hope filled her face, and she straightened in the chair. "You're right. He's wonderful. The decision is already made. He should go back to *real* school." She shot him a knowing smile. "That was easy."

"I wish mine were."

"Yours?" Meara heard the ominous tone in his voice. "What decisions?" She tilted her head, waiting for his answer yet afraid to hear.

"Decisions about going back to teaching, moving back to Kalamazoo, changing my life."

Cold fear snaked through Meara. "You're leaving Mackinaw?"

"Blair called a couple of days ago. The dean wants me to sign a contract for next September."

"I'm glad for you, Jordan." Her dishonest words lay like putty in her heart.

Chapter Nineteen

Jordan pushed his foot against the accelerator. His own words shot through his head. Words he'd used to lecture Meara—a message he needed to heed.

He'd longed to say "your" God or "Lila's" God while spouting his wise proclamation, but he couldn't. No matter how hard he'd tried to deny "their" God, the Lord had become his. How could he be angry and demanding of a God who wasn't there?

As he expounded about accepting God's will, a will he wanted so badly to understand, he recalled Meara's Bible verse from weeks earlier. "'*Now we see through a glass, darkly,*'" she'd said. He'd plowed through his memory to recall the promise of something better.

Today the rest of the verse hit him in the pit of his stomach: "When we meet God, face to face, we will know all things." That promise wasn't enough. He couldn't wait to reach heaven before understanding life's complex happenings. If God were truly merciful and loving, Jordan demanded to know *why.* Why did children suffer? Why did death snatch innocent babes?

Suffer. The word hung in his thoughts. Jesus suffered. God's only son, pure and sinless, suffered for humanity's offenses so they might have... *They.* No. "So *I* can have salvation," he said aloud. The meaning overwhelmed him. *Me.* And Meara and Mac. Christ was made perfect. Sinless. Total perfection. Yes. Christ was *perfect* so He could suffer for the world's sins and give believers eternal life. Not death, but life.

A glaring red traffic light loomed. Distracted, Jordan slammed his foot on the brake and came to a grinding halt, avoiding an accident by sliding through the intersection. *Close.* A blast of air shot from his lungs.

A healing touch of humor settled over him as he contemplated the horror of what might just have happened. God could have answered his plea at that very moment. A quick, unexpected face-to-face meeting with the Lord.

He sent his thanks heavenward, adding, for good measure, that he'd rather wait for that promised appointment.

A warming calm wrapped around Jordan. God had answered his fervent prayer. In time, Mac would be fine. Jordan also knew he, too, would survive. More than survive. He released his death grip on the steering wheel, washed in God's promise. In this life he would have griefs and troubles, but nothing he couldn't endure. And he *had* endured. Death, loneliness, pain, heartache.

But he was still here and a God-given new life waited for him.

Following the special Saturday-afternoon meeting, a crowd poured from city hall. Jordan stepped exhausted into the brisk November air. Though they'd won the battle to ban the saloon from Mackinaw City, the tension had taken its toll.

"Good job," Otis said, giving his upper arm a friendly shake. "Glad it was you talkin' up there and not me. I'm a glib ol' guy when it's me and someone else, but in a crowd I fade away like a hermit crab."

Jordan shook his head. "I have a hard time picturing you as shy, Otis, but if you want me to believe it, I'll give you a million for the Brooklyn Bridge, too."

Otis chuckled. "You know what I mean. I'm not a smooth talker like you, Jordan."

Jordan gazed at his elderly friend, remembering the telephone call that "sweet-talked" him back to the hospital. And he could never thank Otis enough.

Passersby greeted Jordan with a nod as they left the city building. Others stopped to shake his hand, clasp his shoulder or exchange a few friendly words.

Bernie Dawson hailed Jordan with a wave as he came through the door. "Congratulations," Bernie said. "You made a lot of sense up there." He released a hearty chuckle. "Lot more sense than Dom Lombardi. Didn't you love his comment when they asked him to cite the benefits of Hatcher's proposed saloon?"

Otis slapped his leg. "Never heard anything so funny." He puffed out his belly and cheeks, attempting to mimic Lombardi. "'Gives a man something better to do at night than sit home with his wife.' Bet the women in the crowd loved that one."

"*And* the city council," Bernie agreed. With another shoulder pat, Bernie headed for the parking lot.

"I'm glad it's over," Jordan said. "I think we should send thank-you letters to the churches for their support."

Otis shot him a hearty smile. "Don't ya think they should be sendin' you one?"

Jordan pressed Otis's shoulder. "Not me, Otis. Better you." He ambled to the sidewalk and paused. "I'm heading for the hospital. I promised Meara I'd give Mac a science lesson a while back. Today, I'm keeping my promise."

"Give the lad a hug from me." His devilish eyes sparked. "And you give that lovely woman a big kiss, too." He took a step backward and stopped, tossing out his final comment. "Figured you would, anyway."

Waving, Jordan headed down the sidewalk and climbed into his car.

With light traffic on U.S. 23, Jordan made good time. He turned into his driveway and rushed inside to give Dooley a run before heading to Cheboygan. A little later, on the highway again, he spied the rustic cabins a mile or so down the beach and relived the morning he'd first met Meara and Mac. So much had happened since that day. His life had soared toward heaven like one of his kites.

If he went back to teaching, he'd miss this life. He'd miss everything: the kites, Otis and Nettie, life on the water, Dooley's race for the ducks, even The New Curiosity Shop.

"Thank you, Grandma," Mac said from a seated position in his hospital bed. He turned the pages of his new book, a gift from her.

Meara nodded her approval, and Edna Hayden patted her grandson's hand. "Your mom says you've been very brave."

"Brave," Mac said, his index finger poking his chest. He beamed her a bright smile.

"I'm glad you could come, Mother Hay—"

Edna pressed her hand on Meara's arm. "My dear, with all that's happened in our lives, call me Edna. Let's be friends, not former in-laws."

"I'd love that," Meara said.

She reached forward to embrace the woman, but uncomfortable with her action, she hesitated. Instead, Edna opened her arms, and Meara stepped into them, finally released from the plaguing memories.

"Hug," Mac said, opening his arms to them both.

They laughed, and in a cumbersome circle of arms and contorted bodies, they joined in a huddled hug.

"Interesting," Jordan said from the doorway.

Startled to see him, Meara jerked upward.

Mac let out his yell: "Jor-dan!"

"How are you doing, pal?"

"Good." His gaze aimed at the bag under Jordan's arm.

Pleased, yet puzzled, Meara watched Jordan. She resisted the urge to mention it had been days since she'd seen him. "Jordan, this is Edna Hayden, Mac's grandmother."

"Jordan Baird," he said with smile.

"How do you do?" Edna offered her thin hand and Jordan shook it. "I'm glad to meet you...finally. You seem to be one of Mac's best friends."

"I should hope so. He's certainly one of mine." He gave Mac a wink and tousled his hair. "So what do you think I have here?" Jordan asked, displaying the chunky sack that clunked and chinked when he dropped it on the hospital tray-table next to Mac's bed.

Meara watched the interaction, gladdened at their loving relationship.

Mac stared at the bag and shrugged. "Don't know, Jor-dan."

"It's our science lesson, young man. Are you ready?"

Mac nodded, and Jordan rolled the tray closer and settled it in front of Mac.

Mac eyed the bag for a minute until Jordan gave him a nod. The boy beamed an eager smile and pulled open the sack. He turned over the sack, toppling out a myriad of shells. "Seashells," he cried, and delved into the chalky houses, grabbing them in his hands and spreading them back out on the table.

"That's a wonderful sight to see," Edna said, rising. "And now, I suppose I'd better be on my way. Mac has his lesson."

"Please, don't rush off," Meara said.

Edna eyed her wristwatch. "I've been here nearly two hours. My driver probably wonders if I've been admitted." Her thin lips stretched to a grin, and she lifted her handbag and hung it on her arm.

Mac looked away from the shells to his grandmother. "Going home?"

"I am, Mac, but I'll come and see you again, soon."

He opened his arms wide, and Edna bent and wrapped her arms around him, kissing his cheek. "Be a good patient, Mac. Listen to the doctors...and your mother."

"Listen to Jor-dan, too." His face brightened, and he sent his hero an admiring glance.

"And him, too," she added. Edna turned to Jordan and grasped his hand. "I'm so grateful that Mac found you. And from what I hear, he really did."

"That's right," Jordan said.

"I'm sure we'll meet again," Jordan said, as she headed for the doorway.

"Often, I hope," Edna added. She blew a kiss to Mac and left the room.

"Seashells, Jor-dan," Mac said as soon as Edna was gone, her fragrance lingering on the air.

Jordan winked at Meara. "I've never seen anyone so anxious to go to school."

"Real school," Mac said.

Meara chuckled, hearing Mac's persistence. "Real school and soon, Mac. When you're better."

Mac's eyes widened, and his broad grin filled the room. "Real school, Jor-dan."

"I heard, pal." Jordan tousled Mac's hair and pulled a chair closer to the bedside. He eyed the collection, selecting a few specimens. "Okay, the first thing we'll do is study the shells' shapes and sizes." He held up each so Mac could view them. "Do you see any differences?"

Mac grabbed two shells from the table. "This one. This one," he said, holding a clam shell in one hand and a snail shell in the other.

"Good. Now, let's decide what makes them different."

Watching and listening, Meara treasured the sight. Jordan told Mac about the sea life that lived in the shells and how they were unique, while Mac bent over the samples, his face etched with serious concentration.

Meara slid into the only comfortable chair in the room and marveled at the two most important people in her life. How grateful she was for Mac's improved health. She recalled how many times in the past she had wanted to lasso him or tie a gag around his mouth for embarrassing her with his frankness or for singing his incessant songs. God had mysterious ways of helping people reexamine the important things in life.

Her words brought Jordan's transformation to mind. Since Mac's illness Jordan had struggled, but had grown closer to the Lord and closer to her. Despite her fear, Mac's frightening accident had reaped blessings.

A sweep of white stepped through the doorway. Meara glanced up and gave the doctor a smile.

"I'm Dr. Holland from Dr. Carpenter's office. He's off today, so I'm filling in."

He stepped to the end of the bed. "How's the patient today?" he asked, lifting the chart from its housing and eyeing the tray-table filled with shells. "Learning about the sea?"

"Seashells." Mac selected one and extended it toward the doctor. "Snail."

"Right," the doctor said, circling Mac's bed.

Choosing another, Mac showed the doctor. "Clam," he said, peering at Jordan for validation.

"That's right," Jordan agreed, rising and shifting to Meara's side while the doctor listened to Mac's chest and checked his vital signs.

When he finished, Meara rose. "Is he about ready to go home?"

Jordan rested his hand on her shoulder. "He's in the best hands here, Meara. The doctor's and the Lord's."

Dr. Holland grinned. "Your husband's a wise man."

Jordan squeezed her shoulder, and she swallowed the correction that lay on her lips. Apprehensively, she raised her eyes, and Jordan sent her a tender wink that made her shiver.

"Your son will probably be released tomorrow. If not, the next day," the doctor continued. "He's doing very well. Dr. Carpenter will talk to you in the morning." He replaced the chart and left.

Meara averted her eyes, embarrassed at the doctor's error. She moved closer to the bed and put her hand on Mac's arm. "Sounds like you'll go home soon, Mac."

"I...can go home," Mac agreed, preoccupied with reorganizing the shells into piles.

Warm breath whispered against her cheek, and Jordan's hands captured her waist. He rested his chin against her hair. "You heard the good doctor, didn't you?"

A prickling of nerves traveled up her legs and landed in the pit of her stomach. "He said a lot of things."

"I mean the part about your husband being a wise man."

"No, I missed that," she teased, glancing at him over her shoulder.

He caught her chin in his hand and turned her toward him, his eyes tender and warm. "Husband or not, Meara, I love your son. And I love you."

Meara's heart overflowed with emotion. "I love you, too, Jordan."

"I love you, too, Jor-dan," Mac echoed.

He grinned. "I love you, too, son."

Amazed, she shook her head slowly, her heart ready to burst with wonder. "Who would have thought?"

He grasped her two hands in his and pressed them to his heart. "God. I figure He thought up the whole thing."

Chapter Twenty

Leaning against the windowsill, Meara stared out the front window of her apartment and watched the December snow flutter down, thick and feathery like goose down from a torn pillow.

Feeling snug and warm, she moved to the sofa and stretched out, thinking back. Following the hospital vigil—those long days and nights when Meara stayed near Mac's bedside—her son's health had returned to normal. God had answered her prayers...in so many ways.

She glanced at her wristwatch. Within minutes, Mac would bound through the doorway with Jordan, who'd graciously agreed to pick him up from school. They had the Christmas tree to decorate and then Mac's first Christmas concert.

When Mac returned to school at the end of November, Meara was still struggling with the decision. Despite Jordan's logic and her own faith-filled reasoning, she allowed the reality to sail in one ear, bang around against her own stubborn will and limp out the other side.

But she'd caved in to wisdom and Mac's persistence. She'd registered him for the second marking period, and after only a few weeks he had come home telling stories of new friends and exhibiting new skills. His slow but steady progress was more than she had ever hoped for. And she had to admit, Jordan had been correct.

Jordan. Even the thought of his gentle, kind eyes nudged a smile to her face. The image of him standing on the beach, his kite floating high above their heads, lingered in her mind. He'd appeared out of nowhere like a glorious oasis, offering her and Mac sanctuary from a dull, barren life and filling her days with laughter and contentment.

The telephone's ring interrupted her meandering thoughts. Glancing again at the time, a tiny fear jarred her. She'd expected Jordan and Mac by now. Hurrying to the phone, she snatched the receiver. But her worries faded when she heard Roger's excited voice.

"We have a baby daughter, Meara. Melissa Kay. Born late last night. Six pounds, eight ounces. And she's perfect. Absolutely beautiful."

"Roger, I'm so happy for you. And how's Alison?"

"She's wonderful. Thrilled and thankful."

For a dark moment Meara's mind plunged back nearly ten years to when Mac was born, and to Dunstan's angry, unthankful face. She let the thought fade and rallied with Roger's joy. "Tell her how thrilled I am, Roger."

The back door flew open, and Mac's voice drowned out Roger's next comment. Meara lifted her finger to her lips, but Mac seemed to ignore the telephone pressed to her ear, bubbling his own excitement.

"Hold on, Roger. Mac just got home from school." She

pressed the heel of her hand over the telephone. "Mac, hush, please. I'm on the telephone."

The child softened his chatter to no one in particular.

Meara lifted the receiver to her mouth to continue. "Some Sunday afternoon we'll take a ride over to your place. I can't wait to see the baby."

"That would be wonderful."

"Tell Alison I send my love, and kiss the baby for me."

Following her goodbye, Jordan came through the doorway and Meara plopped into a chair.

"Roger just called. Alison had a beautiful baby girl. Melissa. Absolutely perfect." She tilted her head coyly. "Just the way God wanted her to be."

"I'm glad," Jordan said. "God only gives special children to special parents. Did you know that?"

She blinked her eyes playfully. "No, but I'm glad you let me know. I told Roger we would come for a visit some weekend."

"Okay," he said, sliding his arm around her waist and pecking her cheek.

Meara jerked backward. "You're cold. You, too, Mac." She opened her arms and gave him a bear hug, then glanced at the wall clock. "I suppose we should get busy." She grinned at Mac. "We have to go to your concert tonight."

He stood with his chest expanding, stretching his shirt. "And I'm in the front row."

"The front row. Mac, that's wonderful," she said.

"Does that mean you have the best voice?" Jordan asked, ruffling his hair.

"No. I'm the shortest, Jor-dan."

Meara and Jordan burst into laughter.

Jordan gestured toward the door. "I'll bring in the tree. Get the stand ready."

Meara could hear Jordan's footsteps banging down the stairway, and she felt a smile settle on her face. Life had taken a big turn for the better. The best, she thought. "Come here, Mac, and help me."

Her heart lifted, thinking of Christmas with Jordan. She loved him. She loved Mac. She even loved Dooley.

Jordan returned, and after helping him settle the tree in the stand, Meara snapped on her radio, dialing until she found Christmas music. As they strung lights and hung bulbs, she was filled with contentment.

By six o'clock they'd attached the last Christmas decoration—all brand-new, like her life. New and promising. Each ball hung blocked a memory of Meara's past. Each light that twinkled reminded her of God's shining promises. Though the world had crumbled at her feet, God's hand held her firm and sure. Today life held so much hope.

Though he'd made no promises, Jordan had opened a door that filled her with expectation. She'd learned to give him time. God had validated her need for patience. In His time and in Jordan's time. She was a slow learner, too. Maybe slower than Mac when it came to patience.

After their quick dinner, Jordan cleaned the kitchen while she and Mac dressed. When she came from her bedroom, Jordan was clipping Mac's tie to his shirt.

"You look pretty handsome, son." Jordan stepped back and eyed him.

Son. Meara gazed at them both. Both handsome. Both

perfect. Her pulse tripped seeing the two most important people in her life looking happy and content.

Jordan clapped his hands. "Are we ready? The star singer can't be late."

"Me?" Mac asked, looking up at him with loving eyes.

"No one else, Mac," he said with a tenderness that melted Meara's heart.

When they reached the school, they followed the crowds inside. Meara's apprehension faded as she watched the choir line up on the small stage, Mac in the front row, chattering to the boy beside him like one of the regular kids.

Isn't that what Jordan had tried to tell her? Mac had become one of the regular kids. When she looked up, Mac grinned and gave her a little wave. She waved back as Jordan's arm slid around her shoulder and drew her closer.

She glanced up at him, seeing his rugged profile looking ahead at Mac, proud, like a father watching his son's first concert. When the room hushed and the lights dimmed, Mac focused on the director as she lifted her baton, and Meara held her breath, wondering if Mac's singsong voice would stand out from the rest.

"Away in the manger, no crib for a bed..."

Meara's eyes filled with tears. She heard nothing. Only the lovely voices of children, blending together in praise for Jesus' birth.

Jordan gave her shoulder a squeeze.

She turned toward his loving face to hear him say, "Perfect."

Mac jabbed at the packages lying beneath the tree.

"Tomorrow's Christmas Day, Mac. We open our gifts tomorrow morning."

His sad face looked up at her. "But you said today is Christmas."

Meara shook her head at the whiny voice. "Christmas Eve. There's a difference." Looking at Mac's face, she didn't think words would explain.

She heard a noise on the landing and sighed, knowing she would have a reprieve.

The door opened and Jordan appeared carrying a Christmas gift. He stomped his snowy feet on the mat, set the package on the table and slipped off his coat. He hung it over the kitchen chair and drew Meara into his embrace.

His cold hands on her arms made her shiver, and she wiggled away. "You're too icy."

"But not my heart. It's warm as toast," he said, his handsome face sending her heart into a whirl.

"A present," Mac said, pointing to the gift on the table. He eyed Meara, then gave Jordan a plaintive look. "But we can't open it today, Jor-dan."

"We can't?" Jordan said.

"It's only Eve. That's what Mom said."

"Eve? It might be only Eve, but in my family we open our Christmas presents on Christmas Eve, so I think we could make an exception."

Meara grinned. "I don't want to ruin tradition."

Jordan grabbed her hand. "Come on." He motioned to the living room. "Christmas gifts have to be opened by the tree."

Mac's face glowed as he hoisted the package from the table and followed them.

Jordan settled on the sofa and patted the empty cushion. Puzzled, Meara sat beside him. She knew Jordan had something on his mind.

Mac set the package beside the tree and waited.

"It's yours, Mac. You can open it," Jordan said.

Meara gave an approving nod. New life. New tradition. She could handle it.

As Mac tore away the gift wrapping, dowels clanked to the floor and red and yellow tie-dyed cloth unrolled, unveiling the fabric for a kite. A long, multicolored tail slipped to the ground.

A squeal rose from Mac's throat. "A kite!" He clutched the cloth to his chest. "I'm one year older. I can…fly a kite."

Jordan shook his head. "It's too cold now, Mac. You'll have to hang it in your room until spring. Then you can fly it." As he spoke, he stretched open the cloth and held it toward Mac. "What do you see?"

Mac's eyes widened, looking at the letters that decorated the kite. "Me. It's *M-A-C.* Mac."

"You got it. I made this one especially for you."

Meara gazed at Mac's name emblazoned on the kite fabric and touched Jordan's arm, her heart thundering at the special gift and realizing why he'd been so excited to give it to him. "It's wonderful. He's thrilled."

Mac hugged the fabric against his chest, pressed it to his cheek.

"Would you like me to put it together?" Jordan asked.

Without hesitation, Mac handed Jordan the fabric.

Jordan retrieved the dowels that had fallen to the floor and threaded them through the kite seams. With his experienced hand, he wound the heavy cord, pulling the joints together and stretching the fabric tautly across the strips of wood.

Meara watched in amazement, seeing him assemble the beautiful creation. "What do you think, Mac?" she asked, when Jordan handed him the finished kite that was bigger than Mac.

He clutched the kite, grinning. "I think it's Mom's turn."

Meara shook her head. "No, Mac. I don't get a gift today. Jordan was just anxious—"

"Hold on," Jordan said. "I have a little something for you, but first we need to talk."

His sudden seriousness caught Meara off guard. Puzzled, she frowned and searched his face. "Just me?"

"No, both of you."

Both of you. His tone set her on edge. Anticipating the worst, Meara sat stone still, her hands as cold as Jordan's when he arrived. She'd been a fool to think their friendship could be more than that. He'd mentioned the college contract and had talked about moving away. She held her breath.

Concerned, Meara eyed Mac. He'd swiveled on the floor, his eyes following Jordan's every move.

Leaning forward, Jordan rested his arms on his knees and looked from Mac to Meara. "Next September I'm going back to Kalamazoo…to the university. I've given it a lot of thought. Since my old position is open, the time is right, and I've already signed the contract."

Meara's stomach dropped, and she knew her premonition had been correct. Her hidden hopes slipped from her grasp. Unconsciously, she clutched her chest, then slid her trembling hand into her lap, hoping he hadn't noticed. She struggled to control her voice.

"Then, you'll be selling the house?"

"No. I'll close it for the winter like people do with their cottages." He shifted toward her. "And I'm keeping the kite shop. I've asked Otis to stay on as manager. It'll be more work, but if he runs into a problem, I'm not that far away. And I'll spend the summers here."

"The summers," she said, lowering her eyes and fighting back the tears.

Seemingly unaware of her concern, Jordan caught Meara's hand and chuckled. "I couldn't sell the house anyway. It means too much to me...and Dooley. He'd miss the ducks."

Mac giggled, then sidled around to lean on the sofa arm. Jordan tucked his free arm around Mac's shoulders.

"Both of you are my best friends. You know that."

"Best friends," Mac said, shifting to squeeze in beside Jordan. He rested his head against Jordan's shoulder.

Jordan didn't have to say another word. She already understood. Struggling, she swallowed back her tears.

"You helped me learn how to live again," he continued. "And because of you, I found God. My empty life is whole and wonderful. You know I love you both."

Meara's pulse surged. She wanted to scream, telling him to stop. Was he saying goodbye or not?

Jordan squeezed her hand as if reassuring her.

"What is it, Jordan? Just say it."

"I've waited a long time to say this." A shy grin curved his lips. He shifted on the sofa and dug into his pocket. When he withdrew his hand, he placed a small velvet box into Meara's palm. "Will you marry me, Meara? Both of you?" he added, looking at Mac.

Marriage? Her mind swam in confusion. He'd addled her to distraction. With her pulse skipping, she opened the box and held her breath. Gently, she lifted out the solitaire diamond set in gold. So delicate and lovely.

"You frightened me, Jordan," she said, releasing a fervent sigh.

"I'm sorry. I thought you knew."

Cupping the ring in her palm, she gazed at the diamond glinting in the Christmas tree lights and blurring with her tears. With the back of her hand, she brushed the moisture from her eyes, then pressed her hand against his cheek, clutching the diamond ring in the other.

"I'm speechless. I don't know what to say."

"Just say yes."

Mac studied them, eyes shifting from Jordan to her.

Watching his confusion, Meara rose and kneeled at his side. "Mac, Jordan wants us to marry him." She opened her hand, displaying the glistening ring. "We'd live together as a family. What should we say?"

Sensing the seriousness of the moment, Mac lifted his pensive eyes to hers, then reached out and grasped Jordan's hand. "We say...yes, Jor-dan."

Jordan opened his arms and gathered them to his chest. "I'm the happiest man in the whole wide world."

"I'm happiest, too," Mac said.

Stifling her joyful laughter, Meara kissed her son on the cheek. "And I'm the happiest woman in the whole wide world."

Giving Meara his hand, Jordan helped her rise. He took the ring from her clenched fist and slipped it on her finger. "I love you with all my heart." He raised her hand to his lips and kissed her fingers. "God does know what He's doing."

"And aren't we glad He does." With tear-filled eyes, Meara looked down at Mac. Warmth and peace filtered over her, her world complete.

When she lifted her eyes, Jordan caught her chin and lowered his lips to hers. Without fear, she surrendered her love and trust to his care and to God's faithful keeping.

Chapter Twenty-One

Five months later

Meara pulled into Jordan's driveway, stepped out and slammed the car door, waiting for Mac to follow. She glimpsed the lake beyond the house, admiring the May morning sun spreading sparkling diamonds across the water. A warm breeze filled the air with the heady scent of new growth. Meara's life had blossomed as certainly as spring had arrived. Each day something fresh and loving opened to her.

She beckoned, and finally Mac reached her side. With a single rap and "yoo-hoo," she swung open Jordan's back door and peered inside.

Jordan waved to her from the front porch and took a step toward her, stumbling over Dooley, who slid between his legs and bounded to greet them.

Meara chuckled as Jordan's tall, muscular frame avoided an unexpected tumble.

"Dooley," he yelled, but the dog bounded ahead and skidded on the linoleum to Mac's feet, whose giggles nearly drowned Jordan's reprimand.

The setter's long tongue whipped out and swiped a wet kiss across the boy's cheek.

"Dooley," Mac said, his laughter growing. In his excitement he stumbled backward.

Meara snatched his arm and steadied him. "Looks like you were bowled over with love, Mac."

"I love Dooley," Mac sang. "I love Dooley." With the dog tagging by his side, he headed for the front of the house.

Jordan watched him until he reached the screened porch, then turned to face her. "Bowled over with love?"

She laid her head against his chest. "I was thinking the same," she said. She dropped her purse on the kitchen table and slid her arm around his waist, thinking of their wedding day, coming up in another month after Mac finished school. She'd waited a long time for that day, so near now and so perfect.

"Today's the big day," Jordan whispered. "Did Mac bring the kite?"

"The kite. He sure did." She shoved her hand into her purse, then tossed Jordan her car keys.

He snatched them in the air, gave her a wink and headed for her car.

Meara wandered to the front porch. Though Mac had learned to be careful of the water, she still worried. She stood in the doorway and watched Mac roll a ball while Dooley fetched it.

Jordan returned and leaned the kite against the porch wall, then stepped outside.

Surprised Mac had forgotten about the kite, Meara

followed, her heart in her throat, anticipating her son's excitement.

Jordan neared Mac and Dooley and clapped his hands. "Okay, son, you have two choices. You can play fetch with Dooley...or do something with me."

A scowl spread across Mac's face and he hesitated, looking first at the tail-wagging dog, then at Jordan, as if he didn't understand.

"Which is it?" Jordan asked.

He pondered the question a moment before he answered. "Play with Dooley," he said.

Jordan rubbed his hands together. "Okay, then, I guess I'll have to fly the kite by myself."

"Kite!" Mac's eyes widened. "Jor-dan, me. I forgot."

Laughing, Jordan ruffled his hair. "Okay, then, *you* can fly the kite."

"Me," Mac yelled, bouncing in anticipation.

"Remember, I promised you could do it by yourself."

Brushing a tear from her eye, Meara watched Jordan head back to the porch, then return with the canary-yellow kite sporting its long multicolored tail.

Flashing her a tender smile, Jordan turned and concentrated on Mac's attempt to hang on to the kite as they moved away from the house.

"Aren't you coming?" Jordan called.

Still tangled in pure pleasure, Meara followed them down the hill. On the sand, Jordan opened two canvas chairs, and she sank into one, nearly as excited as Mac.

Since the previous year, Mac had grown only a little in size, but much in confidence. More than she had ever dreamed. Now, hearing Jordan's careful instruction, Meara drew her attention back to Mac. She held her breath as the boy clasped the spool of string.

Jordan waited as Mac lumbered along the beach, tilting the kite high into the wind. It lifted, and Jordan darted toward Mac. But too late. A gust caught the fabric, then died away, and the kite flitted and dipped toward the water.

Jordan dashed in for a save, grabbed the spool and ran backward on the grass, avoiding the kite's watery grave. When it touched the sand, he rushed forward and nabbed it before it skittered into the lake.

Mac's expression faded to one of disappointment. "No, Jor-dan." He shook his head as Jordan approached him. "Next year. One more year."

Gazing into Mac's sad eyes, Jordan's heart plummeted. He glanced at Meara, saw her worried face and gave her a brave wink, then kneeled beside the child and wrapped his arm around him. "You can do it, Mac. Now, listen again, okay?"

The child nodded and a faint "okay" fell from his lips.

Jordan began again, explaining in simple terms the tug and ease of the kite on the wind. He gave Mac the string, and he held the kite above his head, pretending he was the wind, jerking the kite one way and dipping it another.

As he listened, Mac raised and lowered his arm, giving more string and drawing back.

"Now, listen carefully. If you pull too hard, the string will break and the kite will fly away. Or it might tip down because it needs more cord. As the wind tugs, give it slack. Relax and let the wind pull it higher."

He pulled and tugged, giving Mac the feel of the wind. "And don't let go or the kite will fly away. Just remember, Mac, it's give and take. Bend with the wind."

In amazement, Jordan paused, gazing at the child and then at Meara. Love was exactly like a kite, giving and taking, tugging and subsiding, soaring and dying. Yet bending with the wind of change made all the difference. And with God, the cord was strong as steel. Gooseflesh spread down his arms. His chest tightened with awareness.

"Jor-dan," Mac said.

He peered down at the child, his expression vacillating between anxiety and wonder.

"Sorry, Mac, you caught me thinking." He gave the boy a reassuring pat. "This time I'll help you until it gets up there. Okay?"

Hesitantly Mac agreed.

This time Jordan ran along the beach, his feet digging through the sand until the wind surged beneath the taut paper and lifted it above his hands.

Playing with the flow and ebb of the wind, Jordan worked his way back to Mac and handed him the spool. Together, they plied the cord until the kite soared higher and higher.

Mac's smile glowed as brightly as the blazing sun, and Jordan eased back, letting the boy control the kite. When Mac felt secure, Jordan retreated farther, and the boy guided the string alone.

"Look at our kite-flyer, Meara."

Mac glanced their way, his face filled with new confidence. "Me," he called. "I'm the kite-flyer."

Meara rushed to Jordan's side. "Just look at him," she whispered, gazing into the sky, her face as radiant as her son's. "Just like you the day we met."

Jordan wound an arm around her waist, reveling in their

shared joy. In another month, Meara would be his wife. Mac, his son. Though he'd turned his back on life, God in His undying love and mercy had prodded him to look toward heaven, and today he'd found a little bit of it right here in his arms.

Lifting his eyes toward the kite against the clouds, he marveled at the colorful spectacle. He nestled Meara's warm, supple body against his side and gazed with joy at God's special gift—his son, Mac. The kite-flyer.

* * * * *